MW00769045

"Although *The Lawmaker* is a novel, it is also an educational work for those who have not experienced the frustrations and setbacks that our justice system can produce for law enforcement. This book addresses many of the problems that produce stress for the dedicated agents and officers doing their jobs."
—Steve Mallory, retired law enforcement officer,
criminal justice professor,
The University of Mississippi (Ole Miss)

"Ward has written a suspenseful and tightly wound novel—the sort of complex and morally ambiguous book that might come from John Grisham."
—Capt. Edward M. Brittingham, author of *The Iranian Deception*

"Wayne Lott is a good example of how even the best of us can be tempted by the corrupting nature of power. *The Lawmaker* is a deeply human story and Rick Ward can be assured of a place among the best Southern writers."
—J. Rye Erixon, author of *The Strip Mall* and *Angel's Milk*

"A blistering thriller of the same caliber as the best of Joseph Wambaugh and James Lee Burke. With his background in law enforcement, Ward understands the gray areas that make politics and life so hard to navigate without losing one's moral compass. A knowledgeable and sizzling portrayal of power's corrupting influence."
—Stephen F. Medici, author of *Adverse Selection*

The Lawmaker

Rick Ward

The Lawmaker

A Novel

Rick Ward

Spring Morning Publishing, Inc.

The Lawmaker
Copyright © 2009 by Rick Ward
Spring Morning Publishing, Inc.

All rights reserved. No part of this book may be reproduced (except for inclusion in reviews), disseminated or utilized in any form or by any means, electronic or mechanical, including photocopying, recording, or in any information storage and retrieval system, or the Internet/World Wide Web without written permission from the author or publisher.

For more information please contact:
info@springmorningpublishing.net

Cover and author photo by Ron Blaylock
www.blaylockphoto.com

Printed in the United States of America

The Lawmaker
Rick Ward

1. Title   2. Author   3. Legal Thriller/Suspense

Library of Congress Control Number: 2009901282

ISBN-10: 0-9823564-0-4
ISBN-13: 978-0-9823564-0-1

Table of Contents

This book is dedicated to the memory of my daughter April Dawn Ward, who was killed in an automobile accident on September 11, 1998. She was headed home on a rainy night when she hydroplaned on a slick road into an oncoming lane of traffic.

April was a wonderful child, loved by everyone and ahead of her time. She was a sixteen-year-old senior at Terry High School in Mississippi. She was working part-time for a CPA firm after school and planned on pursuing a career as an FBI agent after college. She shared my dislike for corruption, was always in favor of the underdog and believed nobody deserved any special treatment over anybody else. She knew no racial boundaries. Many crooks in the future will be glad she never made it but we will love her and miss her forever.

Acknowledgments

I would first like to thank Karen, my wife of over thirty-one years, for all she does, as well as all she has done and continues to do for me. She has encouraged me over the years to write and has reviewed much of my work without hesitation. I would also like to show my appreciation for my entire family, extended family and in-laws for always being there and being a part of my life.

Most importantly, I would like to thank my ninety-two-year-old mother, Emma, a retired seamstress, and my late father, Homer, a self-taught automobile mechanic. They raised me and seven other kids with no education themselves but made sure we went to school every day wearing clean clothes and with lunch money in our pockets. Were it not for them, this book would not be possible.

I greatly appreciate attorney and retired Mississippi Supreme Court Justice Chuck McRae's input on the manuscript and his very valuable comments. Furthermore, I cannot overemphasize the support I received from First Amendment Attorney John Sneed of Wise, Carter, Child and Caraway in Jackson, Mississippi. I can't leave out my long-time friend and Special Assistant to the Mississippi Attorney General, Ed Snyder, for his insight and encouragement as I wrote this book.

I cannot thank my editor, Doreen Michleski, enough. She helped me realize that there are storytellers and there are writers, but few storytellers will go on to be writers without the help of a good editor.

Special thanks to Joel Hochman, James Uttel, Jessica Gorham, Dan Hooks and Olga Vladimirov of Arbor Books in New Jersey for all their assistance in making this book a reality.

Ironically, I would also be remiss if I weren't thankful in my own way for some of the "low-lifes" I have encountered over the years who have inspired me and improved my imagination to write such a book. May justice take its course in their lives.

Last, but certainly not least, I would like to thank all of the American servicemen and women who have given so much in the service of their country in all of the branches, during war and in peace—those who fought, and those in supporting roles for those who did. I only wish we could turn back time and do the same for our Vietnam veterans, my friends who were spit on, mocked, cursed and humiliated by protestors and flag burners. They wouldn't have been able to do any of those things to express themselves had it not been for our fighting forces upholding those freedoms we hold so sacred. In other countries, their abusive treatment could have led to hanging, a firing squad, beheading or loss of limbs. Tell a Vietnam vet how much you care.

Introduction

"I cannot accept your canon that we are to judge pope and king unlike other men, with a favorable presumption that they do no wrong. If there is any presumption, it is the other way against holders of power... Power tends to corrupt, and absolute power corrupts absolutely."
—Lord Action (Libertarian hero)

By the late 2000s, the gaming industry was huge in the state of Mississippi. It started first with bingo and escalated to a multi-billion-dollar industry with many casinos scattered throughout the state's waterfronts. Most of the casinos were reputable businesses that contributed jobs, entertainment and great places to eat. The resulting infrastructures that came with them provided retail goods and exquisite lodging and recreation. Acceptance of the industry was sold to the citizens of Mississippi as a way to improve education, and tax dollars generated would go toward that purpose.

However, many believed that the money found its way into the general fund to be used any way the legislature wanted, instead of being earmarked for education. Still, the jobs created, roads paved, and improved police and fire organizations could not be argued with or overlooked, although the image of crime and corruption in the casino industry has found its way into our history books.

Wherever there is a dollar to be made, there is someone out there seeking to monopolize and make all the money. Those people will stop at nothing, and nobody is exempt from their grasp. They will manipulate the truth and the intent of their actions. They will do their best to hand you a sprig of poison ivy and make you think it is an olive leaf.

In Mississippi, three casinos—Mudbug Gold, Catfish Jack's and Bullfrog Bayou—were believed to be the culprits, and were widely referred to as the "Bogus Trio."

The owners of these casinos, who had done so much for the state, wanted to keep out competition. They wined and dined lobbyists and, before long, had lawmakers trying to sell a new bill of goods in the name of religion, convincing the God-fearing public in Mississippi that more casinos would be unnecessary and immoral.

In order to protect and cater to the Bogus Trio, the handful of legislators supporting them had a duty to keep out any new casinos or new type of gambling, including a state-run lottery. Within years, the Bogus Trio had built its power base by campaign contributions, lobbying funds, and employment and ownership of state politicians. The owners became above the law, exempt from arrest and prosecution at all levels.

They had hit the jackpot.

*"Laws are like cobwebs, where the small flies
are caught and the great break through."*
—Sir Francis Bacon (father of inductive reasoning)

Chapter 1

Aces and Eights

"There can be as much value in the blink of an eye
as in months of rational analysis."
—Malcolm Gladwell

O n the second of August, a few sparse late-summer fireworks
still left over from Independence Day popped in the scorch-
ing afternoon air. The sound made Will Lott jump as he drove
home.

Normally, Will was not a nervous man. His many years as a
cop had hardened his nerves, but had also brought him countless
threats as a well-known enemy of organized crime, illegal gambling and corruption. It was one of those most recent threats that
resurfaced now in Will's memory.

A few days before, he had received an envelope in the mail
with a few playing cards in it: two black aces and two black eights,
known together as the "dead man's hand" because it's what "Wild
Bill" Hickock drew on the day of his murder, August 2, 1876. Will
knew the significance of the cards and their ties to gambling and
death, but had managed to file the incident away in the back of his
mind.

What brought it out again was a strange coincidence over lunch. Will had removed his cell phone from his shirt pocket—he didn't like to keep it clipped to his belt for fear of pulling it out during an emergency instead of the handgun he wore holstered to his right side—and called an old buddy, his ex-partner.

"Murph, want to meet me for lunch at the Chinese Palace?" he asked.

"Sounds good, Will. They have great sushi there, too."

"I ain't eating no fish bait, but you have what you want."

———

In the restaurant, the two men talked about the current state of criminal affairs and caught up on old times. Everything was fine—until Will opened his fortune cookie. "Live each day as if it will be your last," he read.

"What's wrong, Will? You just turned a few shades lighter," Murphy laughed.

Embarrassed, Will threw the fortune on the table. "Huh, I still have a damn sight more color in me than an Irishman." Still, he had to admit to himself that he was a little shaken.

After he said goodbye to Murphy and walked down the street to his car, a passing truck backfired, sounding like a shotgun. A young lady happening past screamed as if she had been shot. It scared the hell out of Will.

Wrong place, wrong time, he thought, trying to calm himself down. But he was breathing hard and clutching his chest as he got into his car.

Just like on any other day, he turned down his street, pulled up into the driveway of his house and saw his rolled-up newspaper lying there. He stopped short—too tired to walk back out and get it later—and opened the driver's side door. Then he unbuckled his seatbelt and leaned out to pick up the paper.

There was a loud cracking noise and Will fell facedown in his driveway. His car continued forward, striking the gas meter on the side of his house and causing an explosion heard by neighbors all around. Within seconds, it was total chaos.

A man mowing his lawn across the street ran over and turned the car off just as flames gushed across the driveway. He found Will lying unconscious with a large pool of blood at the back of his head. Another neighbor managed to shut the gas valve off and call 911. Suddenly, the sirens of fire trucks and ambulances filled the air, and a crowd had gathered on the sidewalk.

Within minutes, EMTs hauled Will away. Nobody knew what his fate would be.

Chapter 2

Tragedy

*"Until the day when God shall deign to reveal
the future to man, all human wisdom is summed up
in these two words: 'Wait' and 'hope.'"*
—Alexandre Dumas

It was a hot, muggy day in Mississippi, just before the sun set over the skyline of Jackson. Even the wide glass doors opened sluggishly at the entrance of Baptist Hospital.

Wayne Lott walked in, stumbling over the upturned corner of the welcome mat. He had no idea whether his father, Will, was still alive. The downcast eyes of the police officers gathered around the nurses' desk gave him little hope that his dad would survive. Less than an hour before, a bullet had creased the back of his skull and lodged into his spine.

Wayne went up to the front desk. His red, swollen eyes were incapable of producing any more tears; he had cried them all out on the car ride over.

"How's my dad? Who did this?"

"Mr. Lott?" asked Jim Long, a state investigator standing nearby.

Wayne nodded. At just twenty-six, he was still a bit baby-faced.

It broke the desk nurse's heart just to look at him, so she occupied herself with the papers in front of her.

"Your father's in surgery now," Long explained. "All we know is it appears he was shot by a long-range sniper as he was getting out of his car after work. We don't have a suspect yet, but we will."

"You damn well better," Wayne said, pointing his finger into the investigator's chest.

"Settle down, Mr. Lott, and have a seat," Long said in a commanding but sympathetic tone.

Long lived up to his surname. He was about six-foot-three and lanky, with a long nose, long fingers and wrists that popped out of his shirtsleeves. Only his eyes were small. Heavy-lidded and close together, they didn't seem suited to a state investigator.

Wayne sat down next to Long on the lobby's lone, unoccupied leather couch that had clearly seen better days. Only then did he register how cold the hospital was, especially compared to the sweltering heat outside. He pulled his suit jacket more tightly around him.

Long took a pen and small notepad out of his shirt pocket. Clearing his throat, he asked, "Can you think of anyone who'd do something like this? Did your father talk to you about any investigations or crooks he was focusing on recently?"

"Knowing my dad, it could be anybody," Wayne said. An unmistakable tinge of pride was mixed with the sorrow in his voice. He rubbed his eyes then ran his hands down his tear- and sweat-streaked face.

The senior Mr. Lott was a big man with a beer gut, who was tough when he needed to be and funny when he wanted to be. He often joked that he had more hair coming out of his ears than he had on the top of his head. But what he did have, in abundance, were enemies.

Will was a well-known figure in charge of the state's Organized Crime Strike Force. Even though he was of retirement age, he insisted on putting away as much "trash" as he could before he died.

"It's the only way I'll rest easy," he had often told his son.

Exhaling deeply, Wayne forced himself to focus on the investigator, who was jotting down notes. "Recently, Dad's been very outspoken about how organized crime has entered all facets of society. *Too* outspoken, some would say. He blamed gambling and corrupt politicians the most."

Wayne knew his father hated politics and most politicians. *Hell, by now I've almost memorized the old man's rants about how they lie, cheat and cover up for each other,* he thought. *The first one came when I was sixteen. His idea of a "facts of life" speech.*

Will put politicians at the top of his "worthless people" list: an actual needlepoint framed and hung over his desk. A gift from Wayne's mother.

Lobbyists were next. "I can never understand how you hold some convicted murderers in higher regard than most members of the legislature," Wayne would argue whenever he saw his dad waving to someone on the street that he'd actually arrested several years earlier.

"At least *they've* paid their debts to society," his father would answer.

Although Will often cursed lawyers, too, he kept them off the "worthless" list, maybe on account of his son. Wayne was just out of law school at Ole Miss University and was now working at a local law firm in Oxford, Mississippi. His father held out hope that Wayne's professional choice was a passing phase and that he'd put his education to "better use" as an FBI agent or federal prosecutor.

Will himself had no formal schooling but was known for being a pit bull in court, capable of embarrassing well-respected—and self-important—attorneys by sparring with them on the witness stand. He never lost a case on its own merits—and the few he did lose he chalked up to "political interference."

"Could you tell me a little more about your father's work?" Investigator Long asked.

"Dad spent his life in different aspects of law enforcement before becoming the top cop of organized crime," Wayne said, repeating the moniker often used by the media. "His strike force is funded by a federal tri-state grant for Mississippi, Louisiana and Arkansas. He reports directly to the state attorney general."

For the first time since hearing the news of his father's shooting, Wayne broke into a smile. "Dad felt pretty confident about the position since the attorney general's an elected Democrat and all the other statewide officials are Republicans. Also thought he'd be free from a lot of local influence due to the federal control that came with the grant money. Feds won't do anyone any favors if a state politician becomes the target of an investigation—which, to hear my Dad tell it, happens pretty often."

Wayne remembered how glad he was when he first heard about his dad's promotion to strike force chief. It meant he rose up the ranks and lived to tell about it, despite all the risks and political pressures.

As a young boy, with help from the local news, Wayne would envision the different dangers awaiting a cop on the beat, and often couldn't fall asleep until he heard the familiar sound of his father's key turning in the door. He never dreamed that one day he'd be shot in his own driveway.

Long looked down at his scribbled notes to avoid eye contact on the next question. "Mr. Lott, I'm informed your mother passed away a few years ago from pancreatic cancer. Were you aware of… Was your father seeing…"

Before he could find the right words, the doors to the emergency room swung open. Wayne practically jumped off the couch, expecting a surgeon to appear. His heart sank when he saw the black garb of a minister.

Wayne walked over, bracing for the worst. "Were you in the ER with Will Lott?"

"Yes," the priest said. His eyes were kind, but his face—like that of many men of the cloth—showed signs of fatigue.

"I'm his son. How is he?"

"It was touch and go for awhile, so they called me in. I hear you're not Catholic, but I'm the best God could send from the duty roster on such short notice. Your father's strong and holding on, but he isn't out of the woods yet. Don't worry, though, young man. He's being attended to by the best neurosurgeons and orthopedic surgeons we have." The priest smiled consolingly.

"Did they tell you what his chances are?"

"The doctors say he has a fifty percent chance of survival. *I say it's in God's hands.*"

Wayne looked down to the floor for a few seconds then turned his eyes up to the priest. "Father, is there a chapel in this hospital?"

"Down that hallway, son."

I wonder if that's the last time anyone will call me that, he thought.

⸻

Wayne excused himself to Investigator Long and headed down the narrow hallway. Stepping into the small, silent chapel, he saw a wooden cross, a ceramic casting of the Ten Commandments, a painting of the Last Supper and, of course, a picture of Jesus. He felt like he was entering any one of his Southern Baptist neighbors' homes. Except he was entirely alone.

Candles were lit at the altar—the only sign that someone had ever been there at all. Standing before them, Wayne watched the wax melt slowly down the sides and couldn't help but wonder as to the outcome of those prayers.

Dropping suddenly to his knees, he began to pray for his father's life.

My dad's a good man, Lord. He does your work here on earth and always stands up for what's right. We need him here...

I need him here.

Wayne hadn't prayed so hard since the death of his mother, a petite, good-looking woman whom he took after. Unlike her husband, who believed that if you looked hard enough, you'd find corruption everywhere, she had believed that if you searched for it, you'd find goodness in everyone—even the most corrupted. It was a trait she passed on to her son, one that often left him bitterly disappointed in the people around him.

The loss of his mom, though heart-wrenching, had brought Wayne closer to his father, as well as to God. Will, however, had never gotten over his wife's death, and Wayne was worried that he'd give up in the operating room to go be with her.

Please don't take him, Lord. Not now... Not until I have the chance to make him proud.

———

The hands on the large clock in the hospital lobby slowly clicked out the minutes. It was the only sound Wayne heard. At first, it was maddening. Now, he found it oddly soothing. Steady. Like a heartbeat.

It was coming up on 2 a.m. Jim Long had left some time ago. Even the desk nurse was gone, replaced by her nightshift counterpart. Only a few of the police officers remained, still huddled together, standing silently off to one side.

Wayne fought off sleep, awaiting word from the surgical staff. He was back on the beat-up sofa, surrounded by Styrofoam cups. Some still contained traces of hospital coffee—the color of which matched the leather couch he was lying on.

The exhaustion of the day washed over him as he closed his stinging eyes. He felt dirty, grimy, and stank of sweat. He realized that the last time he had picked up a toothbrush was almost twenty hours ago, and wondered if that was why the new front desk nurse hadn't spoken more than a few words to him.

At about ten after two, the chief surgeon emerged from the operating room. The front of his scrubs was stained with spots of blood.

He exchanged glances with the night nurse then walked quietly over to the sofa.

"Mr. Lott?"

Wayne sat up, startled and momentarily disoriented.

"Wha…? How is he?"

The look on the surgeon's face was grave. "He's alive."

Wayne hung his head in thanks then took a deep breath. *The worst is over…Dad can handle it from here.* He stood up to shake the surgeon's hand.

"Mr. Lott, I'm afraid it's not all good news. Your father's paralyzed from the waist down. The bullet took a downward trajectory, putting pressure on the areas of the spine and nerves that control the lower body. It's still lodged in there," the surgeon explained. "Any attempt to remove it could cause complete paralysis, leaving him a quadriplegic."

Before he could fully digest the doctor's words, Wayne felt the hot tears springing from his eyes.

"Well, what can we…what happens now?"

"He'll most likely be confined to a wheelchair for the rest of his life. But he'll have complete use of his upper body," the surgeon said, placing a hand on Wayne's shoulder for support.

He's alive but his law enforcement days are over, Wayne thought. *For him, that's as good as being dead.*

His gaze shifted to the well-built young police officers over in the corner, as he remembered how his father had once looked in uniform. Proud. Strong. Ten feet tall.

"Can I see him?" Wayne asked. His voice was trembling.

"Not tonight," the surgeon said. "He'll be in recovery for quite awhile and will remain in intensive care for a few days. You'll be able to see him tomorrow. For now, you should go home and try to get some rest."

"Thanks, doc. I'll do that."

As soon as the surgeon returned to the ER, Wayne headed back down the hallway. He caught a sympathetic half-smile from the front nurse as he passed her desk and tried his damnedest to return it, but couldn't.

In the chapel once again, Wayne lit a single candle among all those that had burned out. Then he went back to the lobby, where he'd wait until morning.

Chapter 3

Run for the Capitol

*"Try not to become a man of success
but rather to become a man of value."*
—Albert Einstein

On September 11, after weeks of grueling physical rehabilitation and intense therapy, Will was finally released from the hospital. When Wayne came in to get him, he saw his father, seemingly in high spirits, saying goodbye to the doctors and nurses.

"Congratulations. You're a free man, Mr. Lott," the doctor said, shaking his hand.

"Now I know what a prisoner feels like after serving his time," Will joked. "Thanks to you, doc, I'm rehabilitated and ready for the outside world."

"Just don't let me see you in here again," the doctor laughed. He patted Will's shoulder then headed out the door with his staff. Wayne stood at the doorway, thanking each of them as they passed.

When everyone had gone, so had his father's smiling expression. He sat silent in his wheelchair, staring out the hospital window one last time.

He looks so small and weak, Wayne thought. Clearing his throat, he said, "Are you ready?"

"Yeah," Will answered, as if noticing for the first time that his son was there. "Just wish I could walk out of here on my own two feet."

Wayne stepped behind the wheelchair and started to push it toward the exit. It was lighter than he expected. "Don't worry, Dad. Julie and I have the place all set up. Ramps, widened doorways… You'll be getting around easy."

"I'll be getting in the way, is what I'll be doing," Will said, holding a bag full of his belongings on his lap.

"Don't be silly. Julie wants you there. Says I've been spending too much time at work and she could use the company."

"Well, I'm sure those pencil pushers and ambulance chasers you work for need you more than your own wife does," Will scoffed. It came out sounding harsher than he had intended. He knew his son was doing his best trying to cheer him up. He was sorry he said it.

Wayne remained silent. He had been struggling to find a way to tell his dad that the law office he worked for was pushing him to run for the state representative seat, recently vacated when the incumbent was killed in a car accident. He knew how his dad felt about politicians. *Hell, everyone in a hundred-mile radius knows how he feels about them*, Wayne thought.

Still, I could become a new breed. One of the few in the legislature standing up for the people instead of for lobbyists and special interest groups. That's one way I could continue Dad's legacy. Write new laws without loopholes that let criminals walk the streets free. Make sure technicalities don't overturn convictions—especially in cases like his, when they finally catch the guy who put him in this chair. But how do I get him to see that he's the reason I'm doing it?

Looking around at his sunny surroundings outside the hospital, Will brightened up. "What do you say, son?" He turned around in his wheelchair and smiled at Wayne. "How about a victory lap, once around the parking lot with your old man?"

When they pulled up to Wayne's Oxford home, his wife, Julie, was waiting outside for them. She came hurrying to the car to help with the wheelchair.

"The house looks great, but I feel so bad imposing on you kids like this," Will said.

"Nonsense, Pop," as Julie called him, "this is your home, too. You're always welcome here, no matter what happens with us."

Will wasn't sure exactly what she meant by that. "Nothing bad will ever happen to you and Wayne. You're the happiest couple I know. But thank you, Julie, for your kindness." He looked into her eyes with tears in his own then grasped her hand and kissed it.

Will felt just as strongly about his daughter-in-law as she felt about him. In fact, he often took her side over his own son's when they'd have friendly arguments or first-year marital spats. He loved her as much as if she had been his own daughter.

"Well, Dad, the boss has spoken," Wayne said, smiling, as he helped his father up the front ramp. "Looks like you're stuck with us. Julie'll show you your room and the bed we put in with a pull-up bar attached."

"I'm an investigator, for goodness sake. I can find my room on my own," Will said. "Look, I appreciate all you've done, but I don't want to be waited on hand and foot. You two do what you need to do. Forget I'm here."

As if to show that he was in complete control, Will rolled down the hallway by himself, peering into the neatly decorated rooms until he found the one that was his. He gave his son a huge thumbs-up, like an astronaut preparing to blast off into orbit. Then with one strong push of the wheels, he propelled himself inside.

Wayne smiled and shook his head. He was happy to have his dad there. Even more important, he felt that he'd be safe in this small town, where it would be hard for anyone to try to hurt him again. But criminals, like rats, could squeeze into the tightest places in the smallest communities—outreaching even the long arm of the law.

———

The next morning, Julie summoned father and son to the porch, where they could enjoy a nice breakfast under the whirling paddles of an old ceiling fan and Wayne could enlighten his dad on his plans to run for legislature, thus making Will lose his appetite entirely. At least that's what Wayne was envisioning.

What'll really happen will probably be a lot worse, he thought.

"Hey, honey?" Wayne asked Julie as she was setting the table. "Do you think I could outrun a man in a wheelchair?"

Julie rolled her eyes and gave her husband a slight smile as if he was being silly. But she quickly disappeared as soon as Will showed up.

"Good morning, Pop," she said cheerfully, kissing the top of his head and walking past him to the kitchen.

"Morning, Julie," he said, looking at her a little curiously.

It had begun to cool off slightly by this time of year, and Will noticed how much quieter it was in Oxford, void of all the traffic and police sirens that usually wailed in his hometown of Jackson.

It was a good setting to break the news, Wayne figured. He poured some steaming coffee into his father's mug then blurted out, "Dad, I wanted to tell you something… I'm going to run for state legislature."

"What?" Will said, nearly spitting out his coffee and jumping out of his wheelchair at the same time. "Are you nuts? With all your talent, you want to be a worthless lawmaker?"

"No, Dad, I want to be a good public servant…and I think I can change your view of the profession," Wayne said with the utmost assurance he could muster.

"Good luck," Will said, laughing in disbelief. "What makes you think you can win a seat anyway? You're just a transplant here in Oxford, barely out of law school."

"I know, but there are extenuating circumstances. The man who held the seat died in an accident. At first, I couldn't understand why no one was interested in the office...I mean, I have only one opponent running. But one of the senior lawyers at my firm explained that no well-established attorney would give up three months of practice to go to Jackson every January for just $30,000 a year and listen to all his constituents complain and all his colleagues argue."

Will laughed. "Finally, a lawyer who speaks sense. Couldn't he talk you out of it?"

"Well, law firms like mine want some influence in the legislature. They can gain that by sponsoring a young, inexperienced candidate with a clean, respectable background," Wayne argued convincingly.

In other words, a patsy, his father thought, keeping his mouth shut.

Despite his inexperience, Wayne would make an attractive candidate, which is just what his father feared. Good-looking, articulate, and earnest to a fault—with religious convictions that would appeal to a wide voter base in Mississippi—he'd also be an ideal frontman for any organization looking to further its cause.

That's not to say that Wayne really was perfect. Like anyone, he had his faults. Though he did excel in his undergrad criminal justice program, he wasn't the best law student. He drank occasionally, took prescription medication for depression and almost ended his short marriage to Julie due to a one-night stand with a blonde—an old high school sweetheart whom he had not seen in five years. He managed to keep that indiscretion from his dad but it had been a painful revelation to Julie; her family, of course, found out about it when she moved back in with them for a few weeks before deciding on a reconciliation. Wayne had begged for—and received—forgiveness from his wife and her parents. But he still hadn't managed to forgive himself.

That, in part, was also a driving force for his seeking office. He wanted to prove—to his wife, her family, his father, himself, and to everyone else in the state—that he was an honest man. Someone they could look up to and trust. It was a public penance for a private mistake.

"Listen, Dad, this is my chance to represent the people and to vote according to their will," Wayne continued pleading his case. "I thought if anybody would understand and respect that, it'd be you."

Will had been around too long and knew the system too intimately to still believe in it, but he tried not to burst his son's bubble.

Wayne had had a hard time dealing with his mother's death; he had slipped in and out of depression and had seemed so lost. His father was hoping that he'd find himself once more. *Preferably in the FBI, fighting organized crime. But if he found himself in the legislature, well...that would have to do. For now, anyway.*

Wayne was getting excited. His father hadn't protested half as much as he had expected him to. Actually, he seemed to be taking it quite well. "I'm still going to continue my job at the law firm," Wayne said, as if that would cheer Will up in any way. "And, of course, I'll be around to look after you as much as possible. If I win, Julie said she'd take care of you during the legislative sessions in Jackson..."

"Wayne, I don't want to discourage you from whatever it is you want to do, but I also don't want you to face the same frustrations I have over the years. I know your intentions are good—and respectable—but I don't know if they're *realistic*. You may be voting according to the people's will, but the guy next to you will be voting for the dollar bill...and the guy next to him and the guy next to him. I'm not sure what your motivations are."

"Can't you understand that *you're* my motivation?" Wayne said. "I want to make a difference, Dad...like you."

Will swallowed hard. He moved closer to his son and put a hand on his shoulder, facing him eye to eye. "Wayne, I am proud of you—and I know you'll always do the right thing. Just watch out for those other sorry bastards. They'd sell their own mothers for a quarter."

From that point on, Will thought it best to let his son be his own man. He had given him the best advice a father could give; now, it was time to back out of Wayne's plans and concentrate instead on assisting investigators in solving his own attempted murder.

"Why waste my time on politics when there's good, honest police work to be done?" he told himself.

Thinking back to what he had been working on shortly before the shooting—several investigations into the gaming industry—he tried to piece two and two together. He'd try tying together the people that he was investigating to see if a pattern emerged or if a covert conspiracy began to reveal itself—anything that could make sense of why he'd been shot. He even made a call to Investigator Long, asking him to stop by on occasion and discuss the details of the case with him.

So far, nothing fit.

But Will was tenacious. With his laptop computer sitting atop his legs, he rolled around the house, from his bedroom to the dining room to the porch, making association charts and recording notes.

"It's my new way of pacing," he told Julie.

She and Wayne were just happy to see him keeping occupied. He seemed to have a newfound sense of purpose and regain some of his old vigor. Shades of his former self began to emerge...even if no answers did.

Chapter 4

Questions of the Heart

"A mind troubled by doubt cannot focus on the course to victory."
—Arthur Golden

October was already nearing, and the legislative election would be held in early November. Several members of the legislature had recently contacted Wayne, assuring him that he would win the seat. Some were so enthusiastic about having him on their team for the first session in January that they were ready to discuss with him upcoming bills they planned to submit and to lobby on his behalf to make sure he'd be put on a couple of important committees.

Wayne, on his part, wasn't sure who to trust.

I haven't even been elected yet and they're already trying to sway me, he thought. *I see what Dad meant. Still, no one's gone so far as to offer to sell me his mother yet, so I guess it's all good.*

Wayne wanted to spend his time stumping and meeting qualified voters in the Oxford area. Instead, he kept getting invitations to Jackson to be wined and dined.

One such offer took him to the Capitol building, where the halls were almost eerily quiet except for the echoes of shoe heels striking the highly polished floors. His meeting was with a couple of legislators, George Quarles and Raymond Wolcott, from the surrounding Jackson area.

Quarles and Wolcott were so similar that they were almost twins. Both graduated from the same law school class at Mississippi College less than ten years ago, and had their own small, struggling law firms in the Jackson area. Quarles mostly handled divorces while Wolcott specialized in bankruptcy and personal injury car wreck cases.

The two men were in their early thirties; Wolcott was five-foot-ten with a medium build and regular features, while Quarles was slightly shorter, skinnier and sharper. Both were clean-shaven with expensive haircuts and clothes that made them look like wannabe male models. Wolcott liked women a little more, and Quarles liked mixed drinks a little more. Other than that, they were cut from the same cloth.

When Wayne met the two in Quarles' richly decorated office in the Capitol, they in turn were being courted by other flashy, cigar-smoking figures that quickly identified themselves by first names only and had little to say about their occupations or intentions.

"Wayne," Quarles said, "these are some of the most important men you'll ever meet."

"That's right," Wolcott boasted. "And they'll do anything for you…anything. Just name it."

"Well, thanks," Wayne stammered, looking around the room at all the anonymous faces. No one seemed too keen on making eye contact.

Quarles and Wolcott both seemed like sleazy used car salesmen themselves, and Wayne was quickly beginning to feel uncomfortable in their presence.

What have I gotten myself into? he wondered, seriously wanting to leave.

"Listen, Wayne, why don't you let us all take you to dinner?

We'll have some drinks, some laughs, maybe talk a little business. What do you say?" Quarles offered.

What kind of business? Wayne wanted to ask.

Something told him that the other guys weren't members of the legislature. First of all, they didn't introduce themselves as senators or representatives, the way Quarles and Wolcott had. And, second, the Rolex watches, large-cluster diamond rings and expensive suits they wore definitely weren't bought on a legislator's salary. These guys had big money behind them.

"Thanks for the kind offer, but I've got to be getting back home. I'll be in touch with you after the election—hopefully," Wayne said, looking at his watch. He realized that he should have already left by then, before he got too aligned with people he didn't know.

Now I know what a beautiful woman must feel like, he thought, as soon as he raced back into his car. *They barely tell me their names, want to take me to dinner then think that I'll just get in bed with them.*

"Well, I'm not that easy," he said out loud as he turned on the ignition.

As Wayne started the nearly three-hour drive back home, heading up Interstate 55 towards Batesville, his thoughts were still on the men he had met. He really did want to know more about those who were courting him—and *why* they were so interested.

First things first, he thought, trying not to get too far ahead of himself. *Go back to Oxford and campaign.*

Just then, his thoughts were interrupted by a call on his cell. It was his father-in-law, Glen Bryant, a retired judge—but still a very busy man. He'd made millions in the stock market by selling out his World Com stock before the company's demise, and he continued to constantly, and obsessively, check stock options. He was also head of the local Republican Party. The legislative position Wayne was seeking had long been held by Republicans—and his father-in-law's assistance would almost assure him the seat. He was an ace in the hole that Wayne hadn't wanted to use.

It was unusual for Glen to be calling Wayne's cell phone—or to be calling to talk to him at all, for that matter—and it made Wayne nervous.

"What's up, Glen? Is Julie okay? Is she with my dad? He's all right, isn't he?" Wayne blurted out.

"Relax. Julie's fine and so is your father," Glen said. "I just talked to her and she told me you went to Jackson to meet with some politicians… I wanted to talk to you before you got in too deep."

"You sound like my dad now," Wayne responded, although he knew Mr. Bryant wouldn't exactly take that as a compliment.

"Listen, Wayne, I expect to get a table by six o'clock for dinner at Taylor's Grocery. As you know, it's now a restaurant visited by prominent people and will be a good place to get you some exposure…"

"I really appreciate that, Glen, but I'm already on my way home."

"So stop here first. It really isn't that difficult," Glen said, getting exasperated.

Wayne checked his watch. It was already past five—plus he really just wanted to get home to his family. He'd had enough of introductions and political wooing for one day. "I'm not sure I can make it on time—and I don't want to get a speeding ticket on I-55. Can't be breaking the law this close to an election," he laughed.

"Don't worry about that, Wayne," Glen explained. "State troopers don't touch members of the legislature. Who do you think gives them the things they need?"

"Technically, I haven't been elected yet," Wayne said. He was getting tired of having to remind people of that.

"That's just a matter of time. If they stop you, tell them you're the newest member of the legislature and you haven't gotten your car tag or window sticker yet. They won't mess with you. And if they do, give me the ticket and I'll call the commissioner. Just get on over here." Glen hung up.

Wayne knew he didn't have a way out of it now. So he floored his trusty old Geo Prism, with almost 200,000 miles on it, and really began to pick up speed. He topped a hill and—*Wouldn't you know it?*—saw a state trooper headed south, the opposite way Wayne was traveling.

As he hit his brakes, he noticed that the long antenna on the back of the patrol car was practically bent over, pointing backwards toward Memphis. That kind of wind power would require a speed of over one hundred miles per hour, which was pretty routine for troopers headed to Jackson for ass-chewings at headquarters, coffee and doughnuts, and other such "emergencies."

I'm convinced they're the biggest speeders in the state, but they act as if the average citizen had committed a deadly sin by driving twelve miles over the speed limit, Wayne thought, shaking his head and glancing at the disappearing patrol car in his rearview mirror, hoping the trooper wouldn't turn around. *Is that a legislative issue I can tackle?*

Even he was beginning to look past the election now, as if it had already been locked up.

Fortunately for Wayne, the trooper passed without turning around and he was again able to punch it in a car that might run ninety miles per hour downhill with a tail wind.

At exactly six, Wayne was just turning on to old County Road 338 a few miles south of Oxford. He knew the restaurant would be packed with its usual hour wait and, although he'd almost make it on time, he didn't like to arrive anywhere even a minute late. He'd rather live by Coach Vince Lombardi's rule that had his players set their watches fifteen minutes back. When it said ten o'clock on their wrist, it would really only be 9:45. If any player showed up less than fifteen minutes early to a practice, the coach would already consider them late.

Wayne was not looking forward to this dinner at all. He parked his car, took a deep breath and headed into the restaurant, an old grocery store that had been converted into *the* place to go for catfish or anything else on their wonderful menu. Wayne usually loved it. It was a unique building made well over a hundred years ago of brick, wood and tin, and had an old general store front complete with gas pumps still in place. The wooden porch with a church pew and bench made of stumps and planks was a great place to sit and talk about politics or ball games while waiting for a table, and there was a visitor registry that almost everyone signed upon entry, which read like a who's who of Southern society. Guests could even sign the walls, as many famous people have.

Wayne walked past the guest registry, disregarding it altogether, and looked through the crowd, spotting his father-in-law's full head of curly, dark brown hair, which conveniently rose above all the others. At six-foot-three, the man was hard to miss. Glen wasn't waiting alone, though. He was hardly ever alone.

Judge Bryant knew everybody in the local area—and when he traveled and met someone he didn't know, he played a game that Julie and Wayne called "Name that Neighbor." He'd keep mentioning names until he hit upon someone who that person knew. Then they'd have a mutual acquaintance—and a basis for conversation.

Walking up to the bar, Wayne shook hands with his father-in-law, ready to apologize for his ten-minute tardiness. Glen didn't give him a chance to.

"Wayne, I'd like you to meet your campaign manager, Danny Magee. Danny will handle everything from here on out. I met with the senior partners at your law firm, and we all agreed that this is what you need," Glen said without reservation.

Danny was a well-dressed, well-groomed, middle-aged man wearing a Rolex watch, a heavily starched shirt with gold cuff links, and shoes polished to a high gloss. He had the look of a successful politician himself, and could have even passed for a televangelist or the CEO of a large corporation.

"Thank you very much, Glen, and you, too, Danny, but I can't afford a campaign manager," Wayne said.

"You can't afford *not* to have a campaign manager," Danny interjected. "Besides, you don't have to pay me anything. That's already taken care of."

"By whom?" Wayne asked.

"Don't you worry about that," Glen said. "It's all taken care of."

The conversation was interrupted on several occasions by well-known businessmen and politicians who walked by and shook hands with Glen, who in turn made sure they knew who Wayne was.

"Wow, this is overwhelming. I don't know what to say," Wayne responded.

"Just say okay and leave the rest to me," Danny replied with the utmost confidence.

Wayne's salary as a junior lawyer wasn't exactly what he wanted it to be, and he still had plenty of student loans to pay. For any kind of campaign that went beyond ringing doorbells, shaking hands and kissing babies, he knew he'd need financial help. He also knew he'd never bring himself to ask his father-in-law for it. Not after what he put Julie and her family through. But Glen just *giving* it to him like that, no questions asked? That was something else entirely. That was a vote of confidence.

When the three men took a seat at the table, Glen spoke up. "Wayne, this election should be a piece of cake. But I insist you follow everything Danny tells you to do. He's a pro...he knows what he's doing, even if you don't. Now, no offense, I know your heart's in the right place. But your opponent's got a lot more experience and isn't afraid to get down and dirty...and you're a part of my family. I can't have you looking like a fool."

Wayne was almost touched. That was the closest to straight-out sentimental that Glen was going to get.

The following Monday morning, Wayne contacted Danny, as per his father-in-law's instructions.

"Wayne, I worked all weekend on upcoming events. Your campaign already has a cash pot," Danny said proudly, "and it'll get even bigger. I contacted Thurman Stroud, a catfish farmer from Tunica, and he's donating over a thousand pounds of catfish for a get-together in your honor this Sunday afternoon at the Rocky Road Baptist Church. Your pastor said all the church wives would bring the fixings and he'd announce the feast at church on Sunday morning. I've already notified the Rotary Club and the Chamber of Commerce, and many members of both will be there."

"You work fast," Wayne said. "I already read about it in the morning paper."

"Oh, yeah," Danny laughed. "I forgot to mention that I contacted the media, too. Hope you like catfish."

"As long as I don't have to kiss them," Wayne joked.

That Sunday, everyone gathered after church for dinner at the Blue Creek Cabin Bed and Breakfast, a fifty-acre estate featuring a square log cabin from the 1800s. Situated in lush green fields with majestic trees all around, it was a perfect setting to reach the old-time religious crowd gathered for a fried catfish dinner. Festivities were opened on the porch with the sound of banjo music and gospel songs from Jason Boone's Bluegrass Band, a local favorite. A few old grandpas stomped their feet while their wives of fifty years or more, clothed in long dresses and supported by walking canes, raised their hands toward the heavens praising God and screaming, "Hallelujah!"

It was a big turnout. People grabbed their plates and quickly filled the rocking chairs, porch swings and old church pews that were set up along the wooden wraparound porch. The porch was covered with tin and supported by rustic old trees, which were finished only by trimming away the bark and standing them up in seven-foot lengths.

Others sat on the rough plank porch in front of walls covered with RC Cola and orange drink signs, their legs dangling off to kick at the ground and occasionally disturb an earthworm. A few times, a red wasp swarmed around, but kept its distance high above the visitors. That porch would become a stage for speakers before the day was done—with well-known locals endorsing Wayne and the candidate himself presenting a grand finale speech—but for now, it felt like a small-town church social.

An old stump was placed in front of the home to give the party the feel of authentic, old-time stump campaigning. Homemade patchwork quilts littered the grassy grounds and were held down from the casual southern breezes by young and old alike. Great care was taken not to place them over red ant hills, but none were found on this gorgeous landscape.

As the catfish disappeared from the large plastic ice coolers and made their way into the pots, Danny had a young man rinse the coolers out with an old hand pump from a well that was still in use. He then turned the coolers into collection boxes for donated cash—the kind that wasn't traceable on campaign finance reports.

Wayne had never seen so much money in his life. The coolers were stuffed to the brim.

"It was a good idea to hold this after church, Danny, while folks are still in the right frame of mind to pass the collection plate," Wayne said.

"There's more to it than that. This establishes you as the candidate of the church—Christ's representative in the legislature," Danny smiled shrewdly.

"But that money's going to my campaign. It's got nothing to do with the church," Wayne said.

"No harm in letting those two images link up in people's minds, now is there?"

After the success of the catfish fry, Danny set up all types of meetings with important people and constantly briefed Wayne on the
major issues that local voters were concerned about, which he
found out through extensive polls.

"This isn't like a general election where potential candidates
have months, if not years, to prepare," Danny stated to Wayne. "And
that works in our favor. It's a special election that caught people off-
guard. Had there been more time to think, there would've surely
been more candidates. As it is, you can just touch on some of the
major issues that people want to hear about, but you don't have to
get bogged down in debates about solutions or long-winded political explanations. You have plenty of time for that once you get
elected. For now, all we have to do is brand you quickly, get your
name out there and keep your image squeaky clean for the next
few weeks."

"Shouldn't be too hard," Wayne said. "I'm living like a Boy Scout
these days."

"Glad to hear it," Danny smiled. "Makes my job that much easier. Just don't get caught out of uniform until *after* the election."

As the weeks passed, Wayne became extremely caught up with the
campaign and felt bad about spending less time with his dad, who
was recovering slowly and starting to show signs of slipping into
a deep depression. His investigation into the shooting had stalled
and he was forced to sit on the sidelines while his son posed and
preened for a job in politics, which he still saw as pointless.

Julie was doing the best she could to keep her father-in-law
occupied, but he was a fiercely independent man now forced to
rely on other people to get around. He wouldn't dare say anything

to Wayne about being away from home too much or his busy pursuit of the office, but he could plainly see that the pressure of taking care of him alone was beginning to take its toll on Julie.

Will also felt like he was starting to lose his dignity, sitting there in his boxers while his daughter-in-law helped him put on his pants, and sometimes urinating on himself when he couldn't make it to the bathroom in time—with only his son's young bride to take care of him.

This is no way to live, Will would often think. But he knew he had to stay strong, especially with everyone else under so much stress.

In one of Wayne's rare moments of relaxation, he sat on the porch of his turn-of-the-century rental house, next to the welcome mat, and read Jackson's *Clarion Ledger* newspaper while he swatted away mosquitoes still lingering from the summer. It was evening, but the sky was still light enough to read by.

As he turned the page, a young man with a pen in one hand and a notebook in the other walked cautiously up the steps beside the wheelchair ramp.

The face looked familiar, but by then, Wayne had seen so many new faces at campaign parties, speaking engagements, civic meetings and churches that *everyone* looked familiar.

"Hi, I'm Jerry Gilliland from the *Oxford Eagle*. I see you're not reading our paper, but the *Clarion Ledger*'s not so bad, either. Can I have a seat?"

"You're not here to sell me a paper subscription, are you?" Wayne asked warily.

"No."

"Then by all means, have a seat," Wayne said, quickly offering him a cane-bottom chair, wobbly and blemished from many years of use.

Wayne sat down in a similar chair next to an old whisky barrel that was cut in half, with a homemade checkerboard covering its open top. Nailed to the wall above the checkerboard was a rusted and bent Coca-Cola sign, complete with a mercury thermometer in the middle.

It was pretty much an ideal country setting, except for the rotted boards at the end of the porch that showed through the gray deck paint, which Jerry was currently staring at. The young man looked cordial, but hesitant.

"I guess you didn't come here to play checkers," Wayne said. "What's on your mind?"

Jerry looked at Wayne, straight into his eyes. "I just wanted to ask you some questions about an alleged fling you had with a former high school classmate after your marriage."

Wayne was devastated. He stared at Jerry's seemingly innocent face for a few seconds in disbelief, unable to speak. Then he rose to his feet. "Where did you get that information?" he demanded.

"The public has a right to know," Jerry shrugged. "So is it true? Do you confirm that you had an affair?"

"Get out, please…just leave!" Wayne backed toward the screen door, hoping his father was not on the other side, overhearing their conversation. In a softer voice, he added, "If you hold off printing anything, I'll contact you soon with the answers you want."

Wayne stepped inside the house, with the front screen door slamming after him. He raced down the hall, stepped inside the bathroom and quickly closed the door. He steadied himself by holding on to the sink. At first he was finding it hard to breathe; then he began gagging uncontrollably. Finally, he vomited.

Staring hard into the mirror at his red face and flushed cheeks covered in tears, Wayne gritted his teeth then cupped some water and rinsed his mouth, washing away the remnants of his dinner.

Even before this bombshell had dropped, Wayne had begun to think that it just wasn't worth continuing his run for office. He had tried to pretend that his dad was adjusting and that Julie was doing just fine without him, but after a full day of meeting new people and looking strangers in the eye, he found it harder to come home and look his loved ones in the face.

My family is more important to me than any public position, he thought. *I'm not going to lose my father's respect, possibly lose my wife or put her through that hell again. Not for some job. Not for the world.*

Wayne opened the door slightly and checked outside the bathroom for any signs of Julie or Will. When he saw that the hallway was empty, he grabbed his cell phone, went straight back outside to the porch and called Julie's father to explain what had happened.

"That's it, Glen," he said after finishing his story. "I'm dropping out of the race."

"Wayne, I understand your feelings," Glen said calmly, when his turn to speak finally came, "but you need to hang in there. We've invested too much in this. Too much time. Too much of the public's money and trust." He knew exactly the right buttons to push with Wayne. "Now, I know the editor of the paper personally, and I'll talk to him just as soon as his office opens tomorrow."

"I can't take any chances," Wayne said desperately. "My father's too sick to handle this and the last thing I want is for Julie to have to relive that nightmare. You've got to make sure…"

"I *will* make sure," Glen insisted. "Wayne, listen to me…she's my daughter. I don't want anything to hurt her. I'll make this go away. I also understand that part of the problem is you're worried about Julie having to look after your dad in your absence. I'll take care of that, too. We'll hire a male healthcare assistant to stay with Will during the day."

"My dad would never allow it," Wayne said flatly. "He doesn't even want family to see him like this."

"Okay," Glen said, "Fine. We'll think of something else. Just don't make any rash decisions before I talk to you. Trust me…I'll handle everything."

"All right," Wayne said with a deep sigh. "I hope so."

He hung up, went inside and walked back to the bathroom. This time, he was too disgusted with himself to even look in the mirror. He opened the medicine cabinet, took two strong sleeping pills, swallowed them and went to bed.

At 8:25 the next morning, after almost ten hours of drug-induced sleep, Wayne was awoken from his bad dreams by a call from Danny, who was obviously upset after speaking to Glen.

"What do you mean you're considering withdrawing from the race?" Danny practically screamed into the phone.

"It's not worth it, Danny…" Wayne said, sounding very much like he had just woken up.

"Tell that to all the churchgoers who thought it *was* worth it to invest their savings into your campaign!" he shouted.

"I know, but…" Wayne tried weakly to argue. "No, you don't know! Your opponent is lagging far behind. Even with a small bump in the road like this, we could make it. If Glen can't keep the story out of the papers, all you have to do is keep denying it. They won't be able to prove anything before the election. Either way, it can't hurt us that much."

"Danny, I don't care if it hurts *my* chances at winning, all right? What I don't want it hurting is my family," Wayne said heatedly.

Just then, his call waiting beeped. When he switched over, he heard Glen's distraught voice on the other end. "Wayne, I just spoke to the editor, and I think you'd better brace yourself. He wouldn't negotiate with me or discuss the issue any further. He's a good man who runs a decent paper, and his position is that he has an obligation to the readers and to the voters. The best you can do is talk to the reporter and try to do some damage control before he digs up anything further."

Wayne was almost stunned. "Damage control?"

"Say you were distraught over your mother's death and taking medication. That you turned to this woman for comfort but didn't have a physical relationship with her," Glen suggested.

"You mean 'spin'? Make excuses? Everything I said I'd never do? Lie…like every other worthless politician!" Wayne shouted. They were his dad's words coming back to haunt him.

Wayne hung up, shut off the ringer on his phone and sat on the corner of his bed, staring down at the floor. He knew Glen was right. He'd have to face that reporter. Even if he dropped out now, they'd still print the story. He could see the headlines now: "Lott Backs out of Race Over Alleged Affair."

If he didn't defend himself, they'd make it sound so much worse than it really was. His family name—his *father's* name—would be dragged through the dirt.

If only I didn't make that stupid mistake, he thought, slamming his fist down hard on the nightstand. He'd later learn that he cracked a bone in the center of his hand that needed steel pins. But now, he was in no mood to see a doctor. A doctor couldn't heal what was really ailing him. And he was certainly in no frame of mind to talk to reporters.

Wayne quickly got dressed, snuck into his father's room and took a couple of Will's prescription pills, hoping they'd relieve the pain in his hand and his heart. By then, he was feeling very hopeless and depressed. The last thing he could do was face his father and his wife over the breakfast table, where he was certain they'd be sitting now, waiting for him.

As he walked out of his house and jumped into the car, he was sure he heard Julie's voice calling to him. "Wayne, where are you go…"

He slammed the car door without looking back, started the engine and lit off.

Although he rarely ever drank recently, especially at this time of day, he needed something else to help him deal with the anxiety.

Just as he was about to stop in a local watering hole—one that he knew would already be open—he thought, *What if someone I know sees me going in there this early in the day?*

Bitterly, he laughed at himself and said out loud, "Huh…I guess there's more of a politician in me than I care to admit."

He spun out of the parking lot and drove towards Sardis Lake, a popular recreational reservoir a few miles out of town that would have few visitors with the fall temperatures approaching. There was little chance he'd see anyone he knew. *Maybe there'll be no one at all*, he hoped.

As he drove, he turned up the volume on the CD player, blasting "Stairway to Heaven," one of his father's favorite songs. When the song speeded up in the end, so did Wayne—showing little regard for his own safety or the safety of others on the road.

When the song was over, Wayne hit the repeat button a couple more times. Driving faster and further, he finally stopped at a local country store, bought a six-pack of beer and began to swig them down in the parking lot.

As he drove towards Sardis Dam, he changed the song selection to "Free Bird" and began driving even faster. He was letting the tempo of the songs that he and his dad loved so much control his mood.

After arriving with only one can of beer left, Wayne parked his car below the spillway and walked up the edge to the highest point he could reach. He looked down at the cool spray, white foam and waves crashing on the large gray rocks just below the water's edge—and thought about ending it all.

He stared for a few minutes longer, as if mesmerized, and contemplated jumping into the rushing water littered with jagged rocks. He thought about what would happen to his body as he crashed into them—what it would feel like, how it would end. *With my luck, I'll be severely injured but not killed…and I'd only add to Julie and Dad's problems.*

Wayne tore himself away from the river and made his way, unsteadily, back to the car. He opened the passenger side door and took a seat in front of the glove compartment, where he kept the old pistol that his dad had given him after retiring as a cop. He had insisted that Wayne always have it with him "in case of emergency."

"Well, Dad, I'd say this is an emergency," Wayne said out loud, staring intently at the glove compartment in front of him. "I either take my own life or have it taken away from me by someone else."

He knew that if he placed a shot directly in the center of his head, he wouldn't become paralyzed or disabled, nor would he be haunted by his past any longer. He visualized exactly how he would do it. It would all be so simple—then it would all be over.

The biggest dilemma he faced was who would look after his father. He knew his dad was strong, and handicapped but not helpless. He was also just as concerned with Julie's welfare but figured she'd be better off without him. Besides, he knew how much she loved Will.

The two of them can take care of each other, he rationalized, *just like they've been doing. Only I won't be around to make things worse.*

His desire to end it all had reached greater heights than his concern for what would happen after he was gone. Wayne reached out and pressed the button on the glove box then banged on the dashboard twice before it opened. He moved some papers out of the way then saw the gun just sitting there, exactly as he had pictured it.

He picked it up, opened the cylinder and found it to be fully loaded. The pistol was cold and heavy in his hands.

He laid it aside on the seat and got out a pen and a piece of paper from the glove box. First, he began to write a letter to his wife, but couldn't finish it. Then he started a note to his father but couldn't even get past the first word ("Dad—"). He put that paper aside also and began to write an explanation to the newspaper reporter, begging him with a dying request not to reveal the story that would be so damaging to those he loved.

Wayne finished that letter and picked up the note he had begun to his wife. As he reread the few short sentences, tears fell from his cheeks and blotted the ink.

I can't do anything right, he thought, looking at the ruined words. *But this…this I'm gonna do. It's the only way. God, please forgive me. Dad, I hope you forgive me, too.*

Desperate, he picked up the gun and placed it in his mouth. The metal felt smooth and tasted acrid. He squeezed his eyes shut but didn't shoot.

He took a few sobbing breaths then suddenly removed the pistol from his mouth and held it hard against his temple. As he began to pull the trigger and cry louder and louder, he heard a buzz.

It was his cell phone, set on vibrate. Wayne picked it up and saw that he had missed several calls due to the loud music. He recognized from the number that it was his father-in-law who was trying to reach him now, but he couldn't bear answering it or talking to anyone.

He laid the phone back on the seat, leaned hard against the headrest and again placed the gun against his temple. Just as he began to squeeze the trigger, he heard the familiar voice mail tone.

Willing to listen to Glen, but not to talk, he placed the gun down and played the message.

"Wayne," the recording said, "you're not going to believe this: Your opponent has dropped out! He just notified the press! The editor called to tell me the good news and that, as far as he's concerned, there's no need to print the story about you now. He feels that regardless of your past indiscretion, you'd get the office by default, so smearing you to the public would serve no useful purpose since the people no longer have a choice." Glen sounded practically giddy.

Wayne threw the gun to the floor of the car and dropped his head against the dashboard, sobbing uncontrollably. When he was all cried out, he pushed the car door open, ran down to the river's edge and dropped to his knees, yelling, "Thank you! Thank you, God!"

He dipped his head into the water time after time like a man being baptized, then jumped up and ran toward his car, screaming with joy. He dumped the empty beer cans into the garbage bin next to his car and headed back to Oxford. The experience cleared his head of any effects from alcohol or prescription drugs—and he swore he'd never abuse either of them again in his life.

When Wayne arrived home, he found Glen, Danny, Julie and his dad celebrating in the living room.

"Where have you been?" Julie asked excitedly. She jumped up and ran over to her husband. "Daddy and Danny were looking everywhere for you. We tried your cell phone but you didn't answer."

Speechless, Wayne went from one person to the other, hugging them tightly, overcome with tears of joy. It was truly the first day of the rest of his life, as far as he was concerned.

Right then and there, surrounded by those he loved, Wayne determined that he would make a difference, make his dad proud and live a life of sincerity, honesty and integrity.

Little did he know that the profession he was about to embark upon was crowded with others who had sworn the exact same oath—at least in public—though few did one damn thing to uphold it.

Chapter 5

Meeting the Colleagues

*"Do not trust all men, but trust men of worth;
the former course is silly, the latter a mark of prudence."*
—Democritus

Wayne was welcomed into Jackson with open arms by the sights of the city itself.

The drive there had been pleasant, as he enjoyed the changing colors along Interstate 55 and gazed at the rolling hills of green, just starting to turn brown, as cattle grazed around large bales of hay. The sky was clear and sunny, and the traffic was light. His mind felt as clear as the beautiful day he observed outside the window of his faded red Prism. He couldn't wait to get started at work, though his agenda was rather light.

When he arrived in Jackson, he first drove past the so-called "new" Capitol, built in 1903, with the beautiful gold-plated eagle resting atop its dome. Ironically, many of its current residents should have felt right at home since it was built on the grounds of the old state penitentiary.

He glanced over at the attorney general's office across the street then made a pass around the back of the building, studying the secretary of state's office as he envisioned how elections were won, bills passed and laws interpreted. Then he drove by the governor's mansion, which was the second-oldest continuously occupied building of its kind in the United States.

If those walls could talk... he thought. *Well, they'd probably have to sign a disclaimer not to.*

Reaching Capitol Street and turning east, he looked directly at the old Capitol building, recalling pictures in history books that showed the majestic structure first with dirt roads— horses and drivers waiting outside—then later with Model-T Fords lining the streets in front.

As Wayne checked into a hotel near the coliseum, he imagined what it would look like under water, the way his dad had seen it when he was on call for emergency assistance during the Easter Flood of 1979.

It was a beautiful city—full of history and full of life—and he couldn't wait to be a part of its law-making body.

———

It was just before Thanksgiving, and Wayne was meeting with several members of his party at a condo that overlooked the Ross Barnett Reservoir in Madison County on the outskirts of the city.

It was a fairly large condo, but had no family pictures on the wall or any other personal décor. It almost looked like a model apartment, with new furniture, artificial plants, lots of mirrors and shiny surfaces. One of the bedroom doors was locked but the other room had the appearance of a small casino: Board games, dice, cases of new decks of cards, and boxes upon boxes of expensive cigars were all laid out.

A large, well-crafted wooden bar separated the living and dining rooms, with scores of stemmed glasses suspended from its top. There was also a large, handmade wine rack with bottles of expensive wine that Wayne had only read about.

The refrigerator was filled with all types of beer from Europe and Asia that Wayne had never seen before and the cabinets contained an enormous selection of chips, nuts and other snacks. It was apparent that nobody really lived there.

In fact, there seemed to be an air of secrecy surrounding the place. "Who owns this condo?" Wayne asked Quarles, one of the few faces he recognized there.

"Oh, it belongs to a couple of judges and a prosecutor," he said, before quickly changing the subject.

"You know, you could stay here any time you want," Wolcott added. "Whenever you're in Jackson. They let us use it, with just a few pre-arranged rules."

"Uh, thanks, but I don't really have a need for this kind of place," Wayne said. But it wasn't the last time he'd find himself there.

In early December, Wayne was summoned to the condo once again—this time to find the glass coffee table covered with draft legislation.

"What's my name doing at the top of this document?" he asked in complete surprise. The way it read indicated that he was the sponsor of the proposed bill—one that he had never seen before.

"Just trying to help out the new kid on the block," Quarles assured him.

"By using me to sponsor legislation that I haven't even drafted?" Wayne asked.

"Well, we knew you'd get around to it but you've got other priorities at home," Quarles started.

"Besides, this is a really good one. Anti-gambling legislation," Wolcott stepped in. "Representative Billy Ray Watson just left—he was the one who asked us to get you to sponsor it."

Though Wayne didn't know Watson personally, he knew of the man. Billy Ray was a powerful member of the Gaming Committee and a gambling proponent in the House. He wasn't quite the committee leader, but he was its public face—the magnetic personality that could rally people around him to support his cause.

"He knew that your constituents in Oxford, in your church and in your entire district don't condone gambling. Said with your religious background, and your father's long career in law enforcement, you'd be the best choice to sponsor the bill," Wolcott explained.

"But…why would a proponent of gambling want me to sponsor anti-gaming legislation?" Wayne asked, truly confused.

"Well, Billy Ray likes a fair fight. He knows that the last bill to try to prevent casinos from building in counties that didn't already have them failed to pass. This one, though, is the bill to end all bills. It wouldn't allow *any* more casinos—in counties that already have them or not—and it would preclude future attempts at any other forms of gambling or lotteries in the state, period. Maybe he figures you'd present your side accurately, and the public—as well as the legislators—could finally get both sides of the story in a balanced portrayal and put the matter to rest. May the better man win, and all that," Wolcott shrugged.

"Or maybe," Quarles interjected, "he figures the new guy would present the least challenge." He grinned. "I'm just playin' devil's advocate."

"Either way, though, it can't be bad for your career," Wolcott said.

———

Wayne drove home that day replaying the scenario in his head. He was pretty convinced that his colleagues were sincere in giving him a great opportunity to make a name for himself while gaining the respect of the constituents in his district and his church—and, most importantly, the respect of his dad. Still, he wanted to discuss the proposed bill with his father and several of his most trusted constituents.

"What do you make of it?" Wayne asked after he had gotten home and explained everything to his dad.

"Well," Will considered, "a bill like this could make you some enemies right off the bat—in the legislature and other low places. Just remember what I always told you: Keep your friends close, but your enemies closer."

"That's great, Dad, except I don't know who's who just yet."

Wayne's constituents, however, were much more enthusiastic. "Wayne, we don't want gambling in our district, and we're very pleased that you'd take on such a large organization as a freshman in the first session of your career. We're proud to have you representing us. We knew we made the right decision."

That was all Wayne needed to hear.

———

Wayne headed back to Jackson with renewed energy and purpose. He'd push for the bill with all his might, though it was co-authored by others in the House with rather shady backgrounds.

"If Billy Ray Watson thinks he can take me down so easily, let him try," Wayne announced. "I've got the will of the people on my side."

Remarkably early in the game, Wayne got appointments to several important committees and became surprisingly popular in his first session. He arrived with the proposed anti-gaming bill in his briefcase—to which he added some strongly worded points of his own—and had already been introduced to the people that could help him make it a reality.

In fact, in January, it was not surprising that Wayne's bill *almost* passed the House of Representatives—and although "almost" doesn't count for bookmakers or lawmakers, it was a resoundingly strong showing…and there would always be next year.

When confronted with news of the defeat, lobbyists from certain factions within the gaming industry could be seen around the rotunda with smirks on their faces. If it had passed, certainly anyone in their right mind in favor of gambling would have been angered by this bill—unlike Billy Ray Watson, who was laughing and socializing in the lobby.

When Wayne saw him in the hallway after the decision, he walked right over and shook his hand. "Mr. Watson, I want to thank you for giving me the chance to present my case on behalf of my constituents."

"Son, that's what democracy is all about," Billy Ray smirked.

It wasn't exactly the response Wayne was expecting. "Well, I hope I presented you with a challenge. I was told you like a fair fight with both sides represented: gaming and anti-gaming," he continued, undeterred.

"I like a fair fight, that's true," Billy Ray smiled. "Just as long as I win."

———

For a while, Wayne considered Watson's attitude. *He seemed pretty sure of winning either way,* he thought. *Like someone playing with a stacked deck.* Besides, he was starting to question if Billy Ray had even been at the condo, specifically asking for him to sponsor the bill, and decided to confront Quarles and Wolcott about it.

"Billy Ray's plan backfired," Quarles assured Wayne. "He didn't expect the vote to be so close and was pissed that you almost beat him."

"But that anti-gaming law wouldn't have done anything about people already in the business anyway. It would just keep more casinos out," Wayne argued.

"Look, Wayne, what do you want to do? Pass a bill tomorrow to blow up all existing casinos?" Wolcott asked. "You start by trying to outlaw any new gaming. Then, little by little, after your foot's already in the door, you can get some legislation passed on the old places. No Sundays, closed by midnight, stuff like that. That's the way it works. It's called progress."

What they said made sense and although saddened by the loss of his bill, Wayne was bolstered by the support he received from his colleagues. After feeling lost for so long, he felt he had finally found himself here, in the legislature—and that he had finally found his fight.

Both proponents and opponents of the anti-gaming bill held Wayne in high esteem afterwards, and he was beginning to be seen as the fair-haired boy among other legislators. He was suddenly showered with new responsibilities and recommended for trips not only outside the state but also outside the country as an ambassador for the great state of Mississippi.

Better yet, Wayne was seen as a hero at home, in his district and in his church for fighting "the good fight" to keep out any new gambling operations. Here he was, a freshman representative willing to take on the casinos (which most people associated with the likes of the Bogus Trio and their owners, who seemed to be above the law) and stand in the way of their potential to spread and develop through the community like a disease. It led everyone to believe that Wayne was the person to watch in the coming year—a superhero in the making and a rising star in the Capitol.

Best of all—to Wayne, at least—people were starting to see him as being just as threatening and fearless when it came to gambling and organized crime as his father had been.

Chapter 6

The Truth Starts
to Reveal Itself

*"All truths are easy to understand once they are
discovered; the point is to discover them."*
—Galileo Galilei

When Wayne returned to Oxford following the end of the legislative session, he was still flush with excitement over his near-triumph.

His father had become a good listener, eager to hear all the details of Wayne's job description and his attempts to pass the bill, but was offering little advice to his son as a member of the legislature. Will had his suspicions about what was going on—but was loathe to dampen Wayne's shining moment by sharing them.

I can't lead him to the answer, Will told himself. *He's got to see reality for himself.*

Will, on the other hand, wouldn't be surprised at any underhanded dealings among certain members of the legislature and lobbyists representing the Bogus Trio of "untouchable" casinos. He wouldn't tell his son—and he had no hard evidence yet—but he even suspected that someone in that circle could have been responsible for his attempted assassination.

I must have been getting close to something, he knew. *But what?*

Nothing had become any clearer since the shooting—and, as Will told Julie, "Without being able to do the proper legwork in this wheelchair, I might as well give up."

Shortly after, she took Wayne aside. "Honey, your dad seems to be getting down on himself again, and with all your new interest in anti-gaming laws, I thought maybe you could get him involved, you know? Talk to him about all his experiences. I'm sure it'd make him feel better, more useful."

"That's an excellent idea, Julie," he said, beaming at her.

"Who knows? With the Lott men working together, you may just get that anti-gambling law of yours passed next year." She smiled deviously and added, "I'd even be willing to bet on it!"

———

As time passed, Wayne drew his father into long conversations about his previous work and interest in organized crime. Wayne wasn't sure why his dad had never talked to him about it before, assuming that he'd just been too busy as the top law enforcement officer in the strike force. But he also liked to believe that by opening up, his father was taking a stronger interest in his legislative career.

One evening, as they were sitting around the table shelling and eating peanuts, Wayne asked Will for his theory of the state of gambling in Mississippi.

"You may want to take notes...and make a pot of coffee," Will said.

Wayne took his dad's advice and brewed a pot. Then he sat and listened attentively.

"Gambling in Mississippi today is a lot like it was in California in the late 1800s, when gamblers had been found to be associated with municipal political corruption and often backed a particular political faction for favor. At first, there were laws allowing the lynching of professional gamblers to take back control of the cities, but not surprisingly the legislature soon passed weaker laws that were difficult to enforce and had little effect on gambling. They only addressed specific games, so gamblers came up with new variants that didn't meet the letter of the law. That's how they got around it until after awhile, nothing could be enforced. Sound familiar, son?" Will asked, throwing up his hands in a gesture of futility.

"Yes," Wayne said. "We still have the same problem in Mississippi."

"That's right, particularly with bingo. That game had been outlawed by the turn of the century, but when churches and charities were hard-hit by the Depression, they had no way to raise funds except relying on people's donations…but people had no money to give. So Massachusetts passed a law decriminalizing bingo, I believe in 1931, and within twenty years it was legal in eleven states, but for charities and churches only."

"Oh, my," Wayne laughed. "My poor little gray-haired granny would've surely spent some time behind bars if it wasn't legal here."

"Don't you talk about my mama that way," Will said, trying to sound tough but smiling the whole time. "The number of states allowing bingo grew, and soon other types of gambling were legalized in the East, like horse racing—and along with legal gambling came illegal gambling and mobsters."

"And don't forget taxes," Wayne interjected.

"Exactly. The government had to get its share, so enforcement agents were funded to go after illegal gamblers since Uncle Sam wasn't getting any cut of their action. That paved the way for supposedly law-abiding businessmen to take over from mobsters. Once casino gambling became legit, Mississippi became the third biggest gambling state between casinos and bingo."

"So that's when our present-day problems started?" Wayne asked.

"Before then. I remember when machines resembling slot machines but with bingo-type games started cropping up in bingo halls—many were never tested by the gaming lab. The days of little old ladies with paper cards wouldn't exactly become a thing of the past, but bingo halls would be greatly enhanced for gambling."

"Why were they illegal?" Wayne asked, pouring himself and his father a cup of coffee.

"They weren't, as long as they were in the bingo halls for charitable purposes, and the state could get their cut off them. But that didn't stop you from walking into almost any convenience store, truck stop or restaurant in the Delta, or elsewhere in Mississippi for that matter, and finding slot-type machines, often referred to as 'cherries.' Machine owners would install them in the establishments and split the money with the storeowner," Will explained.

"Let me guess why those were illegal," Wayne said sarcastically. "The state didn't get any taxes off them."

"Good guess," Will responded. "I remember them as clear as day in the 1970s, and I'm sure they were around earlier than that, probably in a backroom or behind a curtain somewhere so as not to embarrass the good, law-abiding Baptists that dominated those areas."

Will paused so that he and his son could share a laugh.

"Any moron could tell that something was going on that shouldn't have been going on behind that door or behind those curtains, but since you couldn't see it, nobody really made an issue of it," Will continued. "I can't help but think that law enforcement officers, especially those elected to office, turned their heads for political gain or a piece of the pie. Because the state wasn't getting its cut, it started to raid some of those stores—and suddenly nobody claimed to own those 'cherries' or knew how they got there. One attorney general in Mississippi told his agents that the only way to find out who owned the machines was to take trucks, go out and round them up, and see who screamed the loudest."

Wayne smiled and shelled another peanut. "So when did gambling as we know it finally get legalized in Mississippi?" Wayne asked.

"In the early 1990s. The Gaming Commission was established

later for licensure, regulation and enforcement of laws. I think they kept going after some people and certain small establishments with illegal machines because they got no piece of the action tax-wise, but I don't believe the state really cared about what was happening on a large level," Will stated.

"Why do you say that?"

"If you read the early reports by the State Performance Evaluation and Expenditure Review Committee—PEER—they comment on how it seemed that the commission was catering to the gaming industry, breaking the law by doing things, or *not* doing things, that in some way favored the industry. Licenses were given to criminals; background investigations weren't done... This was a state agency telling the legislature that another agency had not only broken the law but kept on breaking it repeatedly. But the PEER Committee was seen as a tiger with no teeth, and instead of making changes in the gambling industry, the legislature carried out action to prevent similar findings in the future by limiting such investigations. Hell, there were only three reports done by PEER in almost fifteen years—and only one applied to bingo."

"Wow, I can see how you could get frustrated," Wayne said.

"'Frustrated' is not the word, son. I'm sickened by this. No owners, operators or senior managers of casinos ever get arrested by the Gaming Commission, but people who victimize casinos by theft or cheating will be arrested in a heartbeat. Usually casinos solve their own crimes and *hand them over* to the Gaming Commission, but in the bingo business, nobody at all ever gets arrested by gaming agents. For a couple of years, there were about two arrests per month on average...but then for seven years, nothing. Not *one* from the Gaming Commission, but less than two a year attributed to the local sheriffs and police. You can thank certain members of the legislature for that. To me, that's just catering to the industry," Will said, spitting out a peanut shell in disgust.

"So you think that has to do with organized crime?" Wayne asked.

"Well, let's just say there are people who claim to be running a legal business, but they're doing it for illegal profits. They surround themselves with politicians and law enforcement to avoid prosecution. Listen, Wayne, I don't believe all casinos or bingo halls are bad—or, for that matter, all politicians. But without proper enforcement of the law, little slaps on the hand with administrative sanctions and fines only worsen our problems with organized crime. Fines are just the cost of doing business for them, just like giving 'contributions' to lobbyists and campaigns."

Wayne looked down. He could see what his father was driving at. "Dad, is gaming the only issue you have with the legislature?"

"No. I just don't trust anything most of those members tell you. It always seems to me that they've got a hidden agenda. When bills are proposed, you need to look beyond the surface and see who really benefits from this legislation. Usually it's somebody who's got to get their cut."

"That's why we need some *new* legislation—to regulate industries and make sure everything's above board."

Will gave his son a small smile. Part of it was out of pity, because he knew what an easy target someone so naïve would make. But part of it was because he took so much after his mother.

"The legislature's *part* of the problem, son. These organizations have actually taken on the motives of organized crime entities by ensuring that they have protection from law enforcement and that there's a lack of stiff laws thanks to certain members of the legislature, who they have as business connections. Members of charity bingo organizations are often also members of the legislature, who are tight with lobbyists representing the casinos. The point, pure and simple, is that gaming is known for corruption and that corruption involves organized crime."

As Will pushed his wheelchair away from the table, ready to retire for the night, he couldn't resist giving his son one more thing to think about.

"Wayne," he said, "Maryland, Missouri, Alabama, Louisiana,

Minnesota, Florida, Virginia, Massachusetts, North Dakota, California, Colorado, and the District of Columbia, just to name a few, have made bingo arrests and seized slot-type machines from bingo halls. In almost every case, there were ties to corrupt public officials and members of organized crime. So you have to ask yourself: Why not in Mississippi?"

After his father went to sleep, Wayne still had a lot of his own questions to consider.

Sure, I had a lot of backers when I targeted the big casinos. But will my constituents and colleagues still stick with me if I go after bingo halls and charities?

It was a gamble Wayne wasn't sure he was ready for.

Chapter 7

The Lessons Begin

*"You learn more quickly under the guidance
of experienced teachers. You waste a lot of time going
down blind alleys if you have no one to lead you."*
—W. Somerset Maugham

The next day, bleary-eyed and exhausted from having spent a sleepless night, Wayne wasn't sure what to make of all the information he had been given—or what to do with it. But there was one thing he did know: He couldn't turn back now. He had to push further.

Wayne approached his father at the breakfast table and poured himself a large cup of black coffee. "Dad, there's so much more I need to learn."

Will tried to hide his smile, obviously pleased that his son had taken such an interest in his life's work.

"You're the most knowledgeable person I know about organized crime, gambling, thugs, corrupt politicians and all that," Wayne continued.

"Thank you, son. I'll take that as a compliment."

"It *is* a compliment, Dad. In fact, I was wondering something… Do you think you could make me your student and spend a couple of hours a week teaching me what I need to know, or at least which direction I should take?" he asked with utmost sincerity.

"Of course I will, but why?" Will said. "You're pursuing a career in law-making, not in fighting organized crime."

"Well, I hope I'm wrong, but I'm beginning to get the feeling that those two issues will come together pretty soon, and I want to know from the best."

"Alright, fair enough. Staring next week, class will convene each Monday at 7 p.m. sharp," Will said sternly. "I'll tell you what I know, and where you should focus."

"Great," Wayne said cheerfully. "And when will they end?"

"They'll end when I say so, son…when I say so."

———

Will began to put together lessons and pull books off the shelf with as much vigor and concentration as if he were recently hired to be a criminal justice professor at the local university. It was serious to him because he knew it could mean the difference between life and death for his son some day.

He was worried about Wayne having to spend so much time in Jackson, and he thought of one of his old sayings: "If you lie around with dogs, you are sure to get fleas." He wanted to make sure that his son was treated for all types of bugs and parasites before he met with that group again—and he figured information would provide the best protection.

The following Monday, Wayne reported to his father's room at precisely seven, as if attending a structured classroom setting. Julie was visiting her next-door neighbor, and all was quiet in the Lott house. Will switched on the lamp in his dimly lit bedroom so that Wayne could read the papers spread across the computer desk.

"The first thing we're going to start with is the FBI's definition of organized crime," Will said. "Pay particular attention to the words I highlighted. They're the most important."

Wayne picked up the Internet printout and read aloud: "Any group having some manner of a *formalized structure* and whose primary objective is to *obtain money through illegal activities.* Such groups maintain their position through the use of *actual or threatened violence*, corrupt public officials, *graft, or extortion*, and generally have a significant impact on the people in their locales, region, or the country as a whole." He looked at his father when he finished.

"There's another one from the U.S. Attorney General's Office. Read it, too," Will said as he quietly rolled his wheelchair back.

"Organized crime groups *seek out corrupt public officials* in executive, *law enforcement, and judicial roles* so that their activities can *avoid, or at least receive early warnings about,* investigation and prosecution."

"Not done yet, son. Keep reading." Will handed him yet another definition—this one written by the California Crime Commission in 1953.

"A technique of violence, intimidation and corruption which, *in default of effective law enforcement, can be successfully applied,* by those *sufficiently unscrupulous, to any business or industry which produces large profits.* The underlying motive...is always to *secure and hold a monopoly in some activity which will produce large profits.* Sometimes the basic business is illegal... *Sometimes the basic activity is legal* and is a racket only because of the *violence and corruption with which the business has become permeated.*"

Wayne put the papers down. "Okay, Dad, I get it. We're not talking about organized crime like John Dillinger, Baby Face Nelson or Bonnie and Clyde. I guess they were just gangsters."

"That's right, son," Will smiled. "It's not like the movies or the famous characters. Al Capone was probably the closest well-known example of someone involved in organized crime, using the definition we use today. But even the mob learned over time that killing wasn't necessarily the answer. That's why you see many of them in expensive business suits, associating with top governmental officials or serving as deacons in church, and appearing to be model citizens."

Wayne thought about the men he met at the condo.

Will continued, "They bought protection through crooked cops who were influenced by big money—especially when their departments paid them pennies for risking their lives. But the gaming industry isn't one that hides underground. It displays bright lights and a flashy appearance, calling attention to itself and claiming to be free of corruption, which, of course, *some* of it is. But remember one thing: Follow the money. Just follow the money."

"And how can I do that?" Wayne asked.

"Anyone can. Go to the legislative website and print out a list of people in the House committee that oversee gaming. Then go to the secretary of state website, find the last election's campaign finance reports and pay attention to any donations from casinos. Taking the contributions isn't illegal, but you have to use your own judgment to determine if you think the practice is worthy of new legislation. We'll discuss it next week."

"You mean you're giving me homework?" Wayne asked in amazement.

"That is exactly what I mean," Will said.

⁓

The next day, Wayne went to work at the law firm. Though he had gotten some requests from constituents, they had not bombarded him, which meant he had time to work on issues handed down to him by the senior partners.

The local mailman dropped off a handful of mail for Wayne then cheerfully walked from office to office inside the suite. Though no longer dressed in his summertime short pants, he was still wearing his "jungle safari" hat as though he were inside the Amazon rainforest instead of a temperature-controlled, bug-free building.

Wayne glanced at his mail and couldn't help noticing an advertisement for a seminar titled "Follow the Money" being sponsored by the Organized Crime Task Force in Memphis. Those expected to attend were mostly prosecutors, senior investigators and certified public accountants, but it was open to any interested professionals.

The seminar was only two weeks away and Wayne was concerned about the short notice, but he immediately got up and got the senior partners' approval to attend. The firm was being very lenient towards Wayne—taking into account his legislative schedule, meetings with constituents and the time he needed to take care of his dad. After all, having one of their employees elected to the legislature was certainly good for business, and they had even rewarded him for it with a small raise.

Things really seem to be coming together, Wayne thought.

As soon as Wayne returned home that evening, he couldn't wait to share the news with Will.

"Dad, check out this seminar I'm going to," he announced excitedly.

"Hey, I know a couple of these instructors," Will said, looking over the brochure. "This guy, Bill Barlow, is a retired IRS agent I used to work cases with, and this one, Lonnie Jackson, is a top-notch former prosecutor for the U.S. Attorney's Office. I worked narcotics with him before he became a lawyer. He's busted a number of high-level businessmen and attorneys for racketeering under the federal RICO act. In fact, I see some outstanding résumés here when it comes to prosecuting white-collar crime. I wish I were going with you."

"I promise to take good notes and tell you everything they say. It'll be like a…a classroom presentation," Wayne beamed.

The next day, Wayne spent most of the time in his office researching the assignments his dad had given him. Printing out the lists of committee members was quick, but the secretary of state campaign finance reports took awhile, with multiple reports filed throughout the year by each candidate for the office.

The task became even more laborious when he started to look through each individual's report. They were voluminous and sometimes hard to read on PDF files that had been generated from hand-written documents. The thought crossed his mind that they may have been purposely illegible.

It didn't take long, though, to find evidence of donations from casinos. Particularly generous were Mudbug Gold, Catfish Jack's and Bullfrog Bayou. He knew that mention of the Bogus Trio would come as no surprise to his father; in his mind, those were nothing but legal payoffs to buy influence directly from the legislature—not to mention the tens of thousands of dollars spent by industry lobbyists wining and dining the legislators. Will had called it "indirect influence peddling," and now Wayne was holding the records that seemed to prove it.

However, between appointments with clients and constituents calling to complain about the need for stiffer penalty on such crimes as stealing goats, it took Wayne days to compile his research on the nineteen members of the legislative Gaming Committee.

It was obvious from first glance that most of the members had received contributions for their campaigns directly from the casinos and their employees, or from their political action committees. Determined to draft legislation on campaign finance reform, Wayne thought, *If they want to make money off casinos, let them put a quarter in the slot like everyone else.*

<hr />

The next Monday rolled around and Wayne met with his dad right on time. Will was already waiting for him in his room, all set to begin class. He had his hand outstretched, ready to collect the homework assignment the second Wayne stepped through the doorway.

"Dad, I'm convinced I should introduce a bill on campaign finance reform," he blurted out, assuming that was the point of his father's assignment.

"Good luck," Will said doubtfully. "You may want to start with something smaller, like maybe term limits. How do you think some of your colleagues get so powerful? By being in the legislature so long! They get in high positions in strong committees and gain absolute power because of their long stints."

"I don't know, Dad. Sometimes I think if I spent a lifetime in the legislature I'd still only accomplish a fraction of what needs to get done."

"But you know what they say about absolute power, don't you, son? Whether you subscribe to the theory that power corrupts or the corrupt are attracted by power, it makes little difference. The two come together to make up the sad world we live in. Corrupt politicians are always on the news for hiding money, pursuing sexual favors, selling political positions, preying on people in bathroom stalls, taking bribes, lying, cheating, stealing, and using others for their own personal gain. Sadly, I'm not sure these are the minority. For every one caught, there are probably at least ten more who aren't. We're losing the battle and empowering those people by making them our leaders," Will stated heatedly. "Of course, that doesn't necessarily *mean* that corruption exists; it's just that the *propensity* and *opportunity* for corruption is there…"

"And that may be reason enough to consider new legislation," Wayne said, finishing his father's thought.

~~~

The next week, Wayne went to Memphis for the seminar on organized crime. During the first break, he couldn't wait to go up to the staff of instructors and introduce himself to the two men his father knew quite well.

"Mr. Barlow, Mr. Jackson, I'm Wayne Lott, Will's son," he said proudly.

"Old 'Bulldog Will'?" Jackson smiled broadly. "How's he getting along? I heard about…what happened."

"He's doing fine, sir. Better than could be expected, considering."

"Well, if I know Will," Barlow said, "he's having a hard time accepting his limitations…but I'm happy to see he's continuing the fight through his son."

For the rest of the day, Wayne sat in awe as he listened to the presentations, learned to draft conspiracy charts, got a copy of the federal racketeering act and participated in group projects, where they did indeed follow the money, just as his Dad had told him.

He learned about intelligence information that banks turned over on cash deposits of over ten thousand dollars on suspicious transaction reports, as well as a multitude of information from the El Paso Intelligence Center (EPIC), and left there just as excited as he was when he arrived. He couldn't wait for next month's seminar on money laundering.

Wayne returned home that Friday night and told his dad every little detail. He also showed him a picture on his cell phone camera of his father's two friends that he had met. "They must've been your old beer-drinking buddies, right?"

"What makes you say that?" Will responded, refusing to give a straight answer.

"They wanted me to stop at a bar near Eudora called The Hand-shake on my way home and sing karaoke with them and The Lynn and Willie Band. I thanked them for the offer but told them I had to get back."

"You made the right decision," Will laughed. "I've heard those two sing."

Wayne laughed, too. "Well, they may be lousy singers but those guys were great speakers. And, man, were they sharp. I think I learned almost as much about criminal law in that one week as I did in all of law school."

That's the difference between learning it in school or living it on the streets, Will thought. But he decided to keep that comment to himself.

Chapter 8

Records Tell the Story

"Get the facts, or the facts will get you.
And when you get them, get them right,
or they will get you wrong."
—Dr. Thomas Fuller

Over the next few weeks, Wayne continued his Monday night sessions with Will. He was inspired and re-energized by the seminar and much more willing to examine a broken system.

"Dad, I decided to take a look at the record of each member of the House and Senate to see how successful that person has been, based on the number of bills they presented compared to those that actually became law. In last year's session alone," Wayne continued, "gaming legislation was introduced that would protect the Gaming Commission, and one benefited bingo operators and employees with increased pay. Over the past fifteen years, things have been good for the gaming industry. Laws that favored gambling were often passed; those that limited the industry were overwhelmingly shot down, or what we call 'died in committee.'"

Will shook his head. The information wasn't new to him, but he was deeply satisfied to see that his son was starting to truly know his colleagues and what he'd be up against.

"It's not that unusual for legislation not to get passed, Wayne," Will said for the sake of argument.

"I know... Take that short, fat Billy Ray Watson from northern Mississippi. He's one of the members of the Gaming Committee, not a statesman. Hell, he's a used car dealer from the Delta, and his effectiveness at getting his proposed bills passed is probably less than one percent. The number of new bills he introduces each year is roughly seventy-five; on average, he gets about three approved," Wayne said.

"It's a double-edged sword. With Watson, we should be thankful that laws are hard to pass."

"I also went on the secretary of state site that lists campaign contributions," Wayne continued, "and found donations from casinos in the maximum amount allowed by law from corporations. But there were additional contributions to members of the Gaming Committee from casino operators and senior employees, as well as from their families. It appears to be a way of getting around the law and giving a larger contribution as an aggregate."

"That's the way politics run here in Mississippi," Will said with some disgust. "First, it's not illegal in itself to take combined campaign contributions from a family or corporation that exceeds individual limits, and, secondly, that law applies only to justice positions. Most of the time, there's no crime committed at all in doing something like that, but in my opinion it has the appearance of impropriety."

"I agree," Wayne said.

"Until our U.S. attorney sends FBI agents out to follow the money, it will never change. Of course, we have to remember who writes those laws and how difficult they are to enforce sometimes—maybe even by design. In most cases, violating campaign finance laws is a misdemeanor, which goes to show that legislators write laws to protect themselves. It's what you'd call 'home cooking.'"

Wayne smiled at his father's turn of phrase.

"The legislators are only part of the problem, though," Will continued. "The agencies themselves are run so piss-poor it's no wonder they're not effective. The State Audit Department only did two audits on the Gaming Commission in the last ten years. They first cited some findings, but didn't address the fact that many law enforcement officers were employed who never performed the job of law enforcement—they only evaluated applicants for licensure approval and performed the duties of administrative regulators. And the second report was absolutely glowing, not reporting anything wrong at all."

"Strange," Wayne said.

"The State Audit Department thinks that's 'discretionary' on the Gaming Commission's part. So taxpayers go on paying for law enforcement officers and end up getting regulators and administrators—but it's not the law enforcement officers' fault. It's the way the commission works."

"Or *doesn't* work," Wayne commented.

"The governor appoints commissioners on a 'staggered term' basis to allow bipartisan membership. But since our governors often serve two terms, by the time they leave office, all three commissioners can be from his own administration—and they ultimately decide who gets a gaming license."

"What's the procedure for getting a gaming license?" Wayne asked.

Will counted each step on his fingers. "The applicant submits a request for a license and the agents conduct a background investigation. If they find them suitable, they're recommended up the chain for a license. But if the agent finds cause for denial, the supervisor himself may overturn it or the executive director may disregard it entirely and recommend approval to the commissioners, who may never have even seen the agent's original findings since they rely solely on the executive director's recommendation."

"Sounds like the whole structure is flawed," Wayne said.

"As a lawmaker, you may want to draft new legislation to change and separate the overall structure," Will said. "As for now, the legislature controls the Ethics Commission, the PEER Committee, the budgets, the laws... If a complaint is filed about performance, budgets, conduct, ethics, or anything, there's a legislative committee or commission with oversight. I think you can see where that much power can potentially become harmful in the wrong hands."

"It's that absolute power thing again," Wayne said.

"Plus the Mississippi Gaming Commission has a problem with transparency," Will said, growing more frustrated. "You won't find their actions, particularly as they pertain to bingo, listed on their websites like you will with other states. Hell, there have been times they wouldn't even tell you if a particular type of document was public record or not unless you told them which specific one you were looking for. I guess it depends on *whose* record it was, which is a little fishy to me."

"So the problem with politics in this state comes down to legislative structure and agency transparency?"

"Is it any wonder so many of us Mississippians get disgusted and don't vote?" Will asked. "Which leads us to the next problem: Our apathy allows friends and special interest groups to get anyone with enough money and involvement into office. That's how we get so many potentially corrupt officials."

"So we're all to blame," Wayne said.

"I'm afraid so, son. It seems to have become a social norm and maybe our acceptance of these practices is the fruit of our labors. We elect governors and lieutenant governors who appoint the gaming commissioners and legislative committee leaders respectively, then they appoint the leaders of the commission, so everybody's conduct must be acceptable. Seems like you and I are the only ones in disagreement with what they do or don't do. If you don't believe it, look at the blogs and letters to the editor and count the responses to the lack of gaming arrests as compared to those about the red light cameras." Will sighed. "Doesn't matter how much difference somebody like you wants to make. You'll most likely get nowhere if you don't play the game."

"But, Dad, I'm *anti*-gaming," Wayne joked. "Besides, I didn't want this job to take on the system or become part of it. I just want to improve it a little."

Chapter 9

Summertime

"The first sign of corruption in a society
that is still alive is that the end justifies the means."
—Georges Bernanos (French author, WWI soldier)

Almost a full year had gone by since Will's shooting. The Fourth of July was fast approaching again and Wayne received an invitation to go out on a large, luxurious houseboat located on the Ross Barnett Reservoir in Madison County. Many of his colleagues would be present, so it would be a good time for him to find out more about them before the next session began.

Hopefully, it'll just be a good time, period, Wayne thought, looking forward to a rare day of relaxation.

He assumed his colleagues had chartered the boat for their enjoyment; what he didn't know at the time was that the boat belonged to Chuck Shyster, one of the state's top casino lobbyists who got his start as a bingo lobbyist. Shyster's name fit him well. Around the Capitol, he wore expensive business suits with his initials embroidered on his shirt cuffs or pocket and gold cufflinks to stand out from and look more impressive than the average legislator.

After work, Shyster was even more flamboyant: a fifty-five-year-old wheeler-dealer who often wore silk shirts, half-unbuttoned, with a large gold chain. His appearance was out-of-date by today's standards, almost as if he had so much fun in the '70s that he decided to stay there. His hair was dirty blond, long on the sides and nonexistent on top. He wore a comb-over to hide his baldness, which only made it that much more noticeable.

Broke as a youngster, Shyster made big bucks later on doing who knows what. He loved expensive toys, and the houseboat was his baby—responsible for his standard of living in the long run. It was quite a sight, big enough for an ocean excursion, with a live band onboard and beautiful young ladies serving all the champagne and finger-food Wayne could imagine.

As soon as Wayne stepped on board, Representative Wolcott yelled out over the crowd: "Wayne! C'mon and let me show you around."

Wolcott took him for a personal tour of the boat as if he owned it. He showed Wayne three plush bedrooms, two large bars, whirlpool tubs, an afterdeck with a large deep-freezer filled with prime filet mignon steaks, located next to a grill so big he could cook a side of beef on it.

"This is really something," Wayne said. The opulence made him think back to the condo he had been in—the one whose owner he still wasn't sure of.

"Just wait," Wolcott grinned lasciviously. "I saved the best part for last."

As they went back through the cabin, Wolcott took him up a set of steps that led to the upper deck. It housed the master bedroom, which was twice as large as the others and had a huge movie screen at one end. A remote-controlled projector was attached to the ceiling above the bed, in the middle of a large array of mirrors. It was a high-tech showroom, with buttons for everything and a built-in stereo/CD player in the headboard of the large, wood-frame waterbed. The room had a smell of lavender due to the mist emitting from some aromatherapy device. The whole room was designed with one thing in mind: to put a person in the mood.

"Nice," Wayne said out of politeness. "Very James Bond. What's it all for?"

"Are you kidding?" Wolcott laughed. "Have you seen the servers?"

It was hard not to notice them. The serving staff seemed to be handpicked based on how close they looked to Las Vegas showgirls. They were even dressed in similar costumes. The guests, however, looked like a legislative roll call. Even those that *didn't* show up for votes at the Capitol were sure to be in attendance at this gala.

Other than the servers and a few sharp-dressed lobbyists, the only highly visible things from the boat were the occasional red and green lights from passing vessels and a sky full of stars. The light of the moon was dancing on the water and the speed of the boat, as it headed in a northerly direction, created a breeze that helped make the night heat much more bearable above deck.

For Wayne, it was quite an experience. Very little was discussed concerning politics. The event was mostly for introductions and having a good time, otherwise known as "hobnobbing," something with which he wasn't that familiar yet.

By midnight, Wayne had run out of small talk and was anxious to get back on dry land—specifically, to be home with his family.

Wolcott rejected the idea, explaining, "It's proper etiquette for junior members to remain onboard until the more senior members leave."

Wayne followed their lead, although he found out later that practically everyone there practiced little to no etiquette.

By 2 a.m., the crowd started to thin out as the boat pulled up to the pier at Cock of the Walk restaurant. A decked-out tour bus with personal TV screens awaited most partygoers; it was operated by a contracted designated driver, who happened to be a moon-lighting off-duty cop.

Wayne wanted to leave but, being one of the most recently elected members on board, felt obligated to stay. By the end of the night, there was almost nobody left except for Shyster, a few girls and some state representatives who had appointed themselves mentors to the remaining junior members.

As the boat neared the next dock, Wayne felt it was time to say his farewells. He proceeded politely and with caution, still feeling somewhat awkward among the group of strangers. He was concerned about rubbing elbows with the "wrong" people, or leaving himself open to charges of misconduct or unethical practices.

However, Shyster was extremely nice to him. They exchanged business cards and he seemed to want him as a friend without making any demands or pressuring him on any forthcoming legislative issues. In fact, they shared similar interests—and as long as they stayed on that playing field, Wayne felt pretty comfortable with him.

Before they docked, Shyster said, "I've heard all about the anti-gaming bill you're working on, Wayne, and I admire that. Not many legislators have been eager to take up the cause and compromise their popularity."

"That's nice to hear, sir," Wayne responded.

"I want you to know that you're welcome on my boat any time."

"Thank you." Wayne smiled. "I believe I may take you up on that offer."

⸻

After a few days spent in Jackson, Wayne went back to Oxford to continue his research and as much of his law practice as he could. His days were busy, and it had gotten to the point where he felt like he had two mentors with differing aims: his dad wanting him to go after corrupt gaming that already existed, and a small group of legislators that he befriended who were trying to keep out new gaming. To Wayne, both goals were for the greater good.

Then he got the call in August: A hurricane had hit the coast and there were discussions about holding a special session to help rebuilding efforts.

"These people are in bad shape! They can't wait for the legislature to meet in January and take its time to solve their problems," the argument went—and Wayne agreed.

Politicians were under tremendous pressure because of the impact the storm had on the gaming industry; thousands of people were out of a job and the casinos were losing big money. This had to be fixed. A two-week session was called.

Wayne kissed Julie goodbye and promised her a "real vacation" when he got back.

"I sure could use one," she said, smiling but knowing deep inside that it wouldn't happen.

Wayne went back to Jackson, where an enormous amount of work was done by the committees involved within the first few days. Still, he couldn't help but realize that a lot of the talk was centered around how the gaming industry was being impacted by the natural disaster—there was little discussion about how the citizens themselves had been affected.

"The laws requiring casinos to be on 'boats' in the water had become silly, if not downright dangerous," Quarles argued. It was a refrain Wayne often heard repeated during the emergency session.

"Everybody knew they weren't really boats in the proper sense, they couldn't get underway due to a storm, and they were much more vulnerable on the water. There was no reason, other than some stubborn old tradition, for them not to have been moved across Highway 90 so they could be rebuilt on safer, solid ground. However, once done, the non-river counties have a valid argument in favor of having casinos in their counties."

Wayne was taken aback to hear Quarles go on so passionately about the casinos after all the work they'd done together on the anti-gaming bill. *Granted, there are jobs and safety concerns to consider*, he thought, *and Quarles is certainly playing to public concern in the wake of the storm.*

When Wayne went back to his hotel that night after a long, fourteen-hour workday, he lay on the bed and tried to get some sleep. But his mind was working overtime. He kept thinking back to all the definitions he had read about organized crime, all the seminars he attended about how corruption in high places made it possible for institutionalized crime to exist, and all of the officials with "absolute power" that his father had warned him about. Something started to click.

I'm being played for a chump, Wayne thought, sitting bolt upright.

He became so highly disturbed at the thought of it that he decided to approach Quarles and Wolcott the very next day, although it was a well-earned weekend.

Wayne knew that a lot of the legislators attending the emergency session were staying in a number of apartments just off Lincoln Street in an old area of the city that had been newly renovated. The complexes were just on the edge of the "bad" neighborhoods, but they were comprised of luxury apartments built with a pool in the center courtyard, enclosed by the buildings themselves. The apartments were accessible only through electronic gates opened by cards given to members of the legislature and other carefully screened residents. Some members lived there full-time, while others took up temporary residence on occasions such as this.

By the time Wayne pulled up outside the complex, he was absolutely livid. "What do those two take me for?" he muttered to himself, all the while taking his anger out on Wolcott's buzzer.

After ringing it about a dozen times, there was still no answer. Steaming even more now, Wayne tried Quarles. Again, nothing.

"I'm not giving up that easy," Wayne said, walking determinedly over to a gated area near the pool. Straining his neck, he peered in.

What he saw were dozens of shirtless legislators, splashing around the water like they were happy to be on a two-week holiday, rather than sitting in an emergency session. What he didn't see, however, were Wolcott or Quarles.

"Come on," he hissed, pulling at the gate like a captured animal.

Then he caught a glimpse of Quarles, walking toward the pool with a tropical drink in his hand and wearing a ridiculous straw hat as if he were on some tropical island in the Caribbean.

"Quarles!" he called out, waving frantically.

Quarles peered out over his sunglasses and returned a leisurely wave. He walked over to the fence and unlocked it from the inside.

"Lott! I see you changed your mind and decided to have some fun after all. Good for you," he smiled.

"I need to talk to you and Wolcott right away," Wayne said. His tone was angry.

"What's up, man? Sit down and relax while I get you a drink," he said, ushering Wayne inside.

"I don't want a drink. I want to talk to you both—now!"

"Okay," Quarles said, glancing around embarrassedly. "Take it easy. I'll find Wolcott and we'll talk privately in my room." He headed inside.

Wayne stayed outside, pacing anxiously. After a few minutes, he saw Quarles emerge and wave him into the building. He followed him into his room, where a damp Wolcott was already sitting, looking almost as perturbed as Wayne felt.

"I hope you have a damn good reason to take me away from the most beautiful woman in the state of Mississippi just as we were climbing out of the shower," he demanded.

"I don't care about that," Wayne said. "I've come to the conclusion that y'all are using me to try to get an anti-gaming law passed that would look good to the churches and non-gaming counties of this state. I'm sure you hoped that I wouldn't recognize the fact that although it appears to be anti-gaming, it isn't at all. It's anti-*competition*."

Wolcott and Quarles exchanged a worried glance.

"If this bill passes, those already in power will continue to profit while everyone else is barred from the business. You two have let lobbyists from the industry influence you into forever ridding them of competition—and when that's done, those with the most money will continue to build bigger casinos, on-site hotels and larger gaming floors to attract most of the business. Then the smaller ones will cave in—going bankrupt or selling to the big guys. That's how a monopoly is formed! And in my opinion, that's a picture-perfect case of how organized crime operates," Wayne fumed.

"Okay, so we get a little help from the industry. What's the crime?" Quarles asked.

"What's the crime? What's the crime? Are you kidding me! *You're* the crime." Wayne stood face to face with Quarles, staring him in the eye. "You are being bought and sold by the industry. You take their money and become indebted to protect them. That's corruption—and I want no part of it. If that weren't bad enough, you're trying to sneak this bill in unnoticed during a special session that's supposed to help victims of a disaster." Wayne stormed out of the apartment, slamming the door behind him.

After Wayne left, Quarles and Wolcott sat silently for a few seconds, both in shock. Then Quarles turned to face his friend. "We have problems…worse than the first time."

They both knew that Wayne was their only straight-laced offering to get the job done in the legislature—and he was backing out. The proposed anti-gaming bill would already face a lot of opposition its second time around. This problem had to be fixed before the January term.

Wolcott stood up immediately and pulled his cell phone out of his pocket. His first call was to the girl waiting back in his room.

"Baby, put your clothes on and get out. I got business to work on," he said before abruptly hanging up.

The second call was to Chuck Shyster. "We've got trouble. Wayne Lott's no longer as naïve as he was. Somehow he put two and two together and now he's refusing to cooperate."

Quarles, standing close by, could hear the shouted response. "You two idiots are amateurs! I'll take care of this myself."

"What are you going to do?" Wolcott asked.

"You two just stand fast, stay by the phone and don't worry about it," Chuck said. "I can't believe this! You assholes call yourselves lawyers and legislators? You'd mess up a shit sandwich if you had the chance! You couldn't pour piss out of a boot if there were instructions on the heel!"

Wolcott winced as Chuck slammed down the phone.

———

Chuck walked the floor, rubbing his temples. When his temper subsided, he hit a button on the intercom in his large, glassed-in office atop one of the largest bank buildings overlooking the city. "Get my technicians on the phone," he said bluntly to his secretary.

Less than a minute later, his phone rang. "Yeah, Earl, I need you again right away. Back at the boat. And don't screw anything up. I'm getting sick and tired of incompetence."

He hung up and dialed another number himself.

"It's your dime," the voice on the other end answered by way of a greeting.

"Al, I need your best girl right away," Chuck said quickly.

"Chuck, with all your guys in town, we're having a special show at the club tonight. Former centerfold. The best in the business. Can't you just come down like everyone else?" he whined.

"Trust me, I'll make it worth your while," Chuck said. "Have her meet me at the condo on the reservoir in an hour."

"Okay, boss. Anything you say," Al sighed resignedly.

Al owned the only strip club in Jackson, located in an out-of-the-way area in the west that was striving for business. The joint operated out of an old hotel that still had a few functioning rooms— in case they were needed.

———

Exactly an hour later, there was a knock on the door of Chuck's condo. He opened it and smiled. "Hey, sweetie, come on in. You're even hotter than Al described."

As Chuck leered at the young lady, she stepped into the room and immediately started to get undressed. "I understand you're in a hurry, so let's get down to business. I'm Cindy," she said, not seeming too thrilled about being pulled away from the club.

"Keep your clothes on—this isn't for me. Though I wish it was," Chuck grinned.

Cindy looked at him with a blank expression and snapped her gum, waiting for what was next.

"I have a very important job for you onboard my yacht," Chuck explained. "It's just down the road at the marina. I want you to go there, get undressed and put on one of the white terrycloth robes you find in the master bedroom. A dockhand will be there to meet you and show you around the boat before he leaves. Make yourself comfortable…snort a little coke, open a bottle of champagne, and be ready for your guest."

Chuck reached into his wallet and pulled out five thousand dollars. Cindy's eyes lit up. "This is for you," he said, handing her the money, a small bag of cocaine and a few pills. "There's another five thousand waiting when the job's done. And you don't have to tell Al I paid you anything. I'll square up with him, he'll give you a cut of his, and you can go back to dancing. Consider that your bonus for a job well done."

Cindy's demeanor seemed to change as she counted dollar signs. "Wow, this guy must be some important old geezer," she said with a sexy laugh.

"Important to me, yes. Old, no. But I've heard that he's tempted by beautiful blondes like you."

Cindy smiled flirtatiously.

"Your job is to seduce him no matter what it takes," Chuck said, trying to keep his mind on business. "Just in case, there are some pills in the main bathroom that you can slip in his drink."

"Hard-on pills?" Cindy asked, astonished. "You don't think he'll want to sleep with me on his own?"

"Honey, anyone would have to be crazy not to want to sleep with you. But this guy, I just don't know."

"He's got a wife?" Cindy asked.

"Yeah…and worse. He's got principles."

Chapter 10

The Trap Is Set

*"Man is the only animal whose desires increase
as they are fed; the only animal that is never satisfied."*
—Henry George

Chuck laid out the plan as if he were an expert. There was no telling how many times he had done this before; in fact, he had lost count himself. Blackmail and extortion were his main business; lobbying was more of a lucrative side job—but both had the same objective: to influence legislation.

He would catch Wayne in a compromising position, shot on video for all to see. The six cameras hidden throughout the yacht's master bedroom were specially wired by Chuck's technicians to start filming when the bedroom door closed. For her part, Cindy wasn't shy about starring in a sex tape. After all, it seemed to work wonders for some celebrities' careers.

Once everything was in place, there was only one small detail left to attend to: getting Representative Lott to appear. As Chuck drove off in his yellow Lamborghini Gallardo Spyder convertible, he pulled out Wayne's business card and dialed the number.

"Hello?" Wayne answered. He might as well have been a director yelling, "Action!"

"Wayne? It's Chuck Shyster," he said in a sympathetic voice. "Listen, it's all over town what happened between you and Quarles today. I want you to know that you're not the only one who played into their hands."

"Really?" Wayne said, surprised.

"Yep. Didn't even occur to me that they were trying to stop competition—and with all my years of experience, you'd think I'd know better. Hell, a junior member like you hardly stands a chance," he said.

Wayne was wary about who to trust anymore. But his ego was bruised, and he was glad to hear that he wasn't the only one feeling like a fool. *If a powerful lobbyist can get taken in, anybody could.*

"Listen, son, why don't you come down to my boat where we can discuss this? I don't want a bill passed that's going to form a monopoly. Maybe there's a way we can work together."

Wayne exhaled deeply. He had wanted so badly for the reforms to be passed that he was willing to risk it. *But I'll keep my eyes open,* he told himself.

"Okay, Chuck," Wayne said. "When should I be there?"

"I'm out of town now but should get there by six. See you then?"

"Yes, sir," Wayne answered and hung up. Part of him felt like he was making deals with the devil, but he gave in. He was willing to accept help from this very powerful man because he felt so powerless against the system.

———

Trying to beat the evening traffic, Wayne left a little early and arrived at the boat. He could tell the door was open at the end of the pier but only saw one car parked outside, a red Jaguar with a New York plate he didn't recognize. As his footsteps clomped along the pier nearing the door, a soft voice from inside said, "C'mon in."

He stepped inside cautiously.

"You must be Wayne," a beautiful young blonde said. She was dressed only in a robe that was left partially open down the front, and her hair was wet from the shower, with curls that dangled past her shoulders. "I'm Cindy, Chuck's niece. I'm visiting from New York so he let me stay on his boat. He called to tell me you'd be coming by. That's why I got out of the shower."

"Oh, I'm sorry about that," Wayne said, trying hard not to stare. "So…where is Chuck?"

"Don't worry. He should be here soon—and I won't bother you when he gets here." She crinkled her nose.

"You're not bothering me now," he smiled.

"Good," she chirped. "Then I hope you won't mind helping me out. I just opened a bottle of champagne—there's too much for me to drink alone and I'd hate for it to go flat. What do you say? One drink before I leave you alone?"

"Thank you," Wayne said, not wanting to be rude.

"I understand you're an important member of the legislature and friends with my Uncle Chuck," she said, handing him a drink.

Wayne didn't respond except for a smile.

"Cheers," she said, clinking glasses, which she filled all the way to the brim. "I try not to discuss politics too much myself. Just makes people argue."

Wayne smiled, took a few sips and began to relax.

"So, why don't you tell me about yourself?" Cindy said in a sexy tone, sounding as if her only interest in the world was what he was about to say.

Wayne sat down on one end of the soft, plush couch. She took a seat at the other end, with her tan, long, smooth legs and painted toenails pointing in his direction. Her robe fell slightly open more down the middle, but Wayne thought it might be rude to mention it.

"Well, if you're not too interested in politics, how do you feel about the law?" he asked, getting more acquainted.

"You're a cop?" she squealed.

He laughed. "Not quite so exciting, I'm afraid. A lawyer."

"That's a great job," she said.

Flattered, Wayne tried to turn the subject off of himself. "So what do you do up in New York?"

"Uh…finance," she said. Wanting to avoid any more questions, she popped up off the couch and walked toward him, taking his nearly empty glass. "But I'm on vacation now, so what do you say we celebrate with more champagne?"

Wayne started to loosen up as she brought him another drink. When he was half-way finished with it, she could tell it was beginning to have some effect—with all the erectile dysfunction pills she crushed up in it—but he was fighting temptation.

Just as she moved closer to him on the couch, Wayne's cell phone rang. It was Chuck.

"Wayne? I'm so sorry. I'm stuck in traffic on I-55—it's backed all the way up. There was an accident that they're still cleaning up, so it may take me awhile to get there. Is my niece there with you?"

"Yes, she is—and she's taking good care of me," Wayne said with a bit of a slur.

"Okay. Sounds like you're in good hands," Chuck laughed. "I'll see you in an hour or so."

"Who was that?" Cindy asked as soon as he hung up. "You don't have to leave, do you?" She pouted with disappointment.

"No, no, the opposite, actually. Your uncle's stuck in a bad traffic jam so I have to wait here awhile longer."

"Well, I don't know anyone here in Mississippi, and I don't have any plans…so if you don't mind, I'll keep you company," she said.

"I don't mind at all," he smiled.

Wayne was a young man. He had fallen to temptation before, but was convinced he had learned his lesson. However, alcohol, pills and a naturally low tolerance weren't in his favor. Neither was human nature.

He had already been away from Julie for almost two weeks, and even when he was home, she was too tired from taking care of Will to have as much sex anymore. He'd been feeling lonely lately—and, now, there was a gorgeous girl giving him all the attention he craved.

The next drink did it. Within minutes, he was being led upstairs and undressed by this beautiful woman. The drugs were working and the plan was working. She shut the bedroom door.

By then, Wayne's sexual desires had overcome any thoughts of his wife, his career or the fact that her uncle could be coming through the door at any time. He was putting himself in a danger-ous position—but at least, for the moment, he loved every second of it. Cindy was ravenous and showed him every trick she knew... all while the cameras were running.

Wayne woke up early the next morning in a place he seemed to recognize...but for a few minutes, he was entirely at a loss. He didn't remember much about the night before and had a tremen-dous headache. Then all at once it hit him: Cindy.

He walked across the room, picking up his clothes and hur-riedly putting them back on. He staggered outside to what would normally be a beautiful sunrise, but it was blurry, and he couldn't quite keep his eyes open. He smelled bacon frying and tried to find his way toward the kitchen, expecting to find Cindy, apologize to her, and leave—hoping to forget that this whole thing had ever happened.

However, when he finally made it to the kitchen, to his sur-prise, he saw none other than "Uncle Chuck."

"Well, hello, sunshine," Chuck said, smiling. "And how are you on this fine Mississippi morning?"

"Not so good," Wayne groaned as he rubbed his face.

"Cindy left a note for me last night. Said you got tired of waiting on me and went to bed to get some rest when she was leaving with some friends," Chuck said nonchalantly.

"Is that all she said?" Wayne asked with a surprised look on his face.

"Nooo…" Chuck drawled.

Wayne's heart skipped a beat.

"She also said you were a perfect gentleman and good company," Chuck finished. "By the time I got back, I felt so bad waking you that I figured it could wait 'til morning." With that, Chuck starting to break some eggs. "How do you like yours?"

"Doesn't matter," Wayne grumbled. "Any way you fix them is fine." He sat down at the table, resting his throbbing head on his hands. "I'm not sure I even feel like eating."

"Oh, you'll be fine, son. You're just stressed out is all. Here, have some headache powder," Chuck said in a caring tone as he handed Wayne headache powder and a glass of water.

They only made small talk during breakfast. Wayne couldn't wait to jump in the shower and wash the smell of perfume and sweat from his body.

He felt ashamed as some of his "best" moves from the night before came flashing before his eyes. He tried to scrub the memories away but it didn't work. *Thank goodness Cindy didn't say anything*, he thought, wondering what old Uncle Chuck would do if he found out he'd been to bed with his niece.

"Wayne!" Chuck called from outside the bathroom door.

A slight shiver of panic ran down Wayne's spine, despite the warm water.

"When you get out of the shower, come to the living room. We can discuss the bill in there!"

At that point, the law was the last thing on Wayne's mind. But he was in no condition to put up a fight.

At around ten in the morning, Wayne's headache was finally subsiding—though whenever he thought of Julie, he felt like somebody had torn his heart straight from his chest.

He dried himself off from the shower, got dressed and dutifully met Chuck in the living room, where a copy of his proposed bingo bill was already lying open on the coffee table.

"Where did you get that?" Wayne asked.

"I hope you don't mind," Chuck said innocently. "I got it from the pocket of your blazer when you went in the shower. Figured I'd get a little work done."

Wayne looked down at his draft and saw some recent changes written in red ink. As he read through them, his eyes became wide and he turned toward Chuck as if he'd seen Satan himself.

"With the way I reworded it, you shouldn't have any problem passing it now, son," Chuck said confidently.

"Please don't call me 'son,'" Wayne snapped. "I see what you're doing with these changes. They're about protecting the bingo halls while screwing the charities!" Wayne snatched up his document and walked toward the door.

"Where are you going?" Chuck asked.

"Mr. Shyster," he hissed, "I decided I'm not going to need your help. I'm going to get this passed on my own if I have to. But it'll be for the right reasons and the right results."

"Wayne, are you sure?" Chuck asked mockingly.

"Absolutely! I'm not for sale. I don't make deals when it comes to my constituents and my integrity," he replied, turning to go.

"Why don't you calm down? Have a seat. Let's watch a little TV," Chuck said, picking up the remote.

Wayne turned to look at him with a confused expression. "What are you talking about? I'm not interested in TV. I just want to get out of here."

"You can't," Chuck said, smiling. "You'll miss my favorite show."

Just then, out of nowhere, Quarles and Wolcott stepped through the door, blocking Wayne's exit.

"What...what's going on here?" Wayne asked.

"Sit down and watch the show, Wayne," Chuck said. Suddenly, his voice had become low and menacing.

Wayne stood his ground but glanced toward the TV. On screen, he saw himself and Chuck's "niece" having wild sex in every position known to man—plus a few that they'd invented.

"Oh, my God! What is this? What have I done?" Wayne cried out.

"As I said," Chuck laughed, "it's my favorite show. I call it 'Man of Integrity.' What do you think, Wayne? Should I have Wolcott here fix us up some popcorn?"

Wolcott and Quarles laughed like the flunkies they were.

"Turn it off!" Wayne shouted. "You sons-of-bitches! This is what you think is 'real world politics,' isn't it?"

"I'm afraid so, son...you don't mind if I call you 'son' now, do you?" Chuck asked with a sneer.

"I don't care what you call me," Wayne said, shaking his head. "You called that girl your 'niece.' She isn't, is she?" He already knew the answer.

"Now where would any niece of mine learn tricks like that?" Chuck said admiringly as he watched the screen. "Son, that little slut...she's a professional, wouldn't you say?" He laughed again, and Quarles and Wolcott joined in.

"So, what do you say, Wayne?" Chuck taunted. "Think you'll be ready to work with us next session? That is, if *we're* willing to work with a drug-taking, alcohol-abusing, womanizing, worthless politician." He practically spat the last word out.

Wayne gritted his teeth so hard that he nearly broke a cap. If he could, he would kill the whole thieving, conniving, blackmailing bunch. But he knew he had gotten himself in too deep. Even murder wouldn't solve his problems now. The only thing he could do is throw in the towel and cooperate.

"Go back home to your lovely wife, Wayne, and take a copy of this movie with you. Maybe she'd like to see it," Chuck scoffed. "Next time we meet, we'll have the anti-gaming legislation with us, all ready with your name at the top."

Chuck tossed a copy of the DVD onto the floor in front of Wayne's feet. "How 'bout we let the bingo law stay as it is for now? You see, jackass, I'm a bingo lobbyist, too, and I don't want anyone messing with my nest egg. All that unaccounted-for cash to pay off politicians whenever we need to! Ha! I'm telling you, it's a thing of beauty. We'll just deal with the casinos. Don't want anyone else moving in on our territory," Chuck smirked.

Wayne looked down at the disc lying there. Then he looked directly into Shyster's eyes. "Why me?" he asked, like a broken man.

"You kidding?" Chuck exclaimed. "With your wholesome, religious image and that cop-turned-crippled father of yours, you'll have most of Mississippi eating out of your hand with almost no work at all. Hell, even Cindy seemed to like you."

As Chuck laughed uncontrollably, Wolcott and Quarles moved out of Wayne's way. With his shoulders hunched in shame, he stepped outside into the hot, thick air then took a few mechanical steps forward before realizing that there was nowhere he could go to escape.

"Think he's onboard with our plan?" Quarles asked as he watched Wayne walk to his car and drive away.

"Of course he is," Chuck said, in complete control. "If his brains were in a hummingbird, it would suck a mule's ass right now, thinking it's a morning glory. That kid's so mixed up he can't find a way out. And the truth is, there isn't one."

Chapter 11

The Mole

"Our character...is an omen of our destiny,
and the more integrity we have and keep,
the simpler and nobler that destiny is likely to be."
—George Santayana

The trip back to Oxford was a long one. Thoughts of suicide once again ran through Wayne's mind. However, he quickly dismissed them this time—remembering what his late mother always told him: "God will try you, but never give you more than you can handle." He kept his faith but wasn't sure why he was being tried so much—or just how much more he could handle.

I can't let the criminals win that easily, Wayne thought. *I've got to fight...for my family, for my beliefs. But how?*

Will and Julie noticed a change in Wayne right after he got back and it continued for weeks after. He had almost completely lost his sense of humor. He slept a lot, didn't shave or shower on the weekends and only took phone calls that he absolutely had to take. He lost interest in the Monday night classes with his dad and wouldn't go to church with his wife.

His family was worried about him but didn't know what to do.

They assumed that his depression had come back and begged him to see the psychologist.

"Okay, I will," Wayne said one day in early fall, after weeks of nagging. But he had absolutely no intention of making an appointment. He just didn't want to argue anymore and needed an excuse to get out of the house and clear his head.

Wayne jumped in his car and headed to the doctor's office, passing it by completely. He parked a few blocks away then got out and walked around the town square aimlessly, wondering if he'd have the strength to go home again and face his family.

As he was walking, he thought about the path of least resistance. *Sign the anti-gaming bill. Pretend it's for the good of the public. Watch it pass. By the time the Bogus Trio expands into a monopoly and spreads like cancer through the state, I'll be out of office and all but forgotten. In a few years' time, life will go on as normal and no one will remember that I drafted the law in the first place.*

No one, that is, but my father.

Wayne took a deep breath and stopped in front of a shop window. It was a bookstore, Square Books, advertising its latest batch of crime thrillers. As he walked into the quiet setting and looked around, his gaze fell on a true-life book about an informer. He picked it up and began to read. Before long, he started to get ideas of his own.

———

The next day in his office, Wayne got up the nerve to call the FBI. As he waited for someone to pick up, he realized that this one call could turn his life upside down. He also knew that it just might save it.

A voice answered. Wayne was caught slightly off-guard. He wasn't expecting a woman.

"Are y'all interested in political corruption cases?" he asked with some hesitation.

"We're interested in crime as a whole. Would you like to talk to an agent?" the secretary asked.

"Yes, please," Wayne said, quietly waiting.

"This is Agent Wallace Tischner. How may I help you?" The gruff voice on the other end spoke with the reservation of an older, more experienced agent.

Tischner was a colorful character from the old school of criminal investigation. Most of the other agents were younger than him, but he got a late start after his career as a street cop. His office was decorated with copies of the old fingerprint cards of gangsters, and their mug shots were attached all over the walls: John Dillinger, Pretty Boy Floyd, Baby Face Nelson, Bonnie and Clyde. It was as if Tischner himself had stepped out of the '30s, although he was only in his mid-fifties. His favorite restaurant was right out of the '30s, too, and had changed little over the years.

He even dressed old school, still wearing suspenders and a hat. He had his father to thank for that. Tischner's dad had loved and hated John F. Kennedy. He loved him for what he stood for but hated him for setting the fashion statement of no more hats. The day Wallace Tischner, Sr., saw Kennedy at his inauguration—his hair blowing in the breeze—he knew hats would become a thing of the past. He was right.

If you were lucky enough to go home and have a beer with Wallace Tischner, Jr., you might get to see his prized possession. His den had a big painting—strong brush strokes on canvas—depicting none other than J. Edgar Hoover wearing a dress. Somebody had gone to great pains to make it look like an official portrait. Tischner would have been fired, not to mention tarred and feathered, had he been caught with that when Hoover was still alive. FBI agents, unlike most other federal employees, had no job protection.

"Agent Tischner, I'm Representative Wayne Lott. I'm involved in a political corruption and organized crime case...centered in Jackson...against my will...sir," he stammered. "I...I need help."

"Stop right there," Agent Tischner said. "We need to meet in person—away from Jackson—to have this discussion. Do you know where George P. Cossar State Park is?"

"Of course," Wayne said.

"Let's meet there at 9 a.m. tomorrow. I'll be in a White Ford, just sitting in my car, reading the paper. When you approach me, ask for directions to Greenwood, then follow me."

"Thank you, sir. I'll be there. I will. I feel better already just talking to someone," Wayne said before hanging up.

What could happen? This guy turns out to be some lunatic, or he doesn't show and I get to read my paper in peace for a change, Tischner figured. *Of course, the worst that can happen is he's telling the truth.*

Wayne entered the park and noticed the White Ford sitting in the lot. For a moment, he panicked and thought about driving away. But the moment passed. He pulled up next to the car and looked over at the occupant that he would soon be approaching for directions to Greenwood.

Agent Tischner was in the car, talking on his cell phone. Wayne rolled down his window and could overhear the conversation. He expected to listen in on something official, but it was apparently Tischner's wife on the other end. He was saying, "Yes, honey, I took my medicine. Yes, I took the blood pressure crap, too. I have to go, Ann. I'm working and somebody's here to meet me."

He hung up, looking slightly relieved to have cut the conversation short. Then he tried his best to appear somewhat official as he turned toward Wayne and waited for the cue.

"Excuse me," Wayne called, a little too loudly. He always spoke at a higher volume when he was nervous. "Can you tell me how to get to Greenwood?"

Tischner, on the other hand, answered barely above a whisper.

"Drive a half mile west on this road then turn around and come back. Go to cabin three and park your car. Get out and walk over to cabin eight. The door will be unlocked. Go in, have a seat and wait for me. I'll be there as soon as I'm sure you aren't being followed."

With that, Wayne was about to enter a covert world. He had gotten a taste of it through a series of hidden cameras spying on him onboard the yacht in his most dreadful moment, and he wondered if the FBI would also have the cabin wired to capture his identity. As he thought about it, he realized, *I don't mind if they do. At least I'm on the right side of the law this time.*

Wayne did exactly as Tischner told him. As he drove back toward the park, he found himself glancing in his rearview mirror, trying to get a glimpse of the agent's car tailing him. It was nowhere to be seen. *He's either really good at his job or hanging me out to dry,* Wayne thought. *Guess I'll find out which when I get there.*

Once Wayne parked his car, he walked quickly into cabin eight, an old structure with pinewood floors and exposed beams. He sat on the early American style couch in front of a small fireplace and anxiously waited. He wasn't exactly able to make himself comfortable. Instead, he glanced nervously around, trying to find any trace of a hidden camera.

He saw nothing out of the ordinary. *Maybe this is what they do if they don't believe your story,* Wayne thought. *Leave you sitting out in the middle of nowhere, where you won't be a threat to society.*

He was half-amused by the notion, and wondered what kind of crazies were waiting in cabins one through seven.

Just then, Tischner came through the door, followed by a younger agent. Wayne stood to greet them.

"Representative Lott? As you've already guessed, I'm Agent Wallace Tischner. This agent here is Bob. That's all you have to know about him."

Wayne shook their hands and waited for further instructions.

"Wayne, I understand from your call that you want to work

with us. You don't mind if we record this conversation, do you?" Agent Tischner pulled a small tape recorder, the size of an old Sony Walkman, out of his inside jacket pocket.

"No, not at all," Wayne said, somewhat taken aback. "I'm just a little surprised that you're being so overt about recording me."

Tischner smiled. "You were expecting wiretaps and spy gadgets? Stick around. There'll be plenty of time for all that in the future. Let's just hear your story first."

Wayne spent the better part of the morning going over the details of corruption and extortion in the legislature to the two agents. They listened intently, asked questions and took copious notes. Tischner was particularly impressed that Wayne had the presence of mind to bring the copy of the DVD that Shyster tossed at him, and they watched an excerpt on the cabin's small TV set.

"Nice tits," Tischner commented.

"Yeah, I wonder what she paid for them," Bob laughed.

Wayne, in the meantime, cringed in embarrassment. Tischner glanced over at him, turned off the TV and said, "Well, Wayne, looks like you got us a case. It was good thinking on your part to bring it to the FBI."

"And bad thinking to ever believe that girl was Shyster's niece," Bob said, shaking his head. He shut up the second Tischner shot him a look.

"Listen, Wayne, we've still got a lot of work to do, and it's going to take some time. So Bob here has volunteered to take our lunch orders and drive over to the nearest hamburger joint," Tischner said.

"When did I volunteer for that?" Bob asked.

"Just then, when you opened your mouth," Tischner shot back.

Bob wrote down what each man wanted for lunch in the same notepad he used to take down the details of Wayne's story. Then he headed out. Seconds later, Tischner's cell phone rang. He took a deep breath, rolled his eyes and answered.

"Yes, Ann. I'm going to eat lunch. Bob has gone to get something for us right now. Yes, it's a burger. I told him to leave the bacon off mine. Okay, okay. I have to go. Yes, honey. Love you, too," he added.

He cleared his throat in embarrassment then sat down next to Wayne, who had politely pretended not to listen to his end of the conversation. "How long you say you been married?" he asked.

"About a year," Wayne answered.

"Hmm. That's still the honeymoon stage," Tischner said.

"Not if my wife sees that DVD," Wayne said.

For a few minutes, the two men sat in silence on the sofa. Moments later, Bob returned with the fast food.

They ate quickly and without much talk. After lunch, Bob went out to the car and brought in a large briefcase that doubled as a fingerprint stand and held several plain manila folders.

"Wayne, we're going to 'code' you as an informant and will later refer to you simply as B-32-P-09, for your own protection." When Agent Tischner was in full law enforcement mode, he reminded Wayne a lot of his father.

"Okay," Wayne agreed. He realized that along with his new code name, he'd also be assuming a different, dual life. *My old life won't be worth very much if I don't*, he reminded himself. He complied with everything the agents told him to do.

They took his fingerprints, photographs and all identifying information, and placed them in a manila folder, which was now marked on the tab with his code number, preceded by the letters "CI." Wayne assumed it must have meant something like "criminal informant," "confidential informant" or "coded informant," but he didn't bother to ask. He just wanted to get on with the show.

He'd been missing from his office for hours and hadn't even checked his cell phone for any calls from home. He didn't want his family to worry about him any more than they had been, but he couldn't really think of an excuse for his absence.

"Bob," Wayne asked, as the agent snapped yet another photograph and took down his vital statistics, "how much longer do you suppose this is going to take?"

"First of all, Wayne, I need you to hold still. But I'm going to need you to forget that my name is Bob. If everything gets approved, we're going to wind up working together, and we'll have to make up our own story about who I am and how we know each other. So don't get comfortable with me just yet," he said.

"Is that true?" Wayne asked, turning to the senior agent.

"Yes, son," Tischner said. "I'll be your control agent and he'll probably be...well, for all practical purposes, your co-worker in charge, so to speak."

Wayne was really getting tired of being called "son" by virtual strangers, but at this point he let it pass.

"You mean I'm actually going to be *working* for the FBI?" By then, he was starting to feel like a booked criminal in one sense and like a spy in another. "My *job* is going to be getting those bastards once and for all?" The vengeance in his heart was taking precedence over all of his other emotions.

"Wayne, don't be so quick to drop the gavel," Agent Tischner said. "This will take time, and your three associates will hopefully be the first few in a long string of dominos that will eventually collapse. That's ultimately going to be your job and ours, if it's approved."

"What does that mean?" Wayne asked.

"It means we go back to Jackson, discuss our contact with supervisors then probably meet with the U.S. attorney himself, instead of the usual assistants. That's how high-level and complex this case can become," Tischner explained. "If it's approved, and I'm sure it will be with the evidence you've shown us, it'll take up a lot of your time. You may want to consider resigning from your law firm if the Department of Justice decides to turn you into a paid informant."

"So that's what I'm going to be," Wayne said, mostly to himself.

He was having a hard time believing the sudden change of course that his life had taken.

It started to sink in that his law practicing days would be prematurely over. He'd now be doing the work his father had always wanted him to do—chasing criminals, but in a way he never would have expected.

Although he wanted to make his father proud, Wayne was having some reservations about leaving his chosen profession. *First of all, my firm backed me in the election and gave me ample time off as I needed it. They've been very understanding,* he thought. *Secondly, I spent a lot of time and money in law school—too much to give up after just getting started. And, most importantly, I doubt if I can even tell my dad about my new work, given its sensitive nature.* He made the decision right then and there to try to hold on to his current job as long as he could.

"How will I explain to my family my being able to sit home and not work? They know my salary from the legislature isn't enough to allow that," he asked.

"Don't worry about that now, Wayne. When necessary, we'll arrange a cover for you. You know you'll have to keep the truth from your family, and a lot of paid informants find that to be the toughest part." Agent Tischner looked him squarely in the eyes and sized him up. He knew that with a young wife and a disabled ex-cop father, Wayne would be tempted to spill his guts. And that would put everyone in jeopardy.

"If need be, at the end of all this, you may be placed in a witness protection program," Tischner continued. "Especially if we're dealing with organized crime. But we can't get ahead of ourselves this early in the game. Just go home for now and wait to hear from us."

"How will I know..."

Bob cut him off. "If we need to leave a message for you, it'll be from 'a concerned citizen' wanting to talk to his representative about crop dust poison. Our numbers won't show up on caller ID, so call us back at this cell number." He handed Wayne a small slip of paper. "Memorize that. We won't call you often, but we expect you to get in touch with us every day…if for no other reason than to let us know you're alive."

Tischner jumped in to try to stop his partner from saying the wrong thing and spooking Wayne. "Stay in this cabin until we've been gone an hour. Then leave the key on the coffee table and lock the door on your way out."

Then, as suddenly as they'd come, the two agents were gone and Wayne was once again left sitting alone. He couldn't help feeling that he had just confessed his sins to a priest, although he was Baptist and that wasn't the way things worked in his religion.

Still, he felt somewhere between on the verge of being saved and having bared and entrusted his soul to a higher, unseen force. In this case, the FBI.

———————

Wayne called in dutifully over the next few days, with no new information from the agents. He was resettling into his role at the law firm when, that following Monday afternoon, he received a call from a concerned citizen.

"Meet me at the truck stop near the Greenwood exit on I-55," Tischner said.

Wayne dropped what he was doing and made the drive over as quickly as he could. When he walked into the truck stop, he was overwhelmed by the smell of boiled peanuts, fried chicken and barbeque that filled the air.

A couple of old farmers sat around telling lies and chewing on toothpicks. They weren't lying about farming, but rather about the fish they had caught and, most of all, the huge one that had gotten away due to "the cheap tackle they make these days."

Wayne looked around and saw a young black child, barefoot with a runny nose and short pants falling down from around his waist, approach the counter that he could barely see the top of. He reached into his pockets about fifteen times, pulling out a handful of pennies each time, to buy a soft drink and as many pieces of gum as he could get with the remaining change. An older black man in coveralls patiently waited for a pig's foot, a pickled egg and a can of tobacco complete with rolling papers.

But there was still no sign of Tischner.

It didn't matter. Wayne felt more comfortable around these people than he did among the bunch of stiff shirts with diamond cufflinks in the Capitol. He took his seat at the back table and waited.

Minutes later, Agent Tischner appeared, appropriately dressed for this occasion so as not to stand out. But his demeanor was strictly down to business.

"We got approval from Washington to make you a paid informant," Tischner said, taking a seat. "Your salary will be eighty thousand a year, and your cover story is that the Department of Justice gave you a federal grant to conduct research on the criminal mind."

Wayne barely got the first word out. "How..."

"A half million dollars will be deposited into an account that we'll monitor closely. You'll take monthly draws from there. We'll send you detailed instructions on how to carry out your daily routine, but you'll need to tender your resignation to your law firm right away."

Wayne realized that he wasn't going to be asked his opinion on any of this.

"Take this new cell phone to call us any time you need us, but don't let anyone else use it." Tischner handed him the device. "It has digital scramble capability. When you call our same types of phones, we'll be able to talk just fine. Anybody trying to listen in will only hear garbled gook."

"Okay," Wayne responded, too overwhelmed to think of anything else to say.

"Go home, get some rest, explain your cover to your family and *don't* tell them the truth. Don't even be tempted to. I don't want to sound condescending here, Wayne, but you've screwed up several times in the past and it has almost cost you your career, your family and even your life. It's time you stick with the program," Agent Tischner said in a fatherly but firm tone.

Wayne knew he was right and that it was time to turn over a new leaf. *I may well have an opportunity now to make the difference I wanted to make in the legislature. I won't be instrumental in authoring new laws, but the final result will pay off better than I originally expected, the law will prevail in an even bigger way, and I can earn my dad's respect, even if he doesn't know it yet.*

He shook Agent Tischner's hand. "I won't let you down."

Wayne made his way home while rehearsing his cover story over and over in his mind. To him, it sounded perfect. But he wondered what his family would think.

At dinner, as his father was passing the mashed potatoes and waiting for turnip greens, Wayne decided to make the announcement. "Dad, Julie, I didn't say anything to anybody before because I really didn't think I'd get it, but I applied for a grant through the Department of Justice a couple of months ago to do research on serial killers. I really got more interested in the criminal aspect of my job with the last two seminars I attended. And today I was surprised with a phone call that my grant application has been approved," he said as he bit into a piece of corn bread.

Julie and Will exchanged a wordless glance while sipping on sweet iced tea. Hers was worried; his was full of astonished pride.

"My monthly salary will be more than my law firm pay, and the grant is funded for the first year with a potential for four more years, which are optional depending on my progress and available funding," Wayne continued.

Julie couldn't rein in her emotions any longer. "Oh, Wayne, that's wonderful! As long as it's what you really want," she said, giving him a hug. "Let's celebrate with a big bowl of homemade banana pudding."

"That sounds wonderful," he said, smiling. Then he looked over to his father, who seemed a little choked up.

"So my son, the *ex*-attorney, is going to become a serial killer profiler," Will said. "The world feels safer already."

"Thanks, Dad." Wayne felt torn about getting his father's hopes up like that, but was sure he'd be even prouder if he knew the truth. *Anyway, it's just great to see him so happy,* Wayne thought as he walked toward the kitchen to help Julie with the dishes.

He felt confident that he convinced his wife and dad that this was the best choice for him. However, he wasn't so sure how his father-in-law or his firm would take it. With some reluctance, he left his house early the next morning and made the necessary rounds.

Surprisingly, his bosses at the firm were very supportive about his decision—especially when he explained that he'd remain in the legislature and look out for their best interests. His father-in-law was somewhat disappointed—after all, an attorney in the family was a pretty prestigious thing—but he wasn't suspicious at all.

Most important to Wayne was his wife's reaction—and as far as Julie was concerned, since he'd be working mostly from home, he could spend more time with her and his dad. It was a win-win all around. Sure, there would still be occasional trips to Jackson for legislative sessions, but Wayne felt better that he'd be spending more time in the federal building there.

———

Wayne called his control agent the next morning to explain how well his story was received by all parties. "Now I'm anxious to get to work," he said.

It's exactly what Tischner wanted to hear. "We'll introduce you to a team of strategists to set up the details of a sting operation. Meet me at the Residence Inn off I-55 in Jackson tomorrow so we can issue you some technical equipment and provide training for its use."

"Okay," Wayne said. "I'm ready to get moving."

He arrived at the hotel early the next day and drove around the lot, looking for counter-surveillance as if he were already a seasoned undercover government agent. *Either we're all clear, or I have no clue what I'm looking for yet,* Wayne thought.

As soon as he walked in the room, he realized that the latter was accurate. Wayne was introduced to so many agents, assistant U.S. attorneys, and technicians that he couldn't keep track of how many there were. *There must be at least twenty people crammed into this suite,* he thought, feeling intimidated about his new undertaking.

The technicians were released and told to come back after the briefing. After they left, Wayne was the only one in the room who wasn't wearing a gun on his side. *I'm sure glad these are the good guys,* he thought.

The senior agent spoke up first. "Wayne, we're working with the IRS on a case involving another lobbyist well-known by the one currently in question. We already have a senator snared on a bribery case, but it'll take all the culprits to really blow the lid off this thing. While we work on our end, we want you to go wired and under surveillance to meet with Representatives Quarles and Wolcott. You've got to get them to admit to their knowledge of the houseboat incident and the blackmailing, and to show their culpability in the crime by having willingly participated with Chuck Shyster."

"I can do that, sir," Wayne said.

"Good. We're also sending agents to wiretap Al's Strip Joint," the agent said, checking his notes. "We want to see what we can get on the owner or any of the girls. The woman in your case… 'Cindy'…was probably working under an assumed name, and we can be sure she's from out of state, but we'll need to identify her at some point."

At that point, the technicians came back into the room and broke out the gear.

"Am I going to have to wear one of those stupid wires?" Wayne asked with apprehension.

"You've been watching too much TV, counselor," the lead tech said. "'Wire' is still the term we use, but we've gotten much more sophisticated. It won't be a black box adhered to your side with a long wire and microphone taped to your chest. We're not in the business of body hair removal. We want you to remain anonymous so we're outfitting you with the latest tech. Hopefully, you'll appreciate that."

"Absolutely," Wayne said, feeling put in his place. "Y'all have got more electronic crap in here than Carter has liver pills, as my dad would say."

"It's for your own protection and for our evidence gathering so these guys don't walk," the technician said proudly. "But trust me, you ain't seen nothin' yet."

Wayne could tell those guys weren't quite as polished as the agents, but they definitely knew their stuff. When they showed him their van later in the day, it was filled with bags of tricks that would have made MacGyver blush. There were pin-hole lens cameras that could be placed anywhere; clocks with cameras; thermostats with cameras; electrical receptacles with cameras; alarm clock radio cameras. They even had a TV that could watch *you* while you were watching it. Wayne was most impressed by the eyeglasses and sunglasses cameras that seemed like they were straight out of a Bond film. Of course, there was some top secret stuff that the techs wouldn't show him.

Wayne spent several days a week afterwards getting a crash course in how to be a spy—not against enemy governments but against criminals in our own legislature. He was amazed at the capabilities, as the agents devoted hours upon hours to showing him how to detect counter-surveillance, how to verify that his equipment was working properly and how to use signals without speaking. They also reviewed entrapment laws with him to be sure that the case would not be thrown out of court on that account.

"Hopefully, every case you make against an individual will be repeated with more vigor and significance, so we can show escalating involvement," a senior agent explained. "Multiple cases void any potential requests for leniency from the defense since they can't say their client made just one mistake and was caught because he's such an amateur. In addition, if one of the cases become tainted or lack sufficient evidence, the others can still be prosecuted."

Most of all, the agents stressed how important it was for him to engage the culprits in conversation, pumping them up to encourage "diarrhea of the mouth."

"Juries love to hear criminals brag about all their illegal ventures on video, in contrast to the pictures their defense attorneys paint of them as victims or first-time offenders," the agent explained.

"Video?" Wayne asked excitedly. "Will I get to wear those camera glasses?"

"You already have your camera," the lead tech answered. "What do you think that overcoat I gave you does? It has a wireless camera in one of the buttons. In fact, in a little while, we'll show you a sample video of this conversation we're having now. By the way, you'll need that overcoat in January when the legislative session starts."

"To videotape the meetings?" Wayne asked.

"No. To keep warm," the tech laughed.

Chapter 12

Dirty Deeds

"It is said that power corrupts, but actually it's more true that power attracts the corruptible. The sane are usually attracted by other things than power."
—David Brin (award-winning novelist)

By early December, it was time for Wayne to approach his dreaded colleagues. He'd been trained and briefed, but was still nervous about how everything would go down. Wired to the hilt and surrounded by agents in the distance, he arranged his first meeting with Quarles and Wolcott at their favorite condo on the reservoir.

"Wayne, it's good to see you," Wolcott said, slapping him on the back as soon as he stepped in, like they were best friends. "It's nearing the next session and we need to hammer out some issues on the gaming bill."

"You're not still mad at us, are you?" Quarles inquired with a grin. He was standing at the bar, pouring himself another drink. "Because actually we did you quite a favor."

"What do you mean?" Wayne asked.

"Shyster really is a good guy once you get to know him," Quarles answered. "He'll *definitely* make it all up to you."

"How can you be so sure of that?" Wayne asked. He was taking advantage of Quarles' talkative, semi-inebriated state.

"Because you are looking at two other guys who fell for the same scam," Quarles laughed. "At first we fought it, just like you. We were green…we thought we were above the system. But now, we just go along with it. We still have our families intact, we're much better off financially, and we can use Chuck to help us get bills passed. He has about as much power as the Speaker of the House."

"Not to mention his boat," Wolcott added with a wink. "But you already know all about those benefits."

"Look, Wayne, we all work together," Quarles said with a broad, friendly smile. "That's the only way we get things done. Remember, there's safety in numbers."

"You mean y'all did the exact same thing I did?" Wayne asked.

"Oh, yeah…but we were smart. We took advantage of the situation instead of us being taken advantage of," Quarles said.

"Now we can have any whore we want from the strip joint…and I say 'whore' instead of 'prostitute' because we don't pay a dime," Wolcott bragged. "We use the houseboat as if it was our own—and we know where all the cameras are now. We know how to turn them on and turn them off, just in case we need to run our own scam. Whether you like it or not, you have to agree that it works great," he laughed. "Just give in to it, man. It's bigger than you are. Get with the program and have fun." Wolcott seemed to have accepted the whole twisted program lock, stock and barrel.

"By the way," Quarles added with a mischievous smirk, "Chuck asked us to give you something."

Quarles walked over to Wolcott, who handed him a thick envelope, then went to the sofa and gave it to Wayne. Wayne tore it open and found a key and five thousand dollars in cash with a yellow sticky note that read, "No hard feelings? Come see me at the boat when you're ready to get *onboard*. I'll be here all night. Drop by."

"See, man? This is your opportunity," Wolcott said. "He wants to work with you."

"The key is to the front door of the boat," Quarles explained enthusiastically. "Chuck said you could use it any time you want. Bring anybody you want—for whatever reason." He and Wolcott laughed wickedly.

Wayne stuck the envelope inside his overcoat, right behind the camera on the pocket button. In one of the condo's many mirrors, he could see a slight bulge near his breast pocket, which reminded him that he had just gathered video and audio evidence that would most likely amount to a bribe. Everything was going even better than he had expected.

"Say, Wayne, why don't you give me your coat?" Wolcott asked just then.

Wayne froze, hoping he hadn't called too much attention to the wire.

"Well, what...what for?" he asked.

"Just hand it over," Wolcott insisted.

Wayne didn't know what to do. He was told that the overcoat wasn't to leave his possession, but hadn't asked the agents what to say in such a situation.

If Wolcott discovers the wire, the operation will be blown and my body will be discovered next, floating in the river a few days from now. But if I don't hand it over, it'll raise suspicions and they'll know for sure that something's up.

Wayne was left with no choice and very little time to think. Wolcott had taken a few steps toward him and was waiting impatiently for the coat. Wayne took it off and held it out. He could feel tiny beads of perspiration starting on his forehead as he stood frozen in place, hoping Wolcott wouldn't find the tiny device implanted in the button.

Wolcott grabbed the coat roughly then...didn't even check. He hung it up in a hallway closet and said, "It's time we rolled our sleeves up and got to work on the bill. I've got a date tonight that I intend to keep."

Wayne went through all the motions, helping Quarles and Wolcott with whatever details needed tending to on the anti-gaming bill. As far as they were concerned, he was on their team one hundred percent and ready to reap the rewards.

Two hours later, as previously planned, Wayne left the condo and met Agent Tischner at a nearby restaurant.

"Did y'all get that on video?" Wayne asked, obviously excited about the work he'd done.

"We sure did. Thank God for wireless video," Tischner said. "But, Wayne, before I applaud you on your success, I want to explain a few things to you. We have something called an 'Attaboy' and, conversely, we have an 'Aw-Shit.' Now, it only takes one 'Aw-Shit' to wipe the board clean of ten 'Attaboys,' understand?"

"I think I'm about to," Wayne said disappointedly.

"Yes, you are." Tischner's voice didn't raise one bit, but his eyes locked onto Wayne's and his face darkened menacingly. He leaned in close and hissed, "You never, ever, *ever* give a defendant an article of clothing with FBI gear in it that's capable of recording evidence. You allowed him to put it in a place where no additional evidence could be gathered and left us in the dark as far as protecting you. Why didn't you just say you felt a cold coming on and had a chill or something?"

"But I…" the words died before Wayne could get them out.

"I won't even go into what would've happened if he'd found the device. Suffice it to say you would've been up shit creek." Tischner sat back then and his expression seemed to soften. "That said, we were fortunate to get what we needed *before* this little mishap. And I suppose we'd share some of the blame had this investigation been compromised. The agents and I should've given you a stronger lecture beforehand."

"Well, believe me, sir, I sure won't forget it from now on," Wayne said, finally remembering to breathe.

"Okay," Tischner said, satisfied that he had made his point. "We got the 'Aw-Shit' out of the way. Let's move on to the 'Attaboys.' Son," he paused, "you really did do a great job."

"Thanks," Wayne said, beaming. "So, when do I get to watch it?"

"Oh, you want to see how you perform under pressure, huh?" Tischner laughed. "All right. Come on out to the van and we'll have a private screening."

Wayne and Tischner walked out to the parking lot. The agent took a sweeping look around to make sure nobody was watching then opened the back door of the van. Wayne went in first.

Inside the van were a couple of technicians and more equipment than Wayne would have guessed could fit inside the rather cramped vehicle. From the outside, though, the van looked entirely normal.

"Burns, how about letting Wayne here have a look at his work?" Tischner said.

With the press of a button, a few seconds later, Wayne was watching the video. "I can't believe how good the quality is," he said. "It's like living the whole scene all over again."

He watched in disgust as Quarles handed him the envelope, and was sickened by how the two men assumed that he'd be bought off as easily as they were. The only thing that made it more palatable was knowing that those two clowns would someday soon get theirs for being involved in such a scam, failing to report the blackmail in the first place and becoming thugs themselves.

"I hated having to play along like that," he said.

"I know, son," Tischner said. "Just keep this consolation in mind: With your help, justice will prevail."

"I sure hope so," Wayne said, staring at the video. "Boy, I can't wait to see those two behind bars. Uh…by the way, how will I get to see myself perform?"

"Keep watching, Wayne," the tech answered. "You moved in front of the mirror twice and glanced down at the camera, which wasn't even visible. You gave us all a good laugh in here, but we got some nice shots when you look directly into the mirror."

"Yeah, I guess I did do that," Wayne said, laughing at himself. "What can I say? I'm a beginner. But at least I have some evidence that it was me—and now we've got all that video evidence of what they've done."

"We don't just have *video* evidence, Wayne," Tischner said.

"What do you mean?"

"Sign your initials on this label then we'll bag the evidence and have you initial the seal," Tischner said, passing him the label. "The envelope that the one idiot handed you was passed to him by the other idiot. It should have both of their fingerprints on it. We're also hoping that we can tie it to Shyster through his fingerprints and through his saliva on the seal, which could yield DNA evidence. I have no doubt that we can also compare the writing on the note to other examples of his handwriting."

"Wow, you got all that?" Wayne asked in amazement.

"Not just that," Tischner said. "The Bureau of Alcohol, Tobacco and Firearms' forensic lab can analyze the pigment in ink. They can even identify the year of manufacture if necessary."

"On what?"

"Once he's arrested, the pen he used will be seized and they'll be able to match its ink with that on the note," Tischner said proudly.

"Well, it sounds like we've got everything we need," Wayne said hopefully.

"Not quite," Tischner responded. "The best part comes next. You're on your way to Shyster's boat to tell him you aren't for sale—not for a measly five thousand dollars."

"Huh?" Wayne asked in surprise.

"We're upping the ante. We want to get him giving you the money himself—but remember what we warned you about entrapment. Don't tell him how much you want, but make sure he gets the idea that your help is worth far more than five grand. Then let's just see what happens."

"Right now?" Wayne asked.

"What better time?" Tischner smiled. "He said he'd be there all night waiting on you. Probably expecting you to go thank him in person. That's how those big shots are. They love to have the little guys like Quarles and Wolcott groveling all over them. They get off on the power."

"Only I'm not there to thank him?" Wayne asked.

"Nope. You're there to show him you're worth more than those two combined. Play hardball with him."

"What if he's not in the mood to play?" Wayne asked nervously.

"He will be," Tischner said. "You're the one he needs."

"Okay," Wayne said. "I guess I'm ready, then."

"Oh, and Wayne?" the tech interjected.

"Yeah?"

"Try to resist checking yourself out in the mirror this time," he laughed. "You may have been on camera, but that doesn't make you Brad Pitt."

Wayne quickly drove to the reservoir and parked on the marina near Chuck's yacht. He was aware of a knot forming in his stomach. *Even Tischner said it*, he thought. *Quarles and Wolcott are the small fries. This is the big boss—and a whole new ballgame.*

He kept his nerves in check as he walked past Chuck's sports car and smelled the aroma of an expensive cigar wafting from the boat. Tischner had let Wayne keep the key Quarles had given him rather than include it with the rest of the evidence. Chuck would expect him to use it, and not doing so could raise suspicions.

He unlocked the door, entered and saw Chuck sitting alone by the bar in the cabin. There didn't appear to be anyone else on the boat, but by now Wayne was camera shy and suspicious that someone could walk down one of the boat's many hallways at any moment.

"Come on in, my friend. I was expecting you." Chuck greeted Wayne with all smiles, as he sipped on a glass of scotch in one hand and held a long, lit cigar in the other.

He was dressed in his usual playboy fashion, with his unbuttoned shirt exposing his hairy chest and gold chain. Staring at his comb-over, Wayne couldn't help thinking that a plastic surgeon somewhere could probably transplant some of the hair from his chest and plug it into the top of his head, if he was having that much trouble accepting baldness.

"Make yourself comfortable," Chuck snickered. "Mi casa es su casa. Only I don't know the Spanish word for 'boat.'"

I'm not going to have any problems playing hardball with this asshole, given what he's done, Wayne realized, seething inside. But he showed little emotion, refusing Chuck's offer of a cigar and a drink. *I want full control of my mental faculties in dealing with good ol' Uncle Chuck.* He was too hyped up to even sit down and stood at the far end of the bar from Chuck.

"I guess you got my little package," Chuck said confidently.

"Oh, yeah, Quarles gave me something—and 'little' is right," Wayne snapped back. "You think five grand is enough to buy casino legislation using *my* good name? Not once now but twice? Surely the casinos you represent have more money than that! I busted my ass on this bill last year only to come back and do the same all over again this coming session. I opened that envelope and thought that poor old Baptists must be funding this effort! Your friends in the casinos better open up their wallets a little wider if they want me."

During the whole tirade, Chuck just sat there stunned, the cigar dangling out of his mouth.

"Tell you what," Wayne continued. "I'm about ready to tell my wife everything and let you find another guinea pig."

Now Chuck pounced. He was the one used to giving ultimatums. "You're getting pretty damn cocky for a wet-behind-the-ears lawyer and wannabe politician—especially with that great video hanging over your head, you bastard. Your sweet little wife might forgive you for that, but your constituents won't. You *stand* for something in their eyes—so your laying down in a strange bed would have them mighty damn upset."

The truth of the matter was that Wayne was in fact getting cocky, and tired of being pushed around. All of his work with the agents was helping him come out of his shell, and his newfound sense of purpose as an informant was bringing him out of his depression. He'd become a force to reckon with—unfortunately for these low-life criminals.

Becoming a victim of a scumbag like Chuck changed Wayne; he was no longer a naïve little lawyer. Chuck didn't know it yet, but Wayne was now using *him*. He was Wayne's target, the one he'd use to cut his teeth on and become an experienced undercover agent. He'd hone his skills in the months to come to see that Chuck got what he deserved, and to bring the whole rotten, corrupt conspiracy tumbling down around him.

"That's true, Chuck. My constituents do trust me. That's what you're counting on, isn't it? And that's why you need me so bad," Wayne said coolly.

With a steely look, but without another word, Chuck reached under the bar. Wayne's first thought was that he might be reaching for a gun.

The agents can't possibly be close enough to save me, he realized at that instant. *But at least they'll have it on video and this no-good, corrupt son-of-a-bitch will be somewhere making little rocks out of big rocks in the end.*

As a lawyer, he knew that a sentence for murder would not net Chuck one of the prime, golf course-style prisons meant for non-violent offenders, no matter how high up his connections went—and Wayne was ready to make that sacrifice.

He squinted his eyes and prepared for the bullet to rip through his skin. But to Wayne's surprise, Chuck came up with a small cash box full of hundred-dollar bills. At first he started counting them out one by one. Then he slammed the box down on the bar and began cursing.

He slid the box down the bar toward Wayne like a bartender in Tombstone, Arizona, would have passed a foamy mug of cold beer to a dusty old cowboy.

"I don't know exactly how much is in there—somewhere around twenty grand—and I don't really care," Chuck said, avoiding eye contact with Wayne. "But you better get your smart ass out of here before I change my mind. And you best keep this to yourself."

Wayne walked back across the small wooden pier, prouder than a kid who just rode his first bike without training wheels. No one had been there to help him. He'd done it all on his own. He could hardly wait to get back to the meeting place and talk to the agents.

"This is easier than shooting fish in a barrel," Wayne bragged, as soon as he sat down next to Tischner in the restaurant.

"Well, for one thing," Agent Tischner said, "pure greed helps. These guys pass money around like hotcakes because they know it's only going to bring them more money. For another thing, you've got to look at it like the opening day of deer hunting season. There are deer everywhere since nobody has bothered them all year long. Then all of the sudden, the first shot is fired and you can't find them anywhere."

"What you're saying is they think they're untouchable because no one's bothered to try to touch them or they've been bribed away," Wayne said.

"That's right," Tischner answered. "These damn Mississippi politicians are so proud of carrying on their shady dealings without having gotten caught for so many years. They don't think it will ever happen to them. They have no reason to."

Wayne shook his head in agreement, thinking about all the similar information that his father had shared with him.

"What we have now is 'the low hanging fruit,'" Tischner continued. "Some of the evidence you just got from Shyster makes it easier for us to tie him to the first batch of money. That knot is tied. Now the hard part comes when we try to lure those other worthless worms out of their holes."

"They'll be more wary," Wayne said. "Like deer on the second day of a hunt."

"You learn fast, son," Tischner said, impressed.

Wayne left his meeting with Agent Tischner on cloud nine. He was already beginning to feel vindicated, and was experiencing things he would never have been involved in as a small town attorney chasing ambulances for a living. His only pang of regret came when Tischner called him "son."

If only I could tell my dad, he thought.

Chapter 13

The Mission Continues

"The government is the potent omnipresent teacher.
For good or ill it teaches the whole people by its example.
Crime is contagious. If the government becomes a lawbreaker,
it breeds contempt for law; it invites every man to become
a law unto himself; it invites anarchy. To declare that the end
justifies the means—to declare that the government
may commit crimes—would bring terrible retribution."
—Justice Louis D. Brandeis (U.S. Supreme Court)

Wayne's next meeting with Chuck was more cordial, now that they seemed to have reached an agreement. It was at a social affair just after Christmas, high above Jackson's skyline at the beautiful Capitol Club, a private, members-only dinner club that overlooked the governor's mansion as well as the old and new Capitol buildings. Legislators were coming together in preparation for the upcoming session, but primarily just to blow off some steam.

A few days before Wayne went to the meeting, Tischner had told him, "Make it appear that you've accepted things as they are. Act friendly toward Chuck, no matter how much he makes your skin crawl. It's important to our case that you two continue your relationship."

Wayne concentrated on those instructions as he entered the building. He'd do his part, though it wouldn't be easy—especially since he had begun to take on his father's attitude about "all the worthless bastards" he worked with.

Everybody that was anybody in state politics was there. Even members of the media were walking around with microphones, asking questions about upcoming bills, and cameramen were dutifully trailing along, filming the smiling legislators during their prepared sound bites. Some guests were laughing and joking in the card room while others were showing their lack of skills in the billiards room.

Wayne wasn't wearing his FBI-assigned gear since the agents weren't really expecting him to make any advances in furthering their case at the event. It was unlikely that anyone would make a move in such a public forum. For the time being, it was more crucial for him to simply mix in; he'd have to leave it up to any corrupt politicians and lobbyists to confront him. If that happened, he would then be authorized to continue his efforts with full surveillance.

Wayne saw Chuck surrounded by a group of legislators crowded around the library. He was carrying on, being loud and overall acting like the center of attention. When the group broke up to get drinks from the bar, Wayne saw his opportunity and headed straight for Chuck. He was hoping that not too many people would see them talking, and especially that no news cameras would capture them together.

"Mr. Shyster, nice to see you," Wayne said in a formal but friendly tone.

"Mr. Lott, my pleasure—as always," Chuck said in return. He seemed very happy that Wayne had approached him. It must have fed his ego.

After a few minutes of small talk about fishing and sailing, Chuck spied a potential target across the room and went off to corner him. *He must already feel secure that I'm firmly on his payroll,* Wayne realized. *Guess I should consider myself lucky.*

Wayne didn't talk to too many people after that. He had a few of their delicious hors d'oeuvres then stood awkwardly alone at the window in the atrium, until a couple of representatives came over to talk to him.

"Representative Lott, so good to see you. Tell us, how's that anti-gaming bill of yours coming along?"

Wayne could feel his face flush. He started to cough and excused himself to get a drink of water.

Just as he regained his composure, a senior member of the House came over and greeted him warmly. "So, there's our rising young star. What sort of things do you have planned for us this session?"

"Oh, sir, I…" He reached into his jacket pocket and brought out his cell phone. "I'm sorry. It's on vibrate. You'll have to excuse me, please. I've got to take this call from my wife."

Wayne moved into one of the old private phone booths near the elevator and closed the glass door. He was finding it extremely difficult to trust anyone there, even members that he had worked with closely before. He just couldn't figure out which ones were truly anti-gaming and which ones were on the take. After a few more minutes of torture, he decided it was best not to be there at all, although he was looking forward to trying out the chef's special that everybody always raved about.

However, just as he was about to leave, he couldn't help but notice a gorgeous young blonde hanging on the arm of one of the members. With all the attention she was getting, she didn't see him staring, and he was glad because he recognized her as Cindy, the girl from Chuck's boat.

She was with a representative from the coast. He thought, *Oh, my God, not another victim.*

Wayne walked outside, quickly but without attracting any attention, and called his contact number. He didn't recognize the voice on the other end and asked for Agent Tischner.

"Tischner's on holiday leave. Who is this?"

"This is B-32-P-09," Wayne answered, using his prescribed identity.

"Wayne?" the voice asked.

"Yes…"

"This is Bob. What's going on? I didn't think you were on assignment today."

Wayne was relieved to hear the young agent, even though he still only knew him by his first name. "I'm not on assignment. But I was told that whenever I run into past contacts, I should immediately notify my control agent."

"So who's the past contact?" Bob asked casually.

"The woman that was used to make the run on me," he answered.

"The babe from the boat?" Bob asked. Wayne could tell that he had gotten his attention.

"That's right. She just arrived at a social gathering with one of the other state representatives and is hanging all over him. I don't know him, but I hope they're not planning to do the same thing to him that they did to me," Wayne said angrily.

"It's a good chance to get her real identity. I'll be right there, but I probably won't recognize her with clothes on. How's she dressed?" Bob asked.

"Like a million bucks," Wayne said. "She stands out in the crowd with a red, low-cut cocktail dress. It looks like a couple of the members already know her. They're all talking to her as she passes by."

"Good. Hopefully that means she won't leave any time soon," Bob said. "If you see me, don't let on that you know me."

"I really *don't* know you, Bob."

Wayne took a deep breath then went back inside. He wanted to stay inconspicuous so that Cindy wouldn't see him. At the same time, he wanted to keep an eye on her. *For professional reasons only*, he told himself. He stood off by the lobby and occasionally looked her way.

The entire time that he was watching, Wayne didn't see any interaction between Cindy and Chuck. *It could mean that there's no plot*, he thought, *or she could have already been instructed what to do.*

Less than thirty minutes later, he glanced over in Cindy's direction and happened to notice a florist deliveryman in a white jacket making his way through the crowd. He was holding a large, colorful bouquet of flowers that partially obstructed his face. But when he placed the arrangement on the large round center table in the atrium, Wayne could clearly see that it was Bob.

The agent left for a moment then came back inside with an armful of single red roses, which he gave one by one to every lady in the room, explaining, "Because we were late with the centerpiece, please accept this compliments of the florist."

Finally, he got to Cindy. She put her champagne glass down on a side table in order to accept the rose, and smiled enchantingly at Bob, who seemed to get flustered. As he started to walk away, he bumped into the table and Cindy's glass fell to the marble floor, shattering into several pieces.

"I'm terribly sorry," Bob said, grabbing a nearby napkin and dabbing at her arm.

"It's all right. It was almost empty," Cindy assured him.

Holding the napkin, Bob bent down and picked up the broken glass fragments, one with bright red lipstick on it. He apologized profusely then straightened up and, without anyone noticing, managed to slip the napkin into his jacket pocket.

All out of roses, Bob left with a final apology and a "Happy holidays."

From a distance, Wayne couldn't be sure that the young agent had a chance to collect the evidence he was after. *He was either truly flustered or a hell of a good actor.*

Wayne waited an hour and a half, watching her stealthily while trying to keep out of sight. Once, when a senior member came up to him, Cindy seemed to look in his direction but gave no sign of recognition.

Of course, Wayne thought. *With all the business Chuck sends her way, why would she remember me?*

The girl hadn't touched food at all and, being a professional, was probably instructed to limit her alcohol intake and keep her head clear. Meanwhile, her date appeared to be getting drunk.

Wayne couldn't watch any more. The man seemed to be falling into the same trap that he had—and there was nothing he could do to save him.

As Wayne was walking to his car, dejected, his FBI-issued cell phone rang. "Hello?"

"Wayne, it's Bob. I got the evidence…"

"From the broken glass?"

"Yep. I slipped the fragments into my pocket while no one was looking," Bob said proudly.

"That's great," Wayne said. "I wasn't sure if…if you had the chance."

"No," Bob said, "be honest. You weren't sure which of my heads was doing the thinking."

Wayne laughed. "Something like that."

"The big head always wins out," Bob said. "It's FBI training. Anyway, I'm going to rush the evidence to the lab for fingerprints and DNA so hopefully we'll know soon who this girl is. I have a feeling 'Cindy' is a stage name and not the one her momma gave her. The vehicle she drives with the New York plate is registered to S.L. Styles and the address is an abandoned house. Her name is probably something like Sherry or Sue. Hell, who knows? It can be 'Sindy' with an 'S,'" Bob scoffed.

"So what can we do in the meantime?" Wayne asked.

"Agents are already on their way to the houseboat to set up surveillance. We figure that's where she'll show up with that date of hers. Are they still at the party?"

"I don't know. I just got out of the elevator. The last I saw them, they…wait!" He saw a woman in a red cocktail dress making her way toward the parking lot; an inebriated man was leaning heavily against her.

"They're coming out now," he said breathlessly. "Bob, is there any way you can catch her before…before they ruin this guy's life? I mean, we don't know if he's married or what."

There was a pause on the other end. Then Bob said, "Sure, Wayne. We'll do whatever we can."

When he hung up, Wayne watched Cindy and the representative get into a black BMW. He assumed it belonged to the man, who was too drunk to drive. Cindy got in the driver's seat and Wayne saw her pull out of the parking lot then started his own car.

At first, he intended to drive right home and wait for Bob's call. Instead, curiosity got the better of him. *I'll just follow a little ways off*, Wayne thought. *After all, I've been trained by the FBI. What could it hurt?*

He tailed the car for a couple of miles before it made a turn—away from the marina.

That's strange, Wayne thought. *I wonder where they're headed.* He didn't have to wait long to find out.

About ten minutes later, they pulled up in front of a hotel and the driver's side door flew open. Wayne watched as Cindy got out of the car and walked around the other side. She opened the door and yanked the incapacitated man out of the passenger seat by his arm. For a second, the representative stood on his own wobbly legs before slumping down into the gutter.

Cindy stood over him, shouting. "Go on up to your room! What good are you in this condition? You'll get about as hard as an overcooked noodle."

She took out her cell phone and dialed a number before storming back into the car and slamming the door. After waiting for the man to make his way inside, Cindy took the car keys and walked up to the front desk clerk. After a brief conversation, she came back outside and waited with her arms folded across her chest.

Within a few minutes, a taxi arrived out front. Wayne picked up his phone and made a call. "Bob, she's not bringing him back to the houseboat."

"What? How do you know that?"

"I followed them from the party to a hotel on the frontage road where she dumped his drunk butt off. She's getting in a taxi now."

"Look, Wayne, I appreciate the info but you aren't a surveillance agent and shouldn't be attempting this on your own. Which way is she heading?" Bob asked.

"Southbound on I-55 back towards town. Maybe she's going back to the party for her car...or to reel in another victim."

"I'll get the agents right on it," Bob said. "Good job, Wayne. Now go home."

Regardless of what Bob had told him, Wayne felt an obligation to keep an eye on Cindy until the agents got to her. He followed her taxi for about fifteen minutes until it pulled into the parking lot by the legislative get-together, where she got out and headed to her car.

Apparently, agents had gotten there first, and they pulled up next to Wayne's car.

"I thought you might be here," Bob said, annoyed. "Get in and brief us."

As soon as Wayne got into the backseat, he saw Cindy's red Jag pull out of the lot—and the agents followed closely behind. She was obviously still pissed about the events of the evening, and her anger was apparent in her driving. She didn't make it too far before being stopped by a Jackson cop for speeding.

The FBI agents passed by, made a loop then came back around and stopped in the distance, about a couple of hundred yards from the police car. Before long, Cindy drove away with only a warning and the cop stayed behind with his interior lights on, writing something down. The agents pulled up behind him and flashed their badges.

"We need to know that woman's identity."

The officer checked his notes. "Her name is Sylvia Lynn Styles, originally from New York, but now she lives about ten miles north of here in Ridgeland." He gave them her apartment number then they thanked him and left hurriedly in that direction.

While en route, the agents ran her name, date of birth and vital stats on their in-car computer and found her to have a record of drug abuse. Bob read the details of her profile off the screen.

"Sylvia Lynn Styles is a former model from Miami who moved to New York, where she got a prior felony drug conviction. She went to rehab then got arrested for trying to sell cocaine to an undercover DEA agent."

Wayne couldn't help feeling a little bit sorry for her. The girl he had met as Chuck's "niece" seemed to have so much going for her. "She would've been better off in finance," he mumbled.

"What?" Bob asked.

"Sorry…nothing. Keep going," Wayne said.

"She was convicted on that drug-selling charge and given a ten-year sentence but was released on parole. She's on federal probation in New York, but an alert says her probation officer hasn't heard from her in months." Bob turned toward the other agent. "She was already violating parole by being out of state and working in an establishment serving alcohol that was also known to be frequented by drug users and other felons."

About two miles down the road, they spotted Sylvia's car at a gas station on the northbound frontage road and pulled in, deciding that they had more than enough information to confront her.

They glanced over at Sylvia, who was pumping gas in her cocktail dress and a thin shawl. Seconds later, the agents got out and approached her; Bob reached into his jacket to get his badge and get her attention as Wayne slumped over in the backseat to keep her from seeing him.

She saw the agent reaching in his jacket, freaked out, dropped the gas hose and jumped into her car. She sped away with her tires squealing.

Wayne ran over to help the agents, who were being sprayed

with gas, and managed to wrestle the hose back into its nozzle. They jumped back into their unmarked car and began to pursue Sylvia up Interstate 55.

Wiping himself off with a handkerchief, Bob turned around to face Wayne. "Thanks," he said, smelling strongly of gas.

"Don't mention it," Wayne said. "So, mind if I smoke back here?"

"Funny," Bob said, turning back around. "But if I were you, I'd put on my seatbelt."

The agent driving floored it to one hundred. They were gaining ground on Sylvia, who was passing everything in sight. Wayne watched in horror as she almost slammed right into the back of a big, slow-moving truck. She swerved to miss it at the last second then screeched off the Lakeland Drive East exit, but continued straight across Lakeland Drive only to re-enter I-55 and continue north.

The agents, in the meantime, had placed their portable blue light on the dashboard and were catching up. From the backseat, Wayne was the first to hear the approaching sirens.

A local police officer was attempting to pull them over.

"What's he doing?" Bob said, straining his neck around. "Can't he see we're on the job?"

Wayne figured it out. "There's been a rash of recent instances where suspected gang members have been posing as policemen, stopping women and raping them. They've got a blue light, too."

"Great," Bob said, shaking his head. "That's all we need."

The driver attempted to switch his radio to the state network and call local dispatch to tell them to call the unit off of them. However, just before he could do so, Sylvia pulled off at County Line Road exit, obviously unaware that the traffic light at the bottom of the ramp was changing. It had just turned red.

"Slow down!" Wayne yelled to the driver.

They heard the screech of tires before they caught a glimpse of

Sylvia's Jaguar. She was forced to jam on the brakes in order to stop, just narrowly missing the car in front of her.

Bob leapt out of the car and ran to her window, flashing his FBI badge. Meanwhile, the driver took out his badge and went out toward the police car that had now stopped behind them to explain that they were in pursuit of a felon.

"Sylvia Stiles, you are in violation of your parole. We need to talk to you," Bob said, quietly but firmly.

Startled, she began to cry. "I didn't know you were law enforcement officers or I wouldn't have tried to run."

"Who did you think we were?" Bob asked, hoping for some names.

She didn't answer, just hung her head and sobbed. "What do you want from me?"

"Are you all right to drive?"

She nodded.

"I'm going to get in with you, and you're going to follow the FBI car back south on I-55," he explained. Bob waved to the driver behind him as a signal then slowly got into the passenger side seat of the Jaguar. "Don't make any sudden moves or try anything stupid," he told her. "We just need to talk to you."

Both cars drove to an undercover office downtown. From the outside, it looked like a local business, located on the third floor of a renovated building just around the block from the Capitol Club. They parked in the garages so as not to be seen by passersby and the agents escorted Sylvia to their office. The building was quiet for the night with no other occupants around.

Sylvia, still nervous but looking more collected now, took a seat across from Bob's desk while Wayne waited in the lobby down the hall, where she wouldn't be able to see him.

"So what do you want me to tell you?" she asked.

"We don't want much, Sylvia. Just everything you know. Starting with the contents of your cell phone. Hand it to the agent here, who'll be in the next room copying down all the numbers while I go over some legal forms with you," Bob said.

She did as she was told then asked, "Are you revoking my parole?"

"That's up to you and how cooperative you are. We want to know everything you know about any criminal activity around here—but trust me, we already know more than you'd like us to. So I'll know if you're telling the truth about other things, too. If you don't, we'll stuff you onto a U.S. marshal contracted airplane and send you straight to New York in handcuffs and leg irons. It's a far cry from class-first," Bob said.

He didn't mention what they already had on her: her involvement in prostitution, drug possession and extortion. In fact, they knew every freckle on her body.

"Somehow I get the feeling that you *already know* everybody I know and everything I've done since being in Jackson for almost a year," she said coolly. "But I'm not about to risk my parole and spend the remaining ten years of my sentence in a federal pen, so I'll tell you what you want to hear."

After that, she sang like a bird, providing the agents with a list of all the members of the legislature that she had been involved with. For the most part, it read like roll call at the Capitol on the first day of the session, and included a well-known asshole, Billy Ray Watson.

With the FBI's video camera set up on a tripod in the corner, running with its red light on, she told them about encounter after encounter with each of those men. She wasn't accustomed to cameras being out in the open, but she was just as open with her stories as she was with her sex.

After awhile, even Bob seemed to get embarrassed and called for a break. While the other agent stayed with her, he received permission for a voluntary search of her belongings in the car, and came back with her little black book—along with another surprise.

"Well, look at this," Bob said, holding a prescription bottle of pills in the air. "Erectile dysfunction medication prescribed to Billy Ray Watson. Now, who would've guessed?" He shook his head then said to Sylvia, "That's a good way to get some of your leading men to perform on camera. You won't mind if we accompany you to your apartment in Ridgeland and conduct a permissive search there as well, would you? See if anything else interesting turns up?"

She took a deep breath. "Okay," she said. "But I want it on record that I'm being cooperative and didn't make you get a warrant." Then she looked straight into the camera. "I also want it on record that I'm agreeing on the condition that you won't wreck my apartment."

Chapter 14

A Woman Scorned

"Strong reasons make strong actions."
—William Shakespeare

Bob and the other agent drove Sylvia to her apartment while Wayne hid down the hallway then got a ride to his car from another agent in the office so as not to be seen by Sylvia. She lived on a quiet street in a good neighborhood and Bob couldn't help thinking how shocked some of the neighbors would be to find out what went on in there.

When they parked out in front, Bob said, "Listen, Sylvia and I will go up first. You come up in about fifteen minutes. We don't want to all walk in together and get the neighbors suspicious."

"Please," Sylvia said. "I've had more than two men up to my apartment before."

Bob shrugged, "Can't argue with that," and they all went in together.

———

Sylvia unlocked the door and walked in first, flipping on the lights. The apartment was elegant and spacious, but there was nothing overtly flashy or obscenely expensive about it, which was consistent with the way the mob operated: Keep the money hidden; don't draw too much attention with big-ticket items or outrageous purchases.

"I know the kinds of things you're looking for," she said, sounding blasé. "I have no drugs but I do have some items you'll be interested in that I kept for personal insurance. I'll hand them over *without* you destroying my place."

She opened a desk drawer and brought out some marked-up draft bills. "These have Billy Ray's hand-written comments all over them." Then she went to a cabinet and retrieved a couple of the earlier "movies" made aboard the houseboat and handed them to Bob.

"I was able to burn a few copies of my own before Chuck took the DVD copier off the boat. The rest are still onboard," she said. "I'm not the only 'actress' you'll see if you watch all the videos. Other girls at the club were doing it long before me. I don't even know what other men are involved other than the ones I've named."

She walked over to a mirror and wiped away the smeared mascara from under her eyes. "That's all I've got."

"Look, it's late…and you've obviously been cooperating," Bob said. "We're going to leave you for tonight but you're to call this number first thing when you wake up in the morning." He handed her a note with a cell phone number on it. "If you try to leave, you know we'll catch you, so let's make it easy on everyone, huh? Oh, and be prepared to run an errand for us tomorrow."

Bob made a call to Wayne as the agents drove away from Sylvia's apartment. "Wayne, we're going to need you on standby to identify some of the representatives in the videos Sylvia just gave us. We've got to find out who's been compromised." He looked at the stack of DVDs sitting on his lap. "It's a dirty job, but somebody's got to do it."

The next morning, Agent Tischner was back on duty. Bob had turned all of the evidence, including the broken glass, over to the senior control agent, who awaited Sylvia's call. She reached him at 10 a.m. on the dot.

"I'm ready to do whatever you want," she said.

"Glad to hear it," Tischner said, taken aback by her abruptness. "Do you know when Chuck's expected back on the boat?"

"He's out of state today and as far as I know, no one's onboard. I was supposed to stay there last night," she said. "We use a secret code to let any of us know if it's being used or not—you know, like roommates do in college. There's an old tin can tied to the pole just to the left of the pier. When any of us go aboard, we turn the can upside down over the top of the pole. If it's just dangling, that means nobody's on the boat. Chuck tells everyone that rule right after they get a key."

"Okay, that's good to know. Meet me at the bottom of the spillway in an hour," Tischner said.

"How will I know who you are?" she asked.

"You won't have to. *I* know exactly what you look like," Agent Tischner said, hanging up.

Tischner had been busy during his alleged "time off." He had already gotten a federal court order allowing agents, or anyone working as an agent for the government, to enter Shyster's boat, install surveillance equipment and record any evidence of a crime. His plan was to collect evidence without Chuck being aware that they had been there at all.

"Don't want to fire the first shot just yet and scare away all the deer," he had explained to the other agents.

The writ also allowed them to return as necessary to perform such functions as battery replacement in surveillance gear, technological maintenance, etc. "So you better have your sea legs ready," he warned them.

A little past eleven, a van pulled up near Sylvia's red Jaguar parked below the spillway. The driver got out dressed in fishing garb and a woman who appeared to be his wife was in tow, carrying a minnow bucket.

As the man walked past Sylvia's open window, he stopped to tie his shoelace and, without turning toward her, said, "I'm the agent you talked to. In a few minutes, the lady with me will go to the bathroom. When she does, pop the hood on your car as if it needs repair, pretend to make a call then follow her into the ladies' room."

A couple of minutes later, the female agent, Kristie, who posed as Tischner's wife, put her minnow bucket down, climbed back up the rocks along the river and headed toward the bathroom. Sylvia saw her and did as instructed, raising her hood and pretending to call someone for help on her cell phone. Then she walked to the bathroom. As soon as she stepped in, Kristie gave her a quick but thorough pat down.

"I have to be sure you're not attempting to introduce any new evidence on to the scene," the agent explained. "For that reason, you're being searched and your car will be searched. Don't try anything. We're maintaining constant surveillance on you."

"Why? I'm cooperating," Sylvia protested.

Kristie ignored her question. "Go back out there and meet the 'mechanics' who are pulling up in a white truck. They're FBI agents who'll search the interior of your car while appearing to work under the dashboard to get it started. They'll place an overnight bag on your seat. It's rigged with a camera. Once they clear you, drive immediately to the boat to retrieve all the DVDs on board. Bring the bag and when you get inside, place the camera in such a way as to capture all of your movements as you remove the discs. We need to make sure you don't hide anything. Put the discs in the bag and come immediately out. Then head back over here near the public restroom and park out front by the spillway, got it?"

"I think so," Sylvia said, trying hard to concentrate on the agent's instructions.

She left the bathroom and followed the plan step by step. After the agents cleaned out her car to avoid any potential planting of evidence, she pulled up to the boat while under surveillance, went onboard for a few minutes and walked out with over twenty discs. When she arrived back at the spillway, she placed the bag on the ground and Kristie picked it up by throwing a blanket over it then putting it in the back of Tischner's van.

The vehicle was equipped with high-speed dubbing machines and, within minutes, all of the discs were copied by technicians then treated with an invisible chemical that could be detected later under ultraviolet lighting. The technicians recorded the entire process inside the van on video. Kristie returned the bag full of DVDs to Sylvia, instructing her to replace them on the boat immediately.

The technicians had also been tracking Sylvia's entire movements throughout the day. They were recorded on video and the discs were maintained for additional evidence.

Once Sylvia came back out of the boat, it was mission accomplished. Kristie met her and told her to contact Tischner the next day before 10 a.m. for further instructions.

"You'll be under constant surveillance," she added. "Don't attempt to leave the area."

Within seconds, the undercover agents pulled away and Sylvia was left "alone," knowing fully well that she was still being watched.

As the legislative session began, the agents spent the next two weeks reviewing the discs to see which other representatives had been caught in the corruption trap. They often asked Wayne to stop by in the evenings to see if he could identify any of the men as members of the legislature; he was able to positively identify fourteen.

As Sylvia had stated, she was far from the only girl to make an appearance in the videos, so she was also brought in, after Wayne had left, to identify the other women, as well as any of the men he didn't recognize. She identified two other men for the agents, but broke into tears as she viewed one of the videos.

"What's wrong?" Bob asked her, hitting the pause button.

"That's Carol," she cried. "A friend of mine who was murdered shortly after that movie was made."

"What do you mean 'murdered'?" Tischner asked.

"On New Year's Eve, we had a big crowd in the club," Sylvia said, drying her eyes. "There was some big bad-ass, steroid freak there who referred to himself as Dog. He was just itching to beat the hell out of somebody. When any of the customers got too close to a girl he liked, he'd push them away. It was ruining our tips! So one of our bouncers followed him into the hallway outside the bathroom, where he was going to try to scare him into leaving. Instead, this guy Dog pushed the bouncer into the bathroom, beat the crap out of him then took his gun and stuck it in his mouth, threatening to kill him. Then he shoved the bouncer's head into the toilet and left him there, bleeding."

"What happened to the gun?" Bob asked.

"Nobody knows what he did with it. But believe me, Dog didn't need it. He was one mean mother even without a weapon. His biceps and triceps were so big they split his shirtsleeves. The bouncer was hospitalized with a broken jaw, a broken cheekbone and a shattered eye socket. He lost several teeth and partial sight in his right eye." Sylvia shuddered.

"And when Dog left the bathroom?" Bob asked.

"He took off almost right away, before anyone even knew he'd almost killed the bouncer. Carol left the club with that bastard," Sylvia said, breaking down once again. "We never saw either of them again. Her body was found on the side of the road the next morning. They referred to her as if she wasn't a person at all. She was only a number." Her sobs shook her entire body. "Number one homicide for that county for the year…and the year was only a few hours old."

"I'm sorry," Tischner said softly. "How was she killed?"

"Shot in the head with what they said 'appeared to be' a forty or forty-five caliber bullet. She also had multiple bruises and abrasions on her face, head and the inside of her thighs. The paper said there were no suspects, but I know Dog did it! She had a four-year-old son at home that Child Services took away," Sylvia said, looking at the agents through red eyes.

"Do you know anything about this Dog?" Bob asked.

Sniffling, she said, "He claimed to be a high-level reserve deputy sheriff from a nearby county, and bragged about his former job as an enforcer for a biker club, where he said he worked with a bunch of drug dealers and loan sharks."

"Was he a regular?" Bob asked.

"He had become one for a couple of weeks, but none of us girls knew much about him. Not even his real name. Afterwards, Al told us not to discuss Carol's murder with anyone. He said that he'd take care of it."

"Is this Dog on the video?" Tischner asked, pointing toward the frozen picture on the screen.

"No. I don't know that man, but it's not him," Sylvia said, growing angry. "That guy's much too sophisticated-looking. I think he's a banker. Dog was just some redneck deputy wannabe."

"Well, if you think you can keep going without a break, we still have three videos left and we could really use your help," Tischner said soothingly.

Sylvia nodded, dabbing her eyes with a tissue as Bob put in the next video, which he had selected carefully. It was time/date stamped for the early morning hours of New Year's Day.

Both agents watched Sylvia closely from the corners of their eyes as the video came on. They wanted to catch her reaction to what she saw.

The man on-screen was burly with oily blond hair. He was

obviously interested in rough sex and cared little for his partner, who he was slapping around brutally.

"No, no! Not Carol! God, please, no! That's him," she screamed. "That's Dog on top of her! Please turn it off."

Bob stopped the video immediately. Tischner walked over to where Sylvia was seated and bent down next to her.

"Why don't you go home and get some rest now?" he said. "You've helped us a lot here—and maybe we can help your friend Carol."

———

By that point, both Bob and Tischner felt that Sylvia was trustworthy and would keep her mouth shut. She knew what she faced if she crossed Shyster, and she knew what she faced if she crossed the FBI.

Keeping in mind that they might need her as a witness later, Tischner and Bob showed up at her apartment a few days later.

"Pack only the essentials," Tischner said. "We want everything left in your apartment to make it look as if you disappeared suddenly under strange circumstances."

"Where am I going?" she asked.

"We're taking you to meet the U.S. marshals who'll place you in the witness protection program. You're getting a new identity."

"You mean I'm getting a new start," she said as a look of hope crossed her face.

The agents had decided to send her to another state with a job already set up. As far as anyone at the club would know, she disappeared off the face of the earth. The agents would even circulate some rumors that the pond near her apartment would be dragged in a search for her body. She left without ever knowing about Wayne's involvement.

Within days, everybody thought she was dead—but she was finally in a safe place known only to the FBI and the U.S. marshals. They would bring her back to testify, if needed, at a later date.

It didn't matter anymore that the agents wouldn't have Sylvia to get inside the boat. They had already installed their own surveillance cameras onboard—each the size of a dime with pin-hole lenses—wired to ultra-slow recording devices that could save months of data.

Sylvia's efforts had also helped the case in other ways. One of the men she identified on the videos was a circuit judge who owned the condo on the reservoir that Quarles and Wolcott used as a meeting place; another was a district attorney believed to share silent ownership.

The agents were seeking a federal court order to place surveillance gear in the condo, and they had already put a wiretap on Al, Chuck and Billy Ray Watson's phones.

"I feel like we're rapidly bringing this investigation to an end," Tischner told Wayne and Bob at their next meeting. "But I'm not ready to stop hunting 'til no more wildlife appears on the scene."

Chapter 15

The Session

*"The government consists of a gang of men exactly
like you and me. They have, taking one with another,
no special talent for the business of government; they
have only a talent for getting and holding office."*
—H.L. Mencken

By mid-January, the legislative session was in full swing, and the FBI was trying to give Wayne the time he needed to rub elbows with lobbyists and legislators since this was only his second year.

"We don't want you to be gone so much as to arouse suspicion, and we certainly don't want you to be seen with anyone who can be tied to the bureau," Tischner told him. So most of their contact at the time was only by phone.

In contrast, Wayne was pretty much joined at the hip with his legislative co-conspirators at that point. Quarles and Wolcott had been working with Chuck for years now and had been involved in no telling how many bills that were bought, paid for and passed due to extortion.

So on the last Monday in January, at seven in the morning, Wayne was surprised to get a phone call on his FBI-issued cell.

They've never called this early, he thought, wondering what was wrong.

"Wayne, this is Agent Tischner. Sorry to call so early, but I wanted to reach you before you got to the Capitol. How are things going?"

"Fine, but not much is happening at this point. I've already begun to push the anti-gaming legislation again, but there isn't much activity on any of the committees," Wayne said.

"Okay. Well, I'm calling about two things. Remember that we were originally thinking about having Bob work with you? We've found a better role for him that will also keep the two of you in contact, so I need to brief you on it. Do you remember a discussion about a case involving a top lobbyist on which we were planning to work together with the IRS?" Tischner asked.

"Yes, I do," Wayne said.

"Do you know Lisa Backman?"

"I know who she is, though I don't know her personally. Seems she's got her fingers in everything, not just gaming. In fact, I think she does a lot of medical industry lobbying," Wayne said.

"You're exactly right. Well, we've got her!" Tischner exclaimed.

"Okay, good. But what does that have to do with me?" Wayne asked, clearly confused.

"We met with her along with IRS enforcement agents, who laid their case out against her and showed her the mandatory sentencing guidelines for bogus filings of millions of dollars. She started to sing like a bird. We've worked a deal with her to 'hire' Bob, who'll be introduced to her associates. We've provided a cover story with credentials, and he's been in training for the last couple of weeks, cramming about the medical industry. Anyway, I have no doubt you'll come into contact with Backman because she lives in the Capitol during the sessions, and her task is to make Bob her shadow. You may see him this morning. Don't act like you know him, but don't shy away from him either if he's introduced to you," Tischner explained.

"You mean you have two separate undercover operations involving two lobbyists going on simultaneously in the legislature?" Wayne asked, surprised.

"That's right. One's a suspect and one an informant. We've already worked a couple of things with Backman to ensure her credibility, but the only problem for the current session is the fact that you're new on the political scene and she's new at working for the federal government and introducing an agent in. It would be helpful for us if you could get to know her, but I'm not sure how many opportunities will present themselves," Tischner said.

"Whatever comes up will be great for me. This legislative stuff is getting pretty boring," Wayne said.

Tischner laughed. "I think I also talked to you about a senator we have a bribery case on. We've been considering trying to flip him and expose more suspects, but our boss doesn't think he'll be cooperative, and we don't want to take a chance. We'll probably hold off and take him down with the rest of these clowns. Everybody can't be a snitch…no offense. I meant criminal informant. That's different from you, a paid confidential informant," he said, trying to cover his slip.

"No offense taken," Wayne said.

"At any rate, it may be some time before we get the results we're looking for. I doubt it'll happen in this session. But it's important for you to get as involved as you can with them and make your willingness to be a 'good ol' boy' known, so they'll seek out your help. Whatever doesn't get passed this session may become a hot issue for the next one. If so, the wolves will be out in force this summer, trying to lobby all the members before next year's session begins."

"I'll do whatever I can," Wayne said, happy to be of service.

<hr>

When the end of the session was near, Wayne realized Agent Tischner was right: *Some bills that might not pass are already gearing up to be next session's hot topics. But he was wrong on one thing: They may not wait until summer.*

The anti-gaming bill was gaining momentum; it passed the House with flying colors but there wasn't enough support in the Senate. There was some talk about another special session this year since the legislature was so far off on several other issues, too. If that happened, the lobbying, back-scratching, deal-making, wining and dining, and payoffs would begin immediately.

Wayne was already disgusted as he saw how taxpayer dollars were wasted. Some members of the legislature who had been around awhile would introduce a hundred bills with little to no support on ninety-eight percent of them. Many of the bills were just plain stupid and didn't stand a snowball's chance in hell of surviving—and they knew that when they introduced them.

These guys are doing nothing but making old "Farmer John" and the likes of him happy by introducing bills they know are going nowhere, Wayne realized. He could spot them by the amount of labor that had gone into them. Some had only one paragraph and no supporters.

The legislators would then go back home and apologize to their constituents, explaining how hard they had worked on getting the bill passed but that "the other damn party just wouldn't cooperate."

What we really need is a bill to be passed that would limit proposed legislation, just like they have for frivolous lawsuits, Wayne reasoned. *Members of the legislature should be paid on a performance basis—receive a smaller salary with bonuses for bills they're successful in getting passed. If they got paid what they're worth, I'm sure the state could overcome the budget deficit in one year.*

Wayne was beginning to think of himself as one of "them" less and less. He was more interested in his duties with the FBI, and more concerned about what was going on at home than in the House.

One evening, he made his normal call to Julie to check on her and Will.

"Honey, things are fine here," she said. "But I think your dad has some wonderful news he wants to tell you when you come home. He wants it to be a surprise so don't say anything when you see him."

"Okay," Wayne said.

But after they got off the phone ten minutes later, he wondered what it was about. *Maybe Investigator Long stopped by to say they had a suspect in the shooting*, he thought. *I hope that's it so Dad can see the shooter brought to justice.*

But Wayne knew even that wouldn't be enough. His father had told him, "I'm convinced it was a paid shooting, and I won't rest until I go beyond the shooter to find the person or people responsible for me being in a wheelchair the rest of my life."

Wayne knew his dad was angry, but had tried to convince him that although it was bad, it could have been worse. He could have been killed.

With all of those thoughts stirred up in his head and a deep curiosity about what the news could be, Wayne finished the last few weeks in the legislature—but he couldn't wait to go home.

Chapter 16

Hope for Recovery

"Even the fear of death is nothing compared
to the fear of not having lived authentically and fully."
—Frances Moore Lappe

In late April, Wayne came home to the great news that his dad was showing signs of recovery from his spinal cord injury. He had been visited twice weekly at home by physical and occupational therapists.

"I didn't say anything at first," Will told his son, "but I started getting feeling back in my lower extremities. First my toes, then my feet. I started feeling pain in my right knee, then spasms in my hamstrings. The sensation came and went and I didn't want anybody to get too excited. But I eventually mentioned it to my physical therapist, who notified my doctor, who insisted I come in for an X-ray. They found the bullet had shifted to one side, relieving pressure off the nerve."

"That's great, Dad," Wayne enthused. "What did he say about your future prognosis?"

"He gave me new medication…" Will started.

"Are you supposed to take it with your methylprednisolone?" Wayne interrupted.

"Son, I haven't taken that medrol since right after I got out of the hospital. I was taking an experimental drug, GM-1 ganglioside, until last week, but now he's got me on tizanidine. Says it helps to control spasticity. He wants to try me out using a combination of drugs and what he calls functional electrical stimulation systems."

"You mean he's going to give you shock treatment?" Wayne asked, truly startled.

"No, I took some notes..." Will said, pulling a small pad from his pocket. It was a habit he learned in law enforcement. "It's a small device that can be implanted under the skin or outside the body, with wires that connect to the nervous system to supplement lost motor and sensory functions. Somehow it controls your arms and legs to help you stand or maybe even walk."

He stopped reading and looked up at his son. "It's computer-controlled and if I understood correctly, I'll press a button to make my legs move since my brain's having problems with that right now. If the pressure stays off my spinal cord, eventually my nerves might start telling my legs themselves without using the device. At least that's the way I understood it," Will said with some degree of optimism.

"Dad, that really is great news. Now that the session's over, I want to start spending more time with you and helping the therapist," Wayne said.

"Good. I'm also going to start going to the doctor more often. He wants to see me walk on a thing kind of like a treadmill. I'll be suspended in a harness, using the electronic nerve stimulation device."

Wayne was less convinced about the treatment technique, but tried hard not to show it for his father's sake.

For the next couple of months, Wayne worked with the therapists when they came to the house and took his dad to a local rehabilitation center for exercise on a treadmill/harness contraption. He was very pleased to see the progress Will was making—besides, it took his mind off the mess in the legislature.

Will was only taking a few steps at a time and most of his weight was supported in the chest harness. He'd hit the switch and his legs would jump forward one at a time. He looked a little like Frankenstein, but at least he was standing to some extent and his legs were moving.

One day, Will insisted, "I want to take off the harness."

"I'm not sure you're ready," his therapist said. "You've progressed, but maybe not enough yet."

"Let me just try. Then we'll know for sure."

"Okay," the therapist said with a deep breath. "Hold on to the handle bars to support your weight."

Will found this to be very difficult because he had to switch the device from one leg to the other using just one hand. He got mixed up and tried to trigger the same leg twice, resulting in a fall that cracked two ribs when he hit against one of the handlebars on his way to the floor.

"It's man versus machine, now," Will said as he was recovering. He had declared war on the contraption and was determined to win.

About a month later, Wayne took him for an appointment in Jackson to meet with Dr. Jonathan Rose. He expected this to be a routine visit, until his father said, "I want to discuss possible surgery to remove the bullet. What are my options?"

The doctor counted them off one by one on his fingers. "Well, you can remain confined to a wheelchair. You can continue with the therapy, which is producing some positive results—but they're minimal and you're aging. Or you can have the bullet removed and, if successful, there's a pretty good chance you may be able to walk again on your own with more therapy," Dr. Rose explained.

"I don't want to remain in this wheelchair, so let's rule that one out," Will said. "I agree that the therapy is helping but progress seems to have stalled. When you say I have a good chance to walk again once the bullet's removed, what do you think my chances are, percentage-wise?" Will asked, cautiously optimistic.

"Your chances are fifty-fifty, but that's not the biggest concern," the doctor said.

"What is?" Wayne chimed in.

"My biggest concern is the risk of damaging the spinal cord during the surgery. Further damage could cause even more paralysis. Your dad's car sat low, and he was leaning out of it, bent over, when he was shot."

The doctor pointed to an X-ray hanging beside him. "Luckily, the bullet creased the skull right at the back, causing a small basil skull fracture, but no permanent brain damage, only bruising. Then it re-entered his body at the base of his neck and ran down the spinal cord, lodging right at the vertebrae that control the coccyx and lower extremities. The nerves and vertebrae that control the upper body are located just above the bullet. If damage occurs in that area, he could become completely paralyzed—a quadraplegic. Of course, that's along with the other risks that must be taken into consideration with any major surgery, a number of which could result in death," Dr. Rose added solemnly.

The room was quiet for several minutes. Wayne looked his father in the eye, and each knew what the other was thinking. *He wants to walk so badly that if there's any chance, he'll take it*, Wayne realized.

I'm the only parent he has left, and he loves me so much that he's not willing to deal with the risk of losing me, Will knew.

After a few more moments of silence, Will turned to the doctor and asked, "When do we start?"

"Dad, you can't be serious," Wayne blurted out. "You're doing fine since your injury and get around great in the wheelchair. It doesn't matter if you don't progress any further."

"Mr. Lott," the doctor interjected, addressing Will. "I won't be doing the surgery. And frankly I don't know another doctor around here who would."

"Why are you getting my hopes up, then, doctor?" Will asked, his voice tinged with anger and disappointment.

"Because there *is* some hope," Dr. Rose said. "Much research is being done on spinal cord injuries. A former associate of mine works for the Spinal Specialty Hospital in Colorado, which treats more spinal injuries than any other facility in the world—they've treated some fifty thousand spinal cord injury patients and remain on the top ten list of rehabilitation hospitals in *U.S. News and World Reports*. I took the liberty to contact him and discuss your case. With your permission, I'll forward your files for his review, but I'll need a new X-ray first. The decision is yours, but I have to warn you that they may not take it."

"What do I have to lose?" Will asked.

"Your life...or at least the use of your upper body, too," Wayne said before the doctor could answer.

"It's *my* life, Wayne. I gave you yours—let me get mine back. I'm willing to take the chance," Will insisted.

Wayne stared at the ground for a few seconds. "It's your decision, Dad," he said, but his tone of voice conveyed that he did not agree.

"Mr. Lott, I'll arrange for the X-ray," the doctor said. "As soon as I have the results, I'll forward them to Dr. Todd Chandler. It will probably take the review board two to four weeks to decide based on your current condition, and since their surgery list is at least six months behind, you'll need re-evaluation when the time comes if you're selected."

"And in the meantime?" Will asked.

"Please continue your medication, therapy and use of the electrical stimulator. Once the pressure's relieved, assuming they get the bullet out successfully, your motor skills may be restored, negating the need for the stimulator soon after. I have confidence in Dr. Chandler and the rehabilitation center, and I think you're making the right decision, even given the risks," the doctor said, shaking Will's hand.

"Thanks, doc," Will said as he rolled away, refusing help from Wayne.

He went to the nurses' station to set up the appointment then waited in the lobby for Wayne to pull the car around. A young lady who was walking past stopped when she saw him.

"Aren't you Mr. Lott?" she asked.

"Yes, I am. And who are you?" Will asked with a smile.

"I'm Sandra, one of the TV reporters that covered your story the afternoon you got shot. I recognized you from one of the photos we ran that we had on file. How are you doing?" she asked.

"I've been in this wheelchair since I got out of the hospital, but my doctor just told me that I might be considered for surgery that would give me a fifty percent chance of walking again," he said.

"That's wonderful. Do you mind if we do a short follow-up story to share what you just told me with our viewers?"

"Sure, no problem. And tell 'em I'll be walking again in no time," Will boasted.

"You betcha. Here's my card. Call me when you recuperate," she said before leaving.

Wayne pulled up outside the hospital and soon the two were headed back to Oxford in silence.

As they got closer to home, Wayne said, "Dad, please give this serious consideration."

"Wayne, I'm sure I want the surgery. And if that doctor in Colorado can't do it, I'll find somebody else that will."

Will stared out at the road ahead, and a steely look came into his eyes. "What I'd really like to do is get the bullet out, get well, then melt it down and have it put into a new cartridge for my gun. Then I'd find the guy who gave it to me and give it back at close range. I won't be a coward like he was and hide hundreds of yards away. No, I want to look him in the face just before I give him that bullet back between his cowardly eyes."

"Dad, I've never heard you talk like that before," Wayne said, somewhat shocked.

"I've never been ambushed by a coward, left for dead, paralyzed, and lost my dignity in front of my family before," Will said as tears welled up in his eyes.

"Have you heard anything new from that investigator in Jackson?" Wayne asked.

"He dropped by a couple of times," Will said, reigning in his emotions. "They've reconstructed the crime scene and interviewed people in the area, but have come up with nothing other than the theory that the shot came from the water tower near the house. I don't think the shooter even knew me. I think some low-life bastard connected with illegal gambling had it done…and I hate to say this, but I also wouldn't put it past some low-life bastard either in or connected to the legislature."

"You mean like a businessman or lobbyist?" Wayne asked.

"That's exactly what I mean. Watch your back, son," Will added quietly.

———

Three weeks later, the phone rang at Wayne's home in Oxford. "Mr. Lott?" the caller asked.

"Yes, this is Wayne. Do you want me or my dad?"

"Hello, Wayne. This is Dr. Rose. I was calling for your father. Is he in?"

Wayne got a nervous feeling in the pit of his stomach. "Yes, hold on, please." He handed the phone to his father. "It's for you."

"Hello?" Will answered. He had been waiting anxiously for the call.

"Mr. Lott, this is Dr. Rose. Remember when I told you it would be about six months before your surgery could be scheduled?"

"Oh, hell, I get it," Will exhaled. "I'll be seventy-five before they finally get around to it."

"No…they can do it and want you there next week!" the doctor said with a great deal of excitement.

"I can leave tomorrow," Will said.

"I think you have more time than that," Dr. Rose laughed. "My secretary will call you back later today with all the information you need. I wish you the best of luck."

"I can't tell you how much I appreciate this, doc," Will said as he hung up the phone.

He looked up at Wayne. "I need a plane ticket to Colorado, and can you take me to the Memphis airport?"

"You think I'm just going to drop you off?" Wayne smiled, knowing exactly what the news had been. "We're going with you, Dad. It's all of us together."

Chapter 17

News from Jail

"He harms himself who does harm to another,
and the evil plan is most harmful to the planner."
—Hesiod

On Friday morning, Wayne called Agent Tischner to explain that he would be out of state for at least a couple of weeks. Tischner was aware that Will was going to have the surgery and added, "Don't worry about what's going on in Mississippi. Just take care of your dad."

That Sunday, Julie's father drove Wayne, Julie and Will to the airport in the church van. The whole community was behind Will and his family as they boarded the plane for Denver and landed later that afternoon in the Mile High City.

The hospital had arranged for a pickup in a van with a wheelchair lift. As Will got in, he said, "Let's hope this is the last time I need that."

It was a less than an hour's drive to the hospital at Starwood, and the driver took them on a short windshield tour of the facility grounds.

The long-term stay hotel was more like an apartment, with

separate bedrooms and a kitchen with full-size appliances. They checked in and made themselves as comfortable as they could, with the worry of surgery hanging over their heads.

"Pop," Julie said, "if you decide not to go through with this, you're always welcome in our home and I'll be committed to your care."

Will said, "I'm touched, sweetheart. But nothing at this point could change my mind."

With the movement of the bullet eliminating some pressure from his spinal cord and nerve, he was confident that complete extraction would further relieve the compression. He knew he'd have to continue with the medication and possibly the electrical stimulation devices, along with occupational and physical therapy, but was motivated to start all of that as well.

The following morning, the family met with Dr. Chandler and a team of other doctors that would perform the surgery later that week. Will underwent some tests and was ready to get with the program.

"I've heard enough medical jargon that I think I could perform the surgery myself," he joked. In truth, he didn't want the risks discussed anymore in front of his son and daughter-in-law.

"I just want you to get it over with, hand me that bullet in a bottle and get me out of this hospital," Will told Dr. Chandler.

"Oh, you want a trophy," the doctor laughed. "Based on the X-ray, it appears you'll have a good one, with surprisingly little damage or mushrooming."

"No, I don't want a trophy," Will said. "I had another use in mind."

"Dad, don't talk like that," Wayne said, stopping his father's talk of revenge. "We just want you to come through this safely."

"You'll check into the hospital the day after tomorrow and we'll conduct the surgery early the next morning," the doctor said. "Get some rest and we'll see you then."

As the doctors walked away, Wayne and Julie each put a hand

on Will's shoulders. They were going to stand strong as a family and face the outcome together.

———

That evening, as Will was lying on the sofa, he started to feel pain in his legs, which he saw as a good thing. "At least I'm having some sensations, whether they're good or not," he said.

Wayne was happy to see him in high spirits, and he and Julie sat with him while he insisted on staying up to watch *The Late Show with Jay Leno*, one of his favorite TV programs. However, he fell asleep after the monologue and Julie quietly turned his TV off. She and Wayne softly kissed him goodnight on his forehead.

"I love you, Dad," Wayne whispered before saying a silent prayer.

He and Julie went to the bedroom, both emotionally exhausted. As his wife took a warm shower before going to bed, Wayne received a phone call.

"Wayne, this is Agent Tischner. I wanted to tell you something I think you might be very interested in. You aren't asleep, are you?"

"No, not yet. But I didn't think y'all worked after 5 p.m," he joked.

"Very funny," Tischner replied. "I do more work by accident than any lawyer or legislator does on purpose."

"Okay, I won't argue. Whatcha got?" He talked quietly so Julie wouldn't overhear.

"We have an informant, an old Vietnam vet who's been on our books for quite some time. He's just bonded out in Biloxi for a DUI, and as you know, when an informant gets arrested for anything, they're required to notify their handling agent immediately," Tischner said.

"Sure, I understand," Wayne said, "but what does that have to do with me?"

"He was in a cell with a young army vet brought in a couple

hours after he got there for public drunkenness, disorderly conduct and destruction of private property. He says the army vet claims to have shot an 'old cop' in Jackson over a year ago and thought he had died. While they were booking him, the dispatcher had the news on TV. Apparently your dad's picture was shown and they ran a story on his upcoming surgery. The kid said he couldn't believe it. Our informant knew that kind of information is important to the FBI, so he told us the story when he called in and said not to worry about the kid getting out because he had no money for bail and would probably have to sell his sniper rifle to pay for damages."

Wayne was stunned silent for a few seconds then asked, "What are you going to do about it?"

"The informant is meeting with a Gulfport agent tomorrow who'll take a complete statement. Normally we don't get involved in murders or even attempted murders because it's a state crime, but there's a possibility that your dad's shooting could be tied in to the overall conspiracy and racketeering case you're working on with us," Tischner explained.

"It would be great if the agent could get this guy on tape or something," Wayne said.

"We're going to take it further than that if his statement pans out. Listen, I just wanted to let you know, but please don't worry about it or tell your dad anything just yet," Tischner cautioned.

"I won't," Wayne said. "We've all got enough on our minds with the surgery. But I appreciate the call…and what you're doing."

The next morning, the interview was about to take place with the FBI informant in Gulfport, Mississippi. He had a grizzled beard and wore a bandana over his long, graying hair.

"Start from the beginning and tell me what was said as soon as this young guy was placed in the cell with you," Agent Byrd said.

"Well, he came in pretty drunk and pissed off. I was drunk also so they made me stay six hours to sober up before I could bond out. The kid just staggered in saying something like, 'I can't believe that old bastard's still alive. He was shot in the head with a 7.62.' He acted as if he was proud of the fact," the informant said.

"Did he ever say he shot a cop?" the agent asked.

"Not at first. He started going off about the military after that. Said he'd been a sniper but was thrown out of school before going to Iraq, where he wanted to blow up Iraqis' heads like pumpkins. He was really pissed about that, too, claiming he was the best shot in his class but they spent most of their time on concealment and stuff like that. Sounded like he had an itchy finger and didn't want to go along with everything else required in sniper school, and they threw him out."

"Go on," Agent Byrd said. "I want to know everything."

"Well, he saw the ink on my forearm," the informant said, showing the agent his Vietnam tattoo, "and started asking me questions about killing gooks. Wanted to know the longest shot I ever made and so on. I told him I was in the marine corps and carried an M-16 since much of our combat was close-in jungle fighting. Then he started describing his sniper rifle to me, saying he had it for less than two years and was probably going to have to sell it to pay for his fines and a bar he tore up. And he gave me a crumbled up business card he had in his pants pocket."

"Did you keep it?" Byrd asked.

"Of course…here it is," the informant said as he handed the agent a battered green business card that read, "Protection Agent—Casino Industry" but had no name, phone number or address on it.

"I asked him his name and he said his friends call him E.B., which stands for Eleven Bravo, an Army MOS," the informant explained.

"We've already checked and placed a hold on him. His name is Gregory Jackson, a former PFC in the army discharged at Fort

Benning on a 'general under honorable conditions' discharge. We've arranged for the damage to the bar to be a civil matter, so he's only charged with two misdemeanors and his bond's reduced to five hundred dollars. We're going to give you the money to bond him out and take him home. You'll be wearing a wire. We want you to get back into a discussion about guns with him, and see if you can take that further. Maybe he'll get diarrhea of the mouth," Agent Byrd said. "I'll call now and take the hold off him."

That afternoon, the informant went back to the jail and paid the army vet's bond. The kid was turned over with a notice to be back in court the following Tuesday.

"Hey, dude, thanks for getting me out. How'd you pull that off?" E.B. asked.

"When I bonded out they forgot to give me my pocket knife back and they hadn't charged me with it. Since my dad gave it to me, I wanted it back. So I went back to the jail to get it and while I was there, I asked them about you and they told me you were still in but your bond was reduced. I went across the street to the titless teller…"

The kid looked confused.

"The ATM, get it? The titless teller," the informant continued, "and got the money out to make your bail. It sounded like you and I had a lot in common, and I just may want to buy that rifle you were talking about or maybe take it in pawn 'til you pay me back."

"I paid over a thousand dollars for that gun," E.B. said. "Well, let's head up to my trailer in Vancleave anyway. It's way out in the country. If it's not too late, I'll let you shoot it. You'll really like it. I have all kinds of rounds—even some old Russian soft lead ammo. Wish I had used that at least once instead of that steel jacket crap. I'll show you the difference when we get out there."

More than an hour later they arrived at the end of a long gravel road. To the informant's surprise, there was a late-model black stretch limousine parked in front of the trailer.

"Wow, that thing's so long you need a Louisiana tag on the front and a Mississippi tag on the back," he said. "Whose is it?"

"Ah, that ain't mine. Belongs to the casino I work for," E.B. answered.

"You're a limousine driver?" the informant asked.

"Not exactly. I do drive it, but I provide personal protection for senior casino weenies when they come to town. I'm pretty much just on call. That's my old GMC truck over there but it's not running right now. A girl I used to know took me to the bar I tore up last night but she split when all hell broke loose, so I didn't have a ride. Thanks for bringing me out here. Hey, why don't you just crash on my couch and we'll get up in the morning and shoot? I've got some sausage and biscuits in the freezer and I'll put on some coffee," E.B. said.

"Sounds good to me." The informant was hoping that the FBI surveillance team was able to follow them and hear the wire out there in the boonies.

When E.B. went into the trailer, the informant stayed outside for a smoke. He whispered into the wire, "I hope you boys can get a relief team. Not much to keep you awake out here. When he starts snoring, I'm going to turn the wire off to save the battery. You probably know this ain't the first time I've worn one of these little jewels. I'll turn it back on as soon as I wake up. This thing's hot as hell anyway."

Early the next morning, E.B. walked into the living room with a large, black plastic gun case in his hand. He set it on the floor next to his guest and broke out the sausage and biscuits while putting on coffee.

"I gotta go piss," the informant said, as he walked down the hall to the bathroom. Once inside, he turned on the wire and said to the agents, "Wake up. If you can hear me, I'm about to go look at the rifle and we'll probably go out shooting soon."

Then he came back into the living room and reached down as if to pick up the case.

"Hold on a minute and I'll show it to you. Let me get breakfast finished," E.B. said.

Within a few minutes E.B. walked over and opened up the case. It was a unique-looking rifle trimmed in wood that looked like oak, with a slight reddish tint. Part of the stock was hollowed out, almost forming a pistol grip. It had a tall front sight and looked similar to what the informant knew as an AK-47, but was much more sophisticated with a big scope and a flash suppressor.

"What the hell is that thing?"

"It's a Dragunov 7.62 X 54. It's very accurate, weighs less than ten pounds with the scope and has a maximum effective range of over nine hundred meters. It's not exactly what I'd like to have for a sniper rifle, but it'll do the job and is much more affordable. Compared to U.S. Remington and Barrett military sniper rifles, which cost thousands of dollars, these things are a steal. Ammo's cheap, too. It'll even shoot the old World War II-era Russian *mosin nagant* ammo you can buy anywhere," E.B. said proudly.

"So this is a Russian gun?" the informant asked.

"Actually, it's Romanian, but I don't care who makes it."

Shortly after breakfast, they went out behind the trailer and approached a wood pile littered with beer cans all around.

"Give me one of those bullets," E.B. said.

"You mean a loaded magazine from the case?" the informant asked.

"No, I mean one bullet from that box. A sniper only gets one shot. I told you I'm a sniper."

"Well, that's not even a hundred yards. Anybody should be able to hit a beer can with a scope," the informant said laughingly.

"I'm not going to just shoot the beer can. I'm going to shoot in the middle of the ring, which is only as big as the end of your little finger. Will that satisfy you, or you think you can do better?" E.B. asked with a certain degree of sarcasm.

"Oh, no…I was just kiddin'. As I told you, I always did close-range shooting and that was a long time ago. As my eyes get worse, I wouldn't mind having a gun like that with a nice scope," the informant said.

As E.B. held the gun up, everything was still—then *BAM!* The sound of the rifle echoed through the trees.

"Let's go see," E.B. said, smiling.

Just as he had said, the bullet had entered the beer can right in the middle of the ring and had blown out its entire bottom and most of the sides.

"Wow, I'm impressed," the informant said. "Not only with your shot, but with what that bullet did to the can."

"That's nothing. Let's fill up some gallon water jugs and you shoot them. We can put a piece of plywood in front of one to simulate bone. The water simulates body mass since our bodies are made up mostly of water. We really need about fifteen percent gel in the water to make it more realistic, but I think you'll get the idea. I'll keep some firewood behind it so we can dig out a couple different kinds of bullets and you can see the difference," E.B. said, really getting into it.

They did just that and the steel jacketed bullets were very much intact even after hitting the hard wood. They passed through the jugs without a lot of blunt trauma. The soft lead bullets had completely mushroomed and, upon impact, knocked the jugs completely over the woodpile and blew out their entire backs.

E.B. handed the bullets to his newfound friend, who acted as if he threw them away but kept them in his pocket along with several spent casings and a sample of the loaded bullets.

"Give me the gun and I'll forget about the bond money," he said.

"You crazy, man? I paid double that," E.B. said.

"I don't think it's worth that," the informant said. "It's foreign made and all."

"Come back in. I want to show you something," E.B. said, and they walked back into the trailer.

"Look at this." He pulled a shoebox from the top of his closet. "Here's the receipt. I bought this at a pawn shop in Jackson. The owner said it was his personal deer rifle and it was already zeroed in when I bought it."

The informant read the receipt aloud so they could hear it over the wire. "Ryan's Pawn Shop, Highway 80, Jackson, Mississippi, July 7, 2008, paid in full $1, 286."

He looked up again. "Well, like I said, it's not worth that to me. So when can you pay the bond money back?"

E.B. ignored the question at first, placing the gun back in his closet and mumbling something under his breath about having to clean it. Then he said, "You know where I live, man. I'll have it this weekend. Here's my cell number. Give me a call late Saturday morning."

"Okay," the informant said as he walked out of the trailer toward his car.

When he drove away, he said into the wire, "I'm going into the truck stop just up the road for gas. Meet me there so I can give you these bullets."

"Who trained you?" the agent asked as soon as he got there. "You did a better job than most of our agents could've done. But I could kick your ass for staying there all night. Don't you ever do that again without prior approval from us. Drop one spent bullet in each of these small zip lock bags, do the same with the casings in the larger bags and put the loaded rounds in this box. Initial these, get out of here and call me in the morning."

"Yes, sir, sir," the informant said, giving the agent a military-style salute and a smart-ass smile.

Chapter 18

Back at the Hospital

*"Victory attained by violence is tantamount
to a defeat, for it is momentary."*
—Mahatma Gandhi

Early the next morning, Wayne and his wife were in the hospital lobby, awaiting any word about Will's painstaking, hours-long operation. As soon as Julie got up to use the restroom, a young, well-dressed man approached Wayne. "Are you Wayne Lott?"

"Yes," he answered.

"I'm Agent Magee of the FBI field office in Denver."

"Am I in trouble for not calling in?" Wayne whispered, though no one was near them.

"Sir, is your dad in surgery?" Agent Magee asked.

"Yes, he is. We're waiting on word from the doctor," Wayne said.

"Well, we're going to have to seize the bullet from your dad's body for evidence," the agent said.

"Don't talk about him like he's dead," Wayne snapped. "The bullet won't be a problem. The doctor said he's putting it in a jar and will give it to him after he gets out of recovery."

"Sir, I'm afraid he won't be able to keep it as a souvenir," Magee said.

"Personally, I'm glad to hear that," Wayne said.

"Our Jackson office has information from the Gulf Coast branch about the alleged shooter, and they've collected some physical evidence," Magee stated.

"You mean they have a bullet for comparison?"

"I don't have all the details, Mr. Lott, but I was told to have you contact Agent Tischner."

"I will. As soon as…" Wayne started.

Just as Julie was walking over to join them, the double doors swung open at the end of the hallway and Dr. Chandler emerged.

"How'd it go, doc?" Wayne ran over and asked immediately.

"How about the bullet? Did you get the bullet?" Agent Magee interjected.

Wayne glared at the agent intently, then repeated, "How did it go? How's my father?"

"He's doing just fine. His vital signs are good and there's no further damage to his spine from removing the bullet. He's being taken to the recovery room right now." Wayne shook the doctor's hand and Julie gave him a big hug.

As Wayne exhaled with relief, both the doctor and Julie glanced at Agent Magee curiously. "I'm sorry," Wayne said. "Julie, Dr. Chandler, this is FBI Agent Magee. He's been tasked with retrieving the bullet for evidence."

"Oh," the doctor said. "Your father's not going to be happy when he wakes up and I don't have that bullet to give him."

"He'll understand," Wayne said.

"When can we see him?" Julie asked.

"It'll be awhile," Dr. Chandler said. "A few hours, at least."

"Doctor, what about the bullet?" Agent Magee asked.

The doctor reached into the front right pocket of his smock and retrieved a prescription medicine bottle with the bullet inside, resting between two cotton balls. He reached out to hand it to the agent.

"Sir, I need you to initial and date it so you can testify later, if necessary, that it's the same bullet you retrieved from Mr. Lott's body," Agent Magee said.

He did so and turned it over to Agent Magee, who left rather hurriedly for the Fedex office.

Wayne and Julie went back to the guest room to rest for awhile before returning to the hospital. As she made tea, he excused himself. "Honey, I'm going to take a short walk and clear my head."

"Want me to come with you?" she asked.

"No. I just need to be alone with my thoughts. You relax a little. Then we'll go back and wait for Dad to wake up."

Wayne walked outside and called Agent Tischner.

"How's your dad?" the agent asked.

"Everything went well, thanks for asking," Wayne said. "But the agent here was more worried about the bullet than about my father."

"Wayne, I apologize for his demeanor, but that bullet's very important. We think we know where the shooter is, and we've retrieved bullets from his gun. Magee's overnighting your dad's bullet to the FBI lab in Quantico, Virginia, where we already sent the suspect's bullets. Our special agent in charge has gotten a priority-one approval at the lab for the comparison. In the meantime, we're keeping the suspect under surveillance," Tischner said with a great deal of enthusiasm.

"That's incredible news," Wayne said. "I can't wait to tell Dad when he wakes up."

Two hours later, Wayne and Julie were back at the hospital. They didn't have to wait too long for Dr. Chandler to come out to find them. "Your dad's awake and doing fine. He's grouchy and a little drowsy, and his voice is hoarse from the tube that was down his throat but he can talk. In fact, he wants to know where his bullet is. I told him he'd have to talk to you about that," the doctor said, smiling.

Wayne practically sprinted to the recovery room, with Julie behind him, trying to catch up. By the time they got to the room, Will had drifted back off to sleep. They quietly sat down and watched him, Wayne with a big smile on his face and Julie with tears in her eyes.

About twenty minutes passed in silence when Dr. Chandler came into the room. "Did you talk to him?"

"No, he's been asleep," Julie said quietly.

"Well, it's time for our best patient to wake up. I wanted to try something anyway." The doctor pulled a pin from his smock, lifted the cover off Will's feet and stuck him in the bottom of his left foot. His foot flopped over to one side.

"Very good. Now let's try the other one."

Dr. Chandler stuck the right foot with the pin and Will almost jumped out of bed.

"Holy shit," he yelled. "What the hell was that?"

"Take it easy, Mr. Lott," Dr. Chandler said. "I was just checking to see if you had any feeling restored. Seems that you do…and you have pretty good reflexes as well."

Julie fell across Pop's chest, crying. "Thank God…thank you, God."

As she moved away, Will caught sight of Wayne. Father and son looked at each other with deep emotion for a few moments. Embarrassed, Will cleared his throat and said, gruffly, "Where's my bullet?"

"That's a long story," Wayne said.

"Well, I have plenty time. I don't think I'll be going anywhere for a while, so let's hear it."

"Honey, would you go down and call your parents and our pastor to let them know how dad's doing while I talk to him?" Wayne asked.

"I'd be glad to," Julie said, kissing Will on the forehead. Then she kissed Wayne on the cheek, whispered, "Good luck," and left the room as if she were waltzing. Dr. Chandler was glad to accompany her out.

"Dad, I have to tell you something. Julie doesn't even know. I've been keeping it a secret for a long time, but if I lost you, and you never knew…" His voice cracked with emotion. "I'm not really working on a federal grant. I work as a paid informant for the FBI."

Will's mouth fell slightly open but no words came out.

"Since I'm a paid informant and a lawyer, they treat me more like an agent than a snitch," Wayne continued. "I'm helping them with an undercover operation aimed at crooked lobbyists and members of the legislator—and you probably won't be surprised to hear that it involves the gaming industry."

"Son," Will said, "I knew you were destined for great things. I always saw you working with the FBI or the U.S. Attorney's Office in one way or another. I guess you fooled me, but in a good way."

"Trust me, Dad, it wasn't exactly by choice," Wayne said.

"You mean you committed a crime and they turned you into a snitch?"

"No. I had a crime committed against *me* when I was somewhere I shouldn't have been, but I have never and won't ever be charged with anything. Please don't ask anything else. I've already told you more than I should have."

"Okay, son, I understand. But just tell me one thing: Are you in any danger?"

"No more than you've been in during your long career. Don't

worry about me, Dad. I'm sure you'll be very pleased with the outcome," Wayne said.

"I knew you'd make your mother and me proud. She's with you—you know that, don't you, son?" Will asked.

"I sure do, Dad. I've known it for a long time," Wayne said, bowing his head.

"Okay," Will said, slapping his hands together to bring the mood back up. "But there's still one thing *I* don't know. Where's my bullet?"

"Dad," Wayne began slowly, "my case agent called and said they had a suspect in your shooting. Somehow they've gotten samples from his rifle, and they picked up your bullet a few hours ago. It's on its way to Quantico, to the FBI lab, for comparison."

"My goodness," Will said, as if he almost couldn't believe the news. Suddenly his expression changed to one of worry. "You're not involved in that investigation, are you, Wayne?"

"Dad, I can't tell you. But I don't want you to worry."

"Okay, okay…I know you know what you're doing and that you can take care of yourself," Will said, partly to calm himself. "And you're sure Julie has no idea about any of this?"

"Yes, I'm sure. That's why I wanted her out of the room," Wayne said.

"Good," Will said. "Don't tell her until you absolutely have to. She'll just worry herself to death like your mother did."

"Don't tell me what?" Julie asked as she walked through the door.

"I wasn't talking about you, sweetheart. We were just having a man to man conversation. How's your dad?" Will asked, trying to change the subject.

"He's fine, but that is just like you. Out of major surgery for a couple of hours and wondering how somebody else is doing," Julie said. "The pastor said to tell you they're having a special prayer on Sunday for your speedy recovery and a safe trip home."

"Call him back and tell him I have room in my closet for another Baptist and a stiff drink when I can stand up on my own and start walking again," Will said, with a big laugh.

"Back to his old self already," Wayne said, shaking his head and smiling.

Chapter 19

Arrest and Relaxation

"There is no den in the wide world to hide a rogue.
Commit a crime and the earth is made of glass.
Commit a crime, and it seems as if a coat of snow fell
on the ground, such as reveals in the woods the track
of every partridge, and fox, and squirrel."
—Ralph Waldo Emerson

On Friday afternoon, Agent Tischner called the lab in Quantico. "Did you get the bullet?" he asked the forensic scientist.

"Yes, sir, it came in just before ten this morning. It's in great shape and we have good 'unknowns' to match it against. We've already been able to determine from the marks caused by the lands and grooves in the rifle barrel that the bullets were fired from a Romanian-made Dragunov, a common, low-end rifle that produces high results for snipers with a small pocket book," the forensic scientist said.

"You said 'bullets.' You mean you've already established that both the suspect's bullets and the known bullet taken from the victim's spine were fired from that same type of rifle?" Tischner asked.

"I certainly do, and I'm not leaving here today until we make a microscopic comparison. I won't be able to get the report out for a couple of days, but I'll call you tonight on my way home with the results."

"You are a God-send, my friend. I'll be waiting for your call," Tischner said as he hung up the phone. He immediately made another call to Agent Byrd of the Gulfport office.

"Agent Tischner," Byrd said, "I've already talked to U.S. Attorney Tyrone about this case, and we're working on the underlying facts and circumstances for a search warrant of the suspect's trailer. He's confident that with the probable cause our agents have gathered, the court order will be no problem. We'll seek a day warrant, and if the information comes back from the lab tonight, it'll be perfect because the suspect expects to see our informant tomorrow morning."

"Good," Tischner said. "I'll let you know when the lab calls."

Tischner was glad to hear that Tyrone was on their side. It didn't surprise him, though. *The U.S. attorney probably knows he'll be selected for a federal judge appointment when this case hits the public,* Tischner thought. *Everyone's got their own agenda.*

At about 8 p.m. that night, Tischner received a call from the forensic scientist in Quantico. "We've got a match on all of the bullets!" he said. "They were definitely fired from the same weapon. Do you have it yet?"

"No, not yet, but we will tomorrow," Tischner said. "And thanks to you, we should also have an arrest then."

He called Agent Byrd, who answered anxiously. "Talk to me, my friend. Tell me we have a match."

"We've got a match, bubba! I'm on my way to the coast," Tischner said.

"Excellent. I've got the warrant. Wanna discuss the plan over breakfast at one of the casinos tomorrow?" Byrd joked.

"I don't think so. I'll grab an egg sandwich or something and head on over to your office first thing. Do you have a team together for the search warrant?"

"Everything's in place. We're bringing agents over from Mobile and New Orleans as well. We don't expect a confrontation, but we'll be ready for one. The plan is to have the informant go over to collect his money and ask to see the gun one last time. He'll be wired, of course, and the code phrase is, 'I better put this thing back in the case.' When he says that, we'll storm the trailer and take both of them down then let the informant walk."

"Sounds good," Tischner said. "See you soon."

At ten the next morning, just as instructed, the informant called the suspect.

"Sure, man, I've got your money. Come on over whenever you're ready," E.B. told him.

Agents put concealed body armor on the informant along with a standard wire, since they didn't like to have criminal informants see their latest technology. Then they left in force, all heading to Vancleave.

"I don't have to tell you that cops don't take kindly to assholes shooting other cops, or people working on their behalf," Tischner said to Byrd on their way to E.B.'s place. "So this old boy has no idea what will happen if he does something stupid."

At exactly 11:14 a.m., the informant pulled into the driveway. Over the wire, he whispered, "The suspect's outside working under the hood of his truck." Then he got out of his car and walked over to E.B.

"Hey, man, c'mon inside," E.B. said in a friendly greeting. "Sure you don't want to come up with a little more money and take that rifle off my hands rather than taking this five hundred dollars?" he added, loudly enough for the agents to hear.

"I doubt it," the informant said, "but I'll take one last look."

The two of them stepped into the living room then the suspect walked toward his back bedroom to get the gun. The informant said quietly over the wire, "He's getting the gun. The front door's unlocked for you. Let's hope he doesn't come out shooting."

"Guess he doesn't know it wouldn't bother any of us one bit to shoot a would-be cop killer," Byrd said to one of his agents. Most of the FBI agents were part-time, collateral duty members of the SWAT team and enjoyed the excitement over their full-time investigative duties.

A few minutes later, as the agents listened intently from only a few hundred yards down the road, they heard the informant open the bolt to make sure it was unloaded, then say, "This is a nice gun, but after paying my DUI fine and tow truck bill, I really need the money worse than I need the rifle right now."

"All right. Let me know if you change your mind," E.B. said as he handed over the cash.

"Here, you've got grease on your hands from that old truck. I better put this thing back in the case for you," the informant said.

The agents heard the snaps close on the case then, moments later, all hell broke loose. Agents came swarming in from the fields out back and from both sides of the trailer as government cars came sliding into the driveway right up next to the limousine.

By the time E.B. looked out the window to see what the noise was, agents were already rushing inside, yelling, "Get down! Get down! Get down!"

The informant hit the floor, landing on top of the weapon case with his hands laced behind his head. E.B. was so stunned that he just stood there with his mouth open in surprise. Agents slammed him to the floor so hard that he never knew what happened.

One agent jumped on his back with his knee out, and E.B. farted so loud it sounded like a buck snort during the rut. When they picked him up with his hands cuffed behind his back, he had pissed all down his leg and was shaking like a leaf. He must have thought they were going to kill him—and they would have, at the drop of a hat.

They decided to let the suspect realize that the informant was working with them so he'd know how much they knew. To show that, they let him hang around for a few minutes and patted him on the back, telling him, "Good job."

By that time, there was no question in E.B.'s mind that he'd been had. He had already made admissions that fell somewhat short of a confession, but the agents had plenty of physical evidence on him. Now they wanted him to talk. Before he "lawyered up" and while he was still in fear, they wanted to know who he was working for and why he shot Mr. Lott.

"Look, we have your gun, we have your expended bullets and we have a positive comparison from the lab. We know this is the gun that shot Mr. Lott over a year ago, and we know you did it," Agent Tischner said.

"I just got that gun not long ago," E.B. said. "Somebody else must have done whatever you're talking about."

Moments later, one of the agents brought the shoebox from the bedroom closet, removed the receipt from the top of the pile and laid it down on the table in front of E.B.

"Look at it," he said, pushing E.B.'s head forward until his eyes were only about three inches from the receipt. "Read the date, you little bastard! Read it, damn it, before I mash your face into this table so hard, you'll look like a dog that's been chasing parked cars."

E.B. remained silent, staring at the receipt.

The agent screamed directly into his ear, "That was three weeks before you shot that cop in Jackson! Don't try to bullshit me."

"Okay, okay…I'll tell you all about it," E.B. said.

"Damn straight you will," the agent said, stepping away from him.

After a search of the trailer for anything that would tie the suspect to a crime, most of the agents began to thin out and head back to the office. A couple of them sat around the table as E.B. signed a rights waiver form and filled out some papers with personal information. His handcuffs had been removed but they kept him behind the table, watching him closely as he signed his name—Gregory C. Jackson.

"Okay, Gregory, we want you to start from the beginning to now," Agent Byrd said. "Tell us about your stint in the army, what happened there. I assume you were infantry, using the name Eleven Bravo, your military occupational specialty."

"Yeah," Jackson said. "I joined after the attacks on 9/11. I was a damn good hunter all my life and a dead-eye shot. I wanted to be in special forces but failed the tryout—though I did make it to sniper school. I was the best shot in my unit. Hell, I don't know how some of those guys even got into sniper school or passed the basic marksmanship skills courses. Some of them couldn't hit a bull in the ass with a bass fiddle, as my grandpa used to say."

Agents Byrd and Tischner exchanged a glance. They knew Gregory Jackson's type. He seemed to enjoy the attention, telling his life story and bragging about his skills.

"I hated all the crap that came with sniper training," he continued. "We spent eighty percent of our time doing physical training, cover and concealment, and crap like that. I got sick of it. I had proven myself with my shooting skills and I wanted to go to Iraq and blow up some heads. They threw me out on a general discharge claiming disciplinary problems after they sent me to Walter Reed Army Hospital and I passed their psychological exam. I was referred there for psychopathic tendencies," he smirked. "I came home with no job and the casinos were the only ones hiring. I told them I'd been in special forces and had been a member of a dignitary protection team in Iraq. They had no way of checking my military records and I said my work was top secret. They hired me to work security but made me a limo driver, escort and executive protection agent. I had to go home and read all I could find on the Internet to learn the lingo, but none of those idiots was smart enough to know the difference. Can I get a bottle of water from the fridge?" he asked.

"We'll get it for you." One of the agents opened the refrigerator door and tossed the plastic bottle to him.

"Go on," Agent Tischner prompted.

"One day just before the July Fourth weekend, I was told to make myself available for some important executives coming from Skylight Casino in Las Vegas. They were spending the weekend on the coast and I had to drive them around, then to Jackson that following week. As I drove, I heard them talking on the cell phone then to each other. They were really pissed off about a guy that, in their words, was getting way too close and making too many allegations about the corrupt casinos being tied to local politicians and lobbyists. I think it was a lobbyist one of them was talking to on the cell because he said something to him about how much money they pay him to get laws passed through those redneck senators." Jackson laughed, looking around at the agents for someone to join him.

"You guys need to lighten up," he said. "Anyway, I couldn't hear the other end of the conversation but it seemed to me they wanted this cop dead. They were so mad it was almost like they forgot I was there. They knew I could hear them. Hell, you could've heard them around the block with the windows rolled up." He paused. "I need a cigarette, man."

One of the agents reached over on the bar, got a pack and threw it on the table.

"Go ahead. Just blow your smoke in the other direction," Tischner said as he lit the cigarette for Jackson. "Finish your story."

"We stopped to eat at some place in Jackson and they put me up in a hotel, telling me to go to my room and keep my mouth shut about what I heard. I told them I was cool with it and if I were them, I'd take this guy out with one shot. I got no response from either of them but they looked at each other as if I'd come up with a great plan. I went to my room and they checked into a suite, I believe. Anyway, about an hour later, the bigger of the two dudes, who went by the name Big Tony, came over to my room. The other guy, Bruno, wasn't with him. I'm not really sure if they were from Vegas or not because every now and then, the word 'Jersey' would pop up and they had those *Sopranos* accents. Anyhow, I thought Big Tony was just checking to see if I did what they told me, which I did 'cause frankly they looked they were with the mob and I wasn't packing my heat. I had a semi-automatic version of an Uzi but it was locked in the car." His eyes gleamed as he spoke of weapons and he grew more animated.

"So Big Tony came into my room and asked me how long I'd been with the company and what I did before. I told him I'd been there a couple of years and was an army sniper in Iraq. He asked what I meant by the comment that I'd take the guy out with one shot, and I told him that's the way snipers do things. Then he asked if I was willing to take on a job like that. Like an idiot, I told him I would. I was afraid that if I didn't, this gorilla was going to kill me with his bare hands…and believe me, he could have done so." Jackson looked around at the agents again but couldn't find one sympathetic expression among them, so he went on.

"He asked me if five grand would be enough to do the job and I said, 'Fine.' Then he said I was to drop them off at the Gaming Commission the next morning for a meeting, where he'd get the money from some lobbyist and give it to me when I picked him up. He said the meeting would last a few hours and that I could take the limo out riding. Guess he didn't want me to stick around. As I pulled up to the Gaming Commission, I felt like I was hauling the president around. Before I could get out and open the back door, some big wigs ran out and opened it for them, treating these two goons like they were kings. Granted, they were dressed that way. I remember pulling away and a guy from the meeting looked like he had his head up one of their asses. If they had stopped short, he would've certainly had a brown nose."

"That's very funny," Agent Tischner said without a smile. "Let's take a short break."

"Good. I need to use the bathroom. I'm about to piss all over myself again," Jackson said.

"Hold on. One of our agents will go with you," Tischner said.

Jackson returned a few minutes later under escort. "Sit back down and let's get this over with," the agent said.

"Well, so then I drove around looking for a gun store. I didn't find one but I did find a pawn shop. I went inside and told the owner I was looking for a sniper-type rifle for hunting but I didn't want the typical old hunting rifle. I wanted a military style. He asked how much I wanted to spend and I told him as little as possible but I wanted a good gun. He said he had his own personal sniper rifle in the back that he used for hunting at first, but had a gunsmith do some work on it to make it match grade. Said he shot it in competition and it was already zeroed in at five hundred meters. He offered me the whole thing with the case, scope and two magazines for fifteen hundred bucks. I told him I didn't have quite that much on me and he asked how much I had. I just got paid so I emptied my pockets. What you see on the receipt is what I gave him. He kept the cheek plate and a sighting scope out of the case since I didn't give him the full amount, but that was okay with me. I knew I was going to get money from Tony and buy some coke."

"You mean cocaine?" Byrd asked.

"Well, I surely don't mean soda," Jackson laughed. "So I filled out all the paperwork, took the gun, walked out and put it in the trunk. I drove around Jackson until they called me to come pick them up. When I arrived, the party seeing them off was just as sickening as the welcoming party. I thought those guys at the Gaming Commission were going to kiss these two goons' asses before they let them back in the car. They looked like a bunch of privates talking to a couple of generals. I couldn't wait to drive away. When I did, Big Tony said something like, 'What a bunch of redneck, kiss-ass, shitheads.'" He laughed again, totally amusing himself.

"As we drove back to the coast, Big Tony called someone—I'm sure it was the same lobbyist as before. He told the guy to get all the information he could on this cop that was causing all the trouble and he'd call him when we got to Biloxi with a fax number to send it to. He told the guy he wanted to know everything: where this cop lived, where he hung out, what he drove and he even wanted a picture of him. When we got to the casino, he went into his office and called the lobbyist, who must've been standing by ready to send the stuff. Tony handed me an envelope with half the money—he was hiding it from Bruno, who I guess didn't know anything about our deal."

Agents Byrd and Tischner were both taking notes, writing furiously to keep up with Jackson's narrative.

"I went over and played a couple of slot machines and Tony came down within a half hour and handed me a thick envelope that had a photo faxed from an old newspaper article, some handwritten notes describing the cop and his every move, and $2,500. He said if I could pull this off in less than a month, he'd give me another five thousand on top of it, which was great but I just wanted to get home and get that gun out of the trunk. So I went home, studied the information, and practiced with the gun out back then went to Jackson a couple of weeks later and rode around in my truck, looking for a good vantage point near the cop's house. The best I could find was a nearby water tower. I stayed there driving around the neighborhood for a few days, watching his house as he came home like clockwork every day at about five-thirty."

At this point in the story, Jackson leaned forward and started talking slowly and intensely.

"I remember it was the first of August. I waited until it got dark and put my gun inside a sleeping bag with some old MREs I had. Then I strapped it to my back, put on my gloves and climbed the tower. I stayed up there all night and all the next day on the back side that faced a field so I wouldn't be seen. It had a platform with a guard rail all the way around. I probably could've made the shot that morning as he left for work but I didn't want to stay up there all day with cops running around. I wanted to climb down in the dark. At about 5 p.m., I looked around the side to see if his car was home yet. It wasn't so I got down low and started to crawl around the side with my gun. It was a good thing I did, because I wasn't there more than ten minutes when he drove up. I wasn't really as ready as I should've been and had to take the only shot I could. He was bent over out of the car, picking up a newspaper. I had the top of his head in my scope when I pulled the trigger. I saw blood splatter, dropped my head and crawled backwards to the other side of the tower where the ladder was. It wasn't long before dark but I waited 'til then before I climbed down. All the fuss was focused around his house with police cars, ambulances and stuff. No one even looked my way. Having been taught to shit in a bag and bury it, I took everything with me—there was not one trace of physical evidence left behind. Guess I didn't kill the guy, but it wasn't a bad shot for seven hundred meters."

Tischner swallowed hard to hide his disgust. "Did you get the other five thousand for doing the job?"

"Only half of it."

"What do you mean?" Tischner asked.

"I was supposed to call Tony in Vegas when the deal was done and he told me to call his friend in Jackson to come by and pay me the rest so I'd have enough to leave town and lay low. The lobbyist, I don't know his name, met me at the coliseum and handed me the money out the window of a beautiful Lamborghini. Said he saw on the evening news that the cop was still alive, but not expected to be that way for long. He said he shouldn't give me a dime but that I'd get the rest when he read the obituary. I can identify him if you show me a picture. He acted like he thought he was a pretty boy but he looked pretty gross, if you ask me."

Tischner opened a movie file clip from the houseboat on his laptop and showed it to Jackson.

"That's him," Jackson said without hesitation when he saw Shyster. "That's definitely him. What a stupid-looking hairdo. Nice car, but a complete asshole."

"Okay," Tischner said, satisfied. "We're going to the federal court house for booking. You need to lock your trailer. I've digitally recorded this conversation on my laptop and I'm e-mailing it now to one of our clerks, who'll have it transcribed by the time we get done with the booking. You'll be given a chance to read it, make any corrections, initial them and sign it. When we're done processing you, be prepared to go to another institution away from this area for your own protection. The location won't be disclosed to anyone other than federal agents. We'll discuss your cooperation with the prosecutor, but are you also willing to help us identify these Vegas guys and testify against them if need be?"

"Only if you put me in that protection program thing and send me somewhere else with a new identity," he said. "Someplace warm. And I want a cool first name."

"I'm afraid that, for now, you're going to be incarcerated. Your helping us identify other suspects is one issue…" Tischner nodded to the agents, who helped a very comfortable Jackson roughly to his feet and re-cuffed him tightly with his hands behind his back. Then he stepped up to Jackson, just inches from his face. "But don't forget you tried to kill a cop. And that's not something we take lightly."

Chapter 20

The Strategic Plan

*"He who every morning plans the transaction of the day
and follows out that plan, carries a thread that will guide him
through the maze of the most busy life. But where no plan
is laid, where the disposal of time is surrendered merely
to the chance of incidence, chaos will soon reign."*
—Victor Hugo

A few weeks after Gregory Jackson's booking, a conference was held in the FBI's Jackson office. Though it was held for the purposes of strategic planning in the corruption case, it also had the feel of a pep rally, complete with "grip and grin" sessions and introductions.

The initial welcome was by U.S. Attorney Tyrone, after which it was turned over to Supervisory Case Agent Wallace Tischner.

"Ladies and gentlemen, I'd like to thank all of you for coming to Jackson today to participate in this strategic planning process to determine our avenues of approach from here. I used to say I'd rather have a sister in a whorehouse than a brother in the legislature, but that was before I met our guest, Mississippi state representative Wayne Lott. His father, Will Lott, is a senior career law enforcement officer shot in the line of duty due to his tenacity in pursuing organized crime and corruption in politics and business. We're happy to report that Will is recovering nicely from surgery and is here with us today, along with his son. Please join me in giving Wayne and Will a roaring round of applause," Agent Tischner said with great pride.

The room was filled with cheers and a standing ovation that lasted several minutes, though many of the agents who attended were not totally aware yet of the significance that Wayne played in the case they were there to discuss.

"It's not often we're able to find a politician willing to offer his or her services against corruption. It's not often we have an informant whose name should be preceded by 'the Honorable.' Nor is it often we're able to place such strong cases, with credible information and participation, on the U.S. attorney's desk with recommendations to go forth. Wayne Lott is not your typical informant, and has and will never be treated as such. He is welcome in my home any time—in fact, he's been there and didn't care much for my artwork."

The crowd laughed, especially Tischner's friends who had seen his painting of J. Edgar Hoover for themselves.

Tischner continued, "Wayne came to me one day after an extortion attempt against him by organized crime figures who wanted him to be their puppet—to turn over and do anything they wanted to influence the laws of this state. Wayne could've chosen the path most traveled but didn't. His unyielding efforts will put corrupt senators, representatives, lobbyists and businessmen where they need to be. He chose not to ignore what was going on around him, as many previously honest legislators have in the past. We thank those who didn't participate in corrupt activities, but applaud those few, like Wayne, who have actually stood up and done something about it."

Once again, the room erupted with praise for Wayne, as he and his dad waved their acknowledgment to the crowd.

"I've prepared a PowerPoint brief for y'all today to bring you up to date on our progress with this case. After, we'll begin a brainstorming effort to try to determine our future methodology, based on our agents' many years of expertise and training. Everyone's input is as valuable as the next person's, and rank does not apply until a final decision is made by the case agent… That's me. Of course, whatever the U.S. attorney decides is what we live by. Anyone have any questions?" Tischner asked.

The room was quiet except for a couple of jokers in the back. "Hey, Wally, I have a message for you from your wife. She says you left your Flintstone vitamins at home. We'll run out and pick them up for you," said one of Tischner's old partners, who was very familiar with *Mrs.* Tischner's phoning habits.

"Very funny…and don't call me Wally. All the starving comedians in the world, and you guys are trying to ruin their reputation. How'd you like to go on surveillance in Siberia?" Tischner asked gruffly. "Let's move on with the presentation. The first thing I'd like to show you is a chronological listing of events that have taken place. Each of you has a copy in your folder in front of you to read more thoroughly during the break. Next is a conspiracy chart showing how each defendant is connected to the other, and includes recent surveillance photographs." Tischner waited a few moments for everyone to study it.

"As we continue, we'll look at each defendant individually and propose potential criminal charges from the United States Code, along with the elements of proof. In some cases, it may be better to flip a defendant either before or after arrest, depending on their role in the crimes or their ability to assist in a follow-up investigation that will lead to additional arrests. We'll then list our defendants by their level of importance in carrying out these crimes and prioritize those we may seek to use for evidentiary purposes. Some of those we'll see later on video may have played the game for the lobbyist willingly. Others may have been extorted. The investigation will have to continue post-arrest to make these determinations without compromising the ongoing cases, the undercover agents or our informants. We'll also need to recommend to the U.S. attorney those we feel should be un-indicted co-conspirators as well as any recommendations for inclusion in the witness protection program."

When Tischner finished his presentation, the agents were assigned break out groups of arrest teams, surveillance teams, evidence collection, and transport officers, and the local/state liaison agents were put with the U.S. attorney on public affairs.

"Tomorrow, all team leaders will give PowerPoint presentations outlining their respective team's role. Team members will also make short, ten-minute presentations concerning their individual responsibilities. At the end of the day, our IT people will merge the slides into one final presentation that I'll present to the boss and U.S. Attorney Tyrone." Tischner concluded, "We've got a lot of work and a long night ahead of us, people."

When the following morning came, Agent Tischner found himself up at the podium again, addressing the agents.

"Ladies and gentlemen, as you know, we're here because U.S. Attorney Tyrone has given his approval and instructions to move forward with the criminal roundup. As you *also* know, this is going to be a media nightmare. But at least in the eyes of the public, we cannot let it appear that there's an issue of 'us and them.' What I mean is that other agencies have had limited involvement in this case, especially as it pertains to the attempted assassination of Will Lott, and we wouldn't be serving the public well if we didn't ask our state counterparts to assist in this roundup. But that doesn't mean we discuss evidence with those groups as we seek their participation. After all, in a roundabout way, these people work for the legislators. They may not want to participate or their agencies may not want them to—and due to the fact that indictments are secret until served, we can't approach them until the absolute last minute. Currently, I plan to contact only the state police investigators and the state attorney general for assistance. Should they choose to participate, they'll be included in a team with specific assignments. Once the indictments are returned, we'll receive packages similar to those the surveillance group received, but also containing the indictments and arrest warrants. Does anyone have any questions or comments before the presentations begin?" Agent Tischner asked.

"What are the chances of interstate flight to avoid prosecution?" one agent asked.

"Most of the defendants are long-time businessmen or politicians, so it isn't likely we need to worry about that. But that's not to say it couldn't happen, especially after the motions for discovery are filed and they see the actual evidence we have against them. At that time, we may want to keep a closer eye on them. Anyone else?" Tischner asked.

When no one else was forthcoming, Will glanced over at Wayne for approval to speak. He knew he was just invited there because of his son and was not expected to participate. Still, he couldn't help himself.

"I know the details of the roundup have not been decided yet, but if it were up to me, we'd wait until the legislative session, stroll in at roll call then snatch each one of these assholes and stuff them into the back of a dirty old van sporting handcuffs and leg irons."

Tischner smiled and said, "It would be effective and easier on all my teams, but it'd turn into a media disaster when these crybaby bastards started calling the governor's office."

Will replied, "True, but on the police department, we used a similar tactic by sending out winners' notices for free gifts. When those we wanted to round up showed up at the hotel and packed into the banquet rooms in droves, they were quickly hauled off in the back of U-Haul trucks. I'm an old street cop," he sighed. "These guys disgust me, running for office in the name of the church, good will, children, education, and effective law enforcement."

"I understand what you're saying, Will," Agent Tischner said, wishing he were on the team. "But this thing has really grown from the bingo corruption as you knew it, and it is big-time. In some ways, it's similar to the indictments in the Tennessee Rocky Top scandal from a number of years ago. In fact, I've got those indictments, as well as some newspaper clippings from the *Commercial Appeal* and *The New York Times*. You and Wayne are welcome to take the material to your hotel room tonight. Might make for good reading."

"Thank you," Will said, satisfied at having said his piece.

"I'm sure all of you recognize the many merits of Mr. Lott's suggestion," Tischner continued to the audience, "but hopefully we won't have to wait until the next legislative term starts and can move quickly since the grand jury's convening on Monday. Our case has priority. The prosecutorial team will advise those needed for testimony, and assuming we get immediate return on the indictments, we may have our roundup near the end of next week. So without further delay, let's get to your presentations."

After all the team presentations had gone smoothly, the IT people merged the slides into a final presentation and gave it to Agent Tischner for his afternoon meeting with the U.S. attorney and special agent in charge of the FBI office in Jackson.

"Sirs, our paid informant, Representative Wayne Lott, identified fourteen members of the legislature other than himself from the twenty-one DVDs, and our second informant, Sylvia Stiles, a co-conspirator, has identified two more, plus a deputy believed to have committed murder. A former Gaming Commissioner, Jack Algood, and a bank president from the Gulf Coast, J. Clyde Davis, have also been identified in the sex videos. There are only four left we haven't identified. If our other informants can't identify them, we'd have to confront the girls at the strip joint to see if they know. However, we feel that's too risky and word might get out, so we're waiting until we complete the investigation and present the cases to the grand jury." The U.S. attorney and special agent both nodded in agreement.

"I believe we should pursue what we've gained through our undercover efforts and interviews or through additional grand jury testimony later to identify the other people and determine whether they were influenced in any way through the sex sting. We have admissions on tape from Representatives Quarles and Wolcott that they'd been scammed just like Lott."

U.S. Attorney Tyrone asked, "What is it that you don't know?"

"Well, besides the other four men in the videos, we haven't ascertained if the other strippers knew they were involved in a conspiracy or whether it was just paid sex for them," Tischner explained. "We don't know for sure who killed that one stripper, but we're pursuing an active investigation against a senior deputy sheriff who calls himself Dog—as in 'top dog.'"

"What are your plans regarding the separate case involving your agent Bob and Ms. Backman?" Tyrone asked.

"We'd like to leave that investigation running and not blow his cover. We're not sure it will be related but we expect a lot of talking and scared people after the roundup, which may net us additional information before the second wave," Tischner said.

"Okay…I'd like your agents to confront Quarles or Wolcott, whichever one is more likely to roll over," Tyrone said. "If one lies to you, pressure him but don't push it too far. Go to the other one; if he lies, too, let him know he'll be charged with lying to federal agents. If he rolls, let him talk. I'd like to know from them first if any of these other legislators were extorted. We may even have them testify for the grand jury and indict others."

"Will do," Agent Tischner replied.

"What about the Will Lott case?" the special agent added.

"We know the casino industry itself isn't behind the attempted assassination on Mr. Lott," Tischner said. "Big Tony's a member of the gaming industry, but his involvement with lobbyist Chuck Shyster wasn't well-known. Let me read you the wiretap transcript: 'Hello, Chuck? This is Tony. Our guy did the job and will call you for the rest of the money. Take care of it yourself. I'm back in Vegas and if my casino finds out I was in on it, they'll fire me.' 'Guess what, Tony? The cop ain't dead yet. But if all goes well, I'll pay the kid the rest of it. I don't need you here raising suspicions—and I don't want your casino knowing about our relationship, either. This deal was between you and me. I want it to stay that way.'"

Agent Tischner looked up from the transcripts. "Our review of Shyster's bank records shows withdrawals in the same amounts that were given to the shooter. So what we've got is the shooter's own admission and strong physical evidence of murder conspiracy and attempted murder against him. Big Tony can be charged with murder conspiracy, and Chuck Shyster with murder conspiracy, extortion and conspiracy to commit extortion. He's also the link between the shooting case and the sex sting. For that, we can get Al the strip club owner on conspiracy to commit extortion and racketeering, Shyster's two technicians on conspiracy to commit extortion and unlawful wiretapping, and Representatives Quarles and Wolcott on conspiracy to commit extortion. Jack Algood and J. Clyde Davis will be un-indicted co-conspirators, and of course we expect additional arrests. In addition, under RICO, we can get the two-million-dollar boat, sports car, strip club building, electronics business and so on."

"I'm pleased with your work," U.S. Attorney Tyrone said. "Let's go ahead with the presentations to the grand jury on Monday."

That's what Tischner was waiting to hear.

At the strategic planning conference the next day, he briefed the agents about those needed for testimony and required them to have their evidence and reports ready for Monday. "I realize that only gives you a few short days to prepare," he said, "but we're not building Rome here, people. More like taking down Sodom and Gomorrah."

Everyone suddenly got very busy—and all personnel would remain in Jackson throughout the following week.

Chapter 21

Stroll Down Memory Lane

"The secret of a good memory is attention, and attention
to a subject depends upon our interest in it.
We rarely forget that which has made
a deep impression on our minds."
—Tyron Edwards

Will and Wayne sat in their hotel room reading over the indictments from the Tennessee Rocky Top scandal that Agent Tischner had lent them. It was a good way of keeping Wayne's mind off the case he was embroiled in and Will's thoughts off the seemingly endless series of doctor's appointments he had scheduled in Jackson within the next few days.

"I remember stories of this scandal from my own days investigating bingo corruption and how it was tied to public officials and lobbyists, bribery, extortion and suicides. These legislative indictments caused the secretary of state to commit suicide. His obituary was printed in *The New York Times*," Will said.

"What happened in Tennessee has an eerie resemblance to what's going on in Mississippi," Wayne said, looking up from his reading to glance at his father.

"That's right, Wayne. Members of the legislature were on boards, bingo halls were almost like casinos clustered with gaming machines, and charities weren't getting what they were entitled to, even though cash money was leaving the halls wrapped in king-sized bedspreads. Enforcement authorities allowed new bingo operations to be licensed though they failed to meet many of the statutory laws or regulations, and charity money was spent on personal use, with board members' and bingo workers' salaries skyrocketing."

"It's the same in this case, only casino owners, lobbyists and lawmakers are the ones profiting," Wayne said.

"The outcomes would be the same, too, if there were ever a prosecutor with enough balls to pursue Mississippi's corruption on a grand scale," Will added. "Tyrone's okay, but we need somebody extremely aggressive and proactive. You know what I mean."

"Hey, Dad," Wayne said, looking through the articles that Tischner enclosed, "this one deals with Indian bingo and gives you an idea of how the FBI sees organized crime as an integral part of the business."

He read the *Time* magazine article from 1989 and paraphrased it for his father. "It says bingo is a $400 million business on Indian reservations, which aren't regulated by the state, so the prize for one game can be as high as $50,000. Dealing with that kind of money, tribes hire management companies to run the bingo operations, but the FBI says they're really just fronts for organized crime. They skim the profits and leave the Indians with almost nothing."

"That's bad," Will said. "But here's one that should upset anyone who likes baseball, especially in Virginia."

He picked up the 1997 article from *The Virginia Pilot* and summarized it for his son.

"The Gaming Commission investigated the ex-manager of the Deep Creek Baseball Association's bingo enterprise for running illegal gambling and stealing hundreds of thousand of dollars from what was supposed to be a charity organization." He shook his head. "Makes me sick. And with America's pastime, too."

"Here's one from the *Chicago Sun-Times* in 2002 that talks

about how bingo used to be for little old ladies but was taken over by big-time gamblers and criminal elements. A federal grand jury found ten men guilty of skimming over $3.2 million in profits from just one 'charity' bingo hall alone." Wayne whistled in amazement. "If only those little old ladies knew where their money was going."

"Well, Chicago always had ties to organized crime," Will said.

"But there are articles in here from Colorado, too," Wayne said. "In 2006, ten people were indicted by a grand jury—most noticeably a city councilman and county commissioner. They took millions of dollars from bingo and pull-tab lottery tickets that were intended for charity. Instead, that money ended up in private hands. Their total of thirty felony counts included violations of the state's Organized Crime Control Act, as well as forgery and theft. And these are supposed to be *public* officials," Wayne said in disgust.

"Yeah, I remember most of that from my research," Will said. "But a lot of the more recent stuff that I found on the Internet dealt with machine seizures, which are happening everywhere as we speak *except* good ol' Mississippi. They don't seize anything here— just reject applications for licensure *if* they're found to have false statements or concealed criminal backgrounds. Of course, those that do get by the investigators have access to millions of dollars in cash a year."

"That's really strange considering that according to our fish and game laws, falsifying an application for a fishing license counts as committing a felony!" Wayne said.

"Hell, there aren't even felonies in the bingo laws. You gotta wonder who the hell is writing them," Will said.

"That's what I'd call the *opposite* of effective regulating," Wayne agreed.

"Look," Will said. "Agent Tischner included a copy of the PEER report that came out on September 11, 1996—but I believe if the same investigation were done today, the findings would be far worse than they were then."

Wayne silently read the Mississippi PEER Report #344, entitled

A Review of the Adequacy of the Mississippi Gaming Commission's Regulation of Legalized Gambling in Mississippi:

"The perception of Mississippi as an industry-friendly state was not limited to academicians and the many casino owners choosing to locate in Mississippi. An affidavit from the FBI dated November 1993 requesting authorization for wire taps on organized crime figures suspected of racketeering and later convicted of conducting a blackjack scam at Mississippi's President Casino in Biloxi noted that the FBI had 'documented the intent of several LCN (La Cosa Nostra) families from around the country to infiltrate the legalized gambling industry in Mississippi.' In attempting to explain this intent, the affidavit included the following quote from a conversation between a 'known' La Cosa Nostra associate and underboss. 'In Mississippi there's no regulations, there's no laws, there's no nothing, you can do anything you want to do.'"

"That's unbelievable," Wayne said, looking directly at his dad.

"To correct the FBI snitch slightly, I'd say there *are* laws that would result in arrest, but years have gone by without anyone using them," Will said. "There are also regulations, but the fines and punishment apply to the charities—not the employees—if, and only *if*, the Gaming Commission decides to use them. In essence, there might as well be no laws or regulations, so I'd have to agree with the La Cosa Nostra associate that pretty much anything goes in Mississippi."

"Don't I know that all too well," Wayne said.

Will noticed that his son was looking tired from all the recent strain. He was sitting with his elbows propped up on the table and was massaging his temples.

"Come on, Wayne, let's hit the sack. I can only handle so many memories and so much dereliction in the performance of duties."

"Okay, Dad. Tomorrow's a big day anyway with Agent Tischner sending agents out to rattle a few cages," Wayne said.

"I'm sure glad you hooked up with him, son," Will said, patting Wayne on the back.

"Me, too," Wayne agreed. "The way he sees things reminds me of you."

"I wish I could say that about the top dogs at the Gaming Commission," Will said. "But they remind me of something else—a quote on a T-shirt I once saw in New Orleans: 'I'd really like to see things from your point of view, but I can't get my head that far up my ass to do so.'"

Will and Wayne shared a laugh, which soon turned into snores.

Chapter 22

The Confrontation

*"A good man would prefer to be defeated
than to defeat injustice by evil means."*
—Sallust

The next morning, Agent Tischner and Bob arrived at Quarles's law office in Flowood. Unlike Quarles himself, the office was conservatively decorated and not at all flashy—though the sparse furnishings had become a bit shabby.

Tischner approached the secretary. "Good morning. We don't have an appointment but are here to see if Mr. Quarles would be interested in representing us on an unlawful death case involving a hospital."

"Oh, I'm sure he'd love to see you. He doesn't have anything on his calendar 'til this afternoon. May I tell him your names?" she asked.

Overhearing them and thinking about hospitals' deep pockets, Quarles didn't wait for his secretary's announcement. He opened his office door and said, "Come in."

The two agents entered and as soon as Quarles closed the door and sat down, they flopped opened the cases containing their badges. "We're with the FBI and would like to talk to you, Mr. Quarles," Tischner said.

Hearing the words that he had so often heard directed at others, Quarles became visibly nervous. "You have the right to remain silent," Bob stated. "Anything you say can and will be used against you in a court of law. You have a right to have an attorney…"

"Damn it, I *am* an attorney," Quarles interrupted. "I know that shit…please."

Bob ignored him and kept reading the rights advisement card.

"Now you're going to ask if I understand my rights," Quarles said. "Of course I understand."

"Mr. Quarles, we know you've been involved in extortion. We're here to see if you want to help yourself," Tischner said.

"What do you mean?" His voice was trembling and the pen in his hand began to shake. "I don't know what you're talking about."

"Mr. Quarles, I'm sure you know that lying to FBI agents about a criminal investigation is a federal offense. We could play this silly-ass game all day, or we could charge you without your cooperation and hope your partners in crime are smarter than you. Quite frankly, I don't have all day, so let's talk about the boat," Tischner said.

"The boat?"

"Shyster's houseboat," Tischner replied. "Let me jog your memory. Ever see the movie *Sex, Lies and Videotape*? Other key words are: extortion, jail, disbarment, removal from office. Last chance… you won't get this opportunity again."

"Oh, my God." Quarles's face went completely white. "What about my House seat?"

"You can kiss that goodbye, counselor. It's in the past. Now, you better worry about your future and how much time you want to do." Tischner walked toward the door with Bob in tow, as if they were leaving.

"Wait, wait, dammit. I'll tell you what I know." He dropped his face on the desk. "I've got a beautiful wife and three kids…one's only a baby." He lifted his head, banged his fist against the desk and screamed, "I don't need this shit!"

The secretary's voice came over the intercom. "Mr. Quarles, are you okay?"

"Hell, yes…I'm just hunky-dory, dammit. Cancel my afternoon appointments then leave for the day," Quarles said, punching the off button on the intercom.

He faced the agents and said, in a much quieter voice, "That was all Chuck's idea. He extorted me. I had to help him with some legislation and the rest of his plan. I *had* to, don't you understand? I didn't have any choice. He was going to send the video to my wife, a Sunday school teacher at the biggest church in the area. It would've killed her."

"Before I ask you the next question, I want you to know that we already know most of the answers. So don't try to lie or protect anybody. Who else was extorted and how much legislation was influenced?" Agent Tischner asked.

"Man, are you kidding? There was so much legislation influenced that I'd have to go back to the docket rooms in the Capitol to make a list," Quarles said.

"Give us the names of the other legislators who were extorted," Bob prompted.

"Senator Boggins, Senator Castle and I think Senator Earhart. The representatives I personally know about are Johnsrud, Wilhelm and Lott. There were more, but I'm not sure who they were. Wolcott worked with me…he had also been a victim himself a couple of years back. I think he set up some more legislators, but you'd have to talk to him… Wait, have you already talked to him?" Quarles asked.

Without answering, Tischner said, "Since we don't have time for you to go to the Capitol to do research, I want you to open the legislative site on the Internet, look at the bills over the last five years that have been sponsored by the men you mentioned, and tell me which legislation was influenced as part of the extortion conspiracy."

Quarles did exactly what he was told, printing off pages and pages of proposed bills, along with the photos and bios of those involved. Tischner took the documents and said, "Be at our office tomorrow morning by 9 a.m. for a further in-depth interview and possible preparation for grand jury testimony."

With that, they left Quarles sitting at his desk in his empty office.

Outside, Tischner called the U.S. attorney's office. "Mr. Tyrone, we got what we wanted from Quarles. There's no need to approach Wolcott before presenting the case to the grand jury. All we have to do now is wait until next Monday."

———

The next morning at exactly 9:19 a.m., the agents were still awaiting Quarles's arrival. Tischner was sitting impatiently at his desk when his secretary poked her head in the office.

"Mr. Tischner, you have a call from an attorney named Shaw."

"You mean Quarles?" he asked. "We've been waiting for him."

"No, he said 'Shaw' very distinctly."

"Patch him through. Maybe he's using a phony name," Tischner said.

When the call came through, Tischner listened to someone speak for only a minute.

"I see...I see. Are you sure?" Tischner said. "Okay." Then he hung up, sighed and called U.S. Attorney Tyrone.

"Quarles has retained counsel with Attorney Shaw and isn't coming in. He's changed his mind and has decided to take his chances."

"Go down to the clerk's office, get that bastard a subpoena for the grand jury and get it served ASAP," Tyrone said, outraged.

"But, sir, he's represented. He'll just plead the fifth," Agent Tischner said.

"No, by God, he will not. He's about to get immunity from

prosecution on the issues we question him about in front of the grand jury, so he won't be able to plead the fifth. He'll be compelled to testify or become a jail bird until he does. Let that son-of-a-bitch screw up one time and he'll be prosecuted on other crimes, too," the U.S. attorney said.

"Yes, sir. Sounds good to me," Tischner said. Before hanging up, he heard Tyrone scream to his secretary, "Get Attorney Kevin Shaw on the phone for me."

Just before lunch, when the subpoena came in, Tischner took a ride to Quarles's office and home to hand deliver it, but couldn't find him at either place. Then he called U.S. Attorney Tyrone, who told him, "Don't worry. I spoke to Quarles's attorney, Kevin Shaw. He was so pleased that his client was getting immunity that he said he'd bring him down personally tomorrow morning at ten."

⁓

The next morning at quarter past seven, after Quarles's two oldest children left for school, his wife lay back down in bed with the baby. Quarles, dressed in a faded blue corduroy bathrobe with two big pockets on the front, went into the bathroom to take his morning shower.

He locked the door, turned on the shower then sat down on the toilet to write a note. He laid the pen and paper next to the sink, stepped into the tub without taking his robe off, removed a small revolver from his pocket, and blew his brains out.

Minutes later, after discovering her husband's body and calling 911 with a shaking hand, Quarles's stunned wife read his final note through eyes streaming with tears.

> Sweetheart, I'm so sorry for what I've done. I love you and
> the kids more than you'll ever know. Please forgive me. I
> just can't stand to do what the FBI wants me to and I can't

face the press when this comes out. Please call Ray Wolcott and tell him that the FBI knows everything. You'll understand it all shortly. Just know that I never meant to hurt you and I'll always love you.

While awaiting the arrival of the police and ambulance, she called the FBI office. "What have you done to my husband?" she screamed like a woman possessed. "Which one of you did it? I'll kill you...I'll kill you! I'll kill all of you!"

The secretary who had answered the call was visibly upset, which Agent Tischner noticed as he walked by. He could hear screaming from the other end of the phone and took it from her.

"This is Agent Tischner. May I help you?"

"You're damn right you can! You can come over here and help me get my dead husband, George Quarles, out of the bathtub! He shot himself," she said, sobbing uncontrollably. "The note he left leads me to believe that somebody there is responsible."

Just then, on the other end of the line, Tischner could hear an ambulance pulling up. "Mrs. Quarles, please put one of the EMTs or officers on the phone. It's important."

"Important?" she asked. "As important as three fatherless children?"

"It may help in a case against a man who has hurt your husband," Tischner replied.

Without another word, she handed the phone to a police officer who arrived on the scene then she collapsed on the couch.

"Officer, this is Agent Tischner with the FBI. Make sure you put the suicide note into evidence. We'll come by and get a copy," he said calmly. What he was thinking, however, was quite different: *Damn it, Quarles, why couldn't you just cooperate?*

Chapter 23

The Grand Jury

"Injustice anywhere is a threat to justice everywhere."
—Martin Luther King, Jr.

By now the agents knew they had to move fast. They were certain Quarles's wife would tell Wolcott about the FBI, but decided to present his case anyway and pursue the other defendants for investigative purposes. Without Quarles's assistance, it would be more difficult to establish guilt—though his own feelings of guilt had gotten the better of him.

The following Monday afternoon, the grand jury convened and the assistant U.S. attorney addressed the members.

"Ladies and gentlemen, I'd first like to thank all of you for being here today and fulfilling your civic duty. The bad news is I expect you to be busy for a while; the good news is that being busy will make time pass more quickly." He motioned to their surroundings: a dreary, closed conference room with no windows.

"I think you'll find this to be a very interesting investigation. Federal agents will testify and present their evidence and conclusions based on a lengthy undercover operation. I'll explain to you the violations committed and you'll be asked to agree or disagree with the findings based on the law. Should you concur, you'll vote 'true bill,' meaning the defendant will be indicted, or 'no bill,' meaning no charges will go forth. You can ask any questions of the witnesses or me. There'll be no defense attorneys or judge present, and with the exception of a few now assisting with the investigation, no defendants will be present, either. So you'll reach your conclusions after hearing each witness—agents, forensic experts and, in limited cases, participants in the crimes—and examining the physical and audio evidence presented only by the prosecution. If indictments are issued, the defendants will be arrested and brought before a federal magistrate for a bond hearing and formal reading of the charges. They'll be released if they post bond after being processed and briefly jailed, and their attorneys will file motions for discovery in order to prepare their defense prior to trial if no plea bargains are reached first. The testimony you hear today must not be disclosed to anyone for six months. Are there any questions?"

"I've been on the grand jury before and have heard lots of different kinds of cases. Am I to understand that this is primarily about one investigation?" the foreman asked.

"For the most part, yes. This is a very high-profile investigation that involves state government officials and businessmen. For reasons that will become obvious, we call the case Operation Sex, Lies and Video. It involves extortion, attempted murder for hire, sex for money, and corruption, and falls under the general category of racketeering," the assistant U.S. attorney explained. "Any more questions?"

"No," somebody in the back yelled out. "Let's get started. This *does* sound interesting!"

"Okay. First I'd like to introduce you to the primary witness, Supervisory Special Agent Wallace Tischner. Agent Tischner, would you please raise your right hand and swear or affirm that the testimony you are about to give before this grand jury today is the truth, the whole truth and nothing but the truth, so help you God?"

"I do," Agent Tischner said without hesitation.

"Please give the grand jury an overall view of how this investigation came about and how some criminal cases materialized."

Addressing the grand jury, Tischner recounted, "I initiated this investigation as a series of proactive offensive cases with anticipation of making each case in the entire undercover investigation with the use of an informant who came to us on his own free will. The informant was not a criminal trying to get a lighter sentence. He is a lawyer and state representative that the perpetrators expected to manipulate into helping with their plan, but he chose to cooperate with us in exposing and pursing those responsible instead—in particular a lobbyist who was using sexual blackmail to extort legislators and influence legislation. We took the complainant on as a paid confidential informant to work as an agent of the government under my direct oversight, having him perform undercover surveillance and secure admissions from the perpetrators."

Tischner braced himself. He knew that the next part would draw gasps from the grand jury members.

"During the conduct of this investigation, we confirmed a lobbyist's use of prostitutes and gained information that led to solving an attempted murder of our informant's father, also perpetrated by the same lobbyist. We discovered evidence of additional crimes, such as violations of the White Slavery Act, bribery, illegal wiretapping, and corruption, which involved approximately twenty people—a criminal enterprise. We hope to address those issues today as a violation of the RICO Act, a federal law under Title 18 of the United States Code, titled Racketeer Influenced and Corrupt Organizations Act. The U.S. attorney has helped us determine the charges against each perpetrator involved for presentation to this body in order to seek indictments that will result in their arrests." Tischner cleared his throat. "We'd like to start this process by seeking an indictment on the kingpin of this investigation himself."

For the rest of the week, a very busy room full of grand jurors saw agents and other witnesses going in and out, systematically and methodically presenting the cases one after another. Agents had filled up one end of the already cramped room with video discs, surveillance video, audio tapes, investigative reports, crime lab reports, audio and video players, monitors, conspiracy charts and on and on. Following their testimonies, additional witnesses included Will Lott (as a shooting victim), Wayne Lott (as an extortion victim), Sylvia Stiles (as an un-indicted co-conspirator in extortion) and Gregory C. Jackson (as the shooter).

One case that wouldn't be presented was Carol's murder. Agent Tischner and U.S. Attorney Tyrone decided that there wasn't enough evidence against "Deputy Dog" to involve him in the racketeering enterprise or as part of the criminal conspiracy. Rather than taking a chance on his being found not guilty, they'd wait for other information gained from the grand jury investigative process and turn it over—along with the New Year's video—to the state for a murder prosecution.

Though Tischner wasn't thrilled about handing over the case, he realized, "I'd rather it be someone else's fight to win than mine to lose. That's the only way that girl is going to get any justice."

⁓

After three more days of testimony and evidence, the grand jury began deliberations. They'd reconvene ready to vote on all the accused persons.

While Agent Tischner waited anxiously for any word, his cell phone rang. "Boss, you need to come down to the cafeteria to see this special news report," an agent said.

When Tischner arrived downstairs, the TV was showing firefighters attempting to extinguish a large fire at the reservoir. It was hardly recognizable, but he could tell that one large boat had exploded and several boats on each side of it were ablaze. Agents dispatched to the scene confirmed it was the infamous boat used by lobbyist Chuck Shyster.

"Well, I'll be..." Tischner said, staring at the screen in disbelief.

Reporters were interviewing bystanders about what had happened. "It sounded like a couple of large bomb blasts, one after the other, then some smaller ones," one witness said. "I'm not sure if anyone was on the boat, but I've heard rumors that someone was."

"We may have another defendant suicide on our hands," Tischner said to another agent standing close by. "Make sure the agents on the scene locate the fire marshal and the police on-scene commander to advise them that the FBI has an interest in this case. A crime scene search team should be arriving soon, as well as agents from the Bureau of Alcohol and Tobacco. Our agents should establish an outer perimeter to make room for the crime scene investigators then have them photograph the crowd surreptitiously and require anyone who doesn't have to be there to move on."

When the agent went to make the calls, Tischner continued watching the surreal scene unfold.

One witness was mentioning "a smell of propane when I arrived earlier," which Tischner knew was explainable due to the large propane tank onboard, plus two more for the grill. But the man also said that "as the fire disbursed and smoke cleared, there was only a smell of bleach," which was unexplainable.

On screen, Tischner could see that the water still had splotches of fire from the fuel oil believed to have come from the diesel tanks for the engines. However, the reporter announced that "a large plastic tank that sat on the after-deck for the launch motor is missing and presumed burned up."

From the initial look of things, Tischner knew it would be difficult to determine whether the cause was arson, a bomb, or accidental. But his hunches told him that this was no accident.

When the crime scene response team and evidence technicians arrived from Quantico, they immediately began searching the marina. The upper half of Shyster's houseboat was blown away and the lower part sunk where it sat. Debris was littered all over the water and pier.

Agents managed to recover the large gas stove and found that all four burners had been switched on. Granular chlorine, like that used in swimming pools, was scattered on either side of the boats and partially on the pier. A large can of brake fluid with scorch burns on one side was found on the deck of a boat four slips away. The top was missing, there was a small amount of fluid still inside, and the can appeared to have only been quickly exposed to the fire but blown away by the concussion.

Agent Tischner contacted the team leader a couple of days later, pressing for a cause.

"Forensic analysis hasn't been done yet," the agent said. But he was willing to theorize. "Somebody put bags of granular chlorine on the after-section of the boat deck above the fuel tanks, perhaps with the large can of brake fluid somehow suspended above the chlorine, leaking out slowly onto it. To create a blast multiplier, they left the gas can, propane tank and bottles in place, but blew out the stove pilot lights and turned on the burners. The explosion caused by the fuel tanks was ignited by the mixture of chlorine and brake fluid, which takes awhile to catch on fire, but will do so without an igniter due to chemical reaction. It probably took long enough for the cabin to become filled with propane gas from the stove. The initial explosion blew the sliding glass door in and the resulting flame ignited the cabin, causing a secondary explosion. The smaller propane tanks probably accounted for the smaller explosions."

"Any evidence of human remains?" Tischner asked.

"None," the agent said, "which leads us to believe that somebody started the fire back-aft in such a way that it'd take a while to catch up, giving the cabin time to fill with gas and the perpetrator time to get away."

"Our agents began their search for Mr. Shyster and found he flew to New York a few days before the explosion, most likely to have an alibi as to his whereabouts when the boat met its final demise," Tischner added.

It was Tischner's belief that Quarles's wife called Wolcott, who then alerted Shyster that the FBI knew everything.

"Shyster most likely had his video technicians do the job in hopes of destroying evidence such as hairs, fiber, fingerprints, DNA or other video evidence," he told the agent. "Of course, he could've also been trying to get the insurance money."

"For what?" the agent asked. "I thought he had money."

"Not enough to pay the legal bills for the defense he's going to be needing."

Chapter 24

The Roundup

"The sword of justice has no scabbard."
—Antione De Riveral

Waiting until after the next legislative session to make arrests was no longer an option. But how to go about making the arrests was an issue of much discussion among agents and investigators. Some wanted a pre-dawn raid, kicking in doors like they had often done on drug indictments. Others wanted to barge into the Capitol during a session and arrest the perpetrators in front of all their colleagues. A few wanted to call them to come down to the federal building to have papers served on them; even fewer wanted to cut the state attorney general in on the action.

There was no question that the U.S. Attorney's Office was going to get a big bang out of the scandal when it showed up in the *Clarion Ledger* and on Channels 3, 12 and 16 just because of the nature of the investigation and those involved.

U.S. Attorney Tyrone decided that there was no need to make the task any more dramatic than it already was. "We need to keep the public on our side and not have FBI agents seen as members of the Gestapo. The focus must be on the bad guys. If we don't give anyone any reason to try to make the feds appear as the enemy, there's no way members of the legislature can publicly condone their colleagues' activities." Still, he wasn't sure exactly how to go about it.

Tischner said, "Agents sometimes confer with their informants for recommendations since they know the group better than anybody else. That's especially true where the informant is a professional."

They decided to talk to Wayne.

"I don't see the need to sensationalize the arrests," Wayne said, sitting in the U.S. attorney's office a few hours later. "The story itself is going to be sensational enough. I know the FBI agents have done a lot of work to perfect a plan to pull this off without losing any defendants or agents. I saw the team presentations, and they all had safety and professionalism in mind."

He nodded at Tischner, who smiled in acknowledgment.

"I don't think bringing in the state attorney general is the best idea," Wayne continued. "I'm not saying he's involved, but he's already been in the public eye due to other corruption cases and documentation has surfaced that he may have received hundreds of thousands of dollars in campaign contributions from at least one of the lawyers recently sentenced to jail time for corruption."

"Good point," Tischner agreed. "I'm not sure how that would be received."

"These arrests could be done at their homes early, but not necessarily pre-dawn with individual teams, as the FBI is planning. I know some of the members of the legislature are shady, but I don't see violence as a major risk. Sadly, most of these guys were victims of extortion, like me," Wayne said. "They just made a different decision about how to handle it. My biggest concern is that all of these members won't be in Jackson, which poses a number of logistical problems."

"Wayne, I think you're right," Tyrone said. "And you've given me an idea. We're going to bring the governor into it. He needs to review the laws that were influenced through this illegal process anyway since he signed them. I'll be notified when the first person is arrested and will immediately go to the governor's office and insist on an emergency meeting. We'll have teams simultaneously arresting members of the legislature all over the state, so about a dozen arrests should be made by the time our conversation's over. In the event one or two defendants are missed, I'll just tell him that of course the indictments are secret until served. Then he can do some of the press conferences and it won't seem like a federal agency like the FBI is out to get state politicians. There'll be no us and them—just right and wrong."

The day had come. Just as planned, the agents made their way to their assigned areas, waiting for word that all teams were in place within blocks of their targets. Tischner gave the signal to go and within minutes, the raid was complete across the state. All but two, who weren't home, had been arrested. Agents would continue surveillance on their houses—one in the Greenville area, the other in the Brookhaven area—and attempt to determine their whereabouts.

The arrests went like clockwork—all without incident. By the time most Mississippians were getting into work, newspaper reporters were already calling the U.S. attorney's office, from the *Sun Herald* on the coast to the *Commercial Appeal* in Memphis and every paper in between, including the *Daily Corinthian, Times Picayune, Greenwood Commonwealth, Mississippi Press, Tunica Times* and Brookhaven's *Daily Leader*. No part of the state was untouched by this investigation.

Even the WLBT helicopter was busy circling the federal building and state Capitol, eager to get the scoop on the most bizarre case in the state's history. Only Operation Pretense, a roundup of county supervisors in the 1980s, even came close. The number of arrests was higher, but they were only county officials.

Agents attending the briefing turned up the TV as a CNN reporter announced, "Mississippi has made the largest single roundup of statewide elected officials ever seen in the history of our broadcasting."

Actors, entertainers, athletes, authors, congressmen and senators from Mississippi were popping up on every national TV channel and being interviewed about their opinions on the state— and its state of corruption.

At noon, Tyrone held a news conference at the federal building. Microphones stuck up like the quills on a porcupine's back as the U.S. attorney, speaking on behalf of the Governor's Office as well, gave a brief statement with promises of a short question and answer period to follow.

"Today is a sad day for the political institution here in Mississippi," he said, standing at a podium in front of the large but densely populated conference room with large windows that looked out at the gold eagle perched atop the dome of the state Capitol.

"Over a dozen members of the state's legislature, lobbying industry and private businesses have been arrested by FBI agents and federal marshals for charges including extortion, wire fraud, racketeering, conspiracy to commit murder and violations of the White Slavery Act. Two are still outstanding and are being pursued by FBI agents. Most defendants have multiple charges of the same offense with mounds of physical evidence. These arrests are the result of a long-term undercover operation, and defendants will be brought before a U.S. magistrate for their initial appearance. We have no objections to them making bond and are looking forward to working with their defense attorneys on evidentiary discovery. After all the indictments are served, they'll be returned to the clerk and as a matter of public record may be obtained for further details by the media. At this time, I'm prepared to answer a few questions."

He pointed to a woman in the front row. "Jackie Rollins from Channel 12 news. Can you tell us how this investigation started?"

"I can tell you that the U.S. Attorney's Office has placed political corruption as one of its highest priorities. We took advantage of an opportunity we had, explored the possibilities and followed every lead. That's all I can tell you at this time," Tyrone said, nodding to another reporter.

"Johnny Williamson, *Clarion Ledger*. Will there be additional arrests other than the two not yet found?"

"Possibly, as we assemble additional evidence, but I won't comment on whether additional suspects will be arrested as part of today's raid." Tyrone picked out another reporter.

"Wilbert Montgomery from the *Vicksburg Post*. You said this was a result of a long-term undercover investigation. Was any member of the legislature an inside informant?"

"No comment," Tyrone quickly responded. "We don't disclose the identities or activities of our informants." He pointed to a woman in a business suit.

"Maggie Johnson from the *Mississippi Business Journal*. Since you indicated there were businessmen involved, can you tell us whether the gaming industry was targeted? We're hearing rumors that it was."

"No charges have been made at this time against any member of the gaming business. Some are connected to the industry, but you'll have to wait until the indictments are provided by the clerk's office. We only have time for one more question," Tyrone said hastily, pointing to his final pick.

"Brendan Yorke from the *Hattiesburg American*. Sir, can you tell us who the target of the attempted murder was?"

"I can tell you it was a high-ranking police officer, but other details will be in the indictment. That's all I'll answer today. Thank you for your attention and participation," the U.S. attorney said before quickly exiting the conference room, folders firmly in hand.

Tyrone hadn't had a chance to speak directly to Tischner yet, but he was interested primarily in one person who wasn't even a politician. He wanted to know how Chuck Shyster reacted to his arrest. As soon as he got to his office, he called Agent Tischner to inquire.

"We've processed him and begun an initial interview," Tischner said. "Surprisingly, he didn't ask for an attorney at first, but he didn't give any information, either. He wanted to know what we were interested in and we asked him who was behind the murder-for-hire job and which casinos paid him to influence legislation outside the bounds of the law. We already knew from the wiretap that he had ripped off the casinos, but we wanted to see if he'd take the normal criminal stance of trying to make someone else look more guilty than himself."

"How did that go?" Tyrone asked.

"All he said was, 'Life's a bitch and I ain't no snitch.' Then he laughed and asked for his attorney. We're recommending no bond on him," Tischner said.

By the time the six o'clock evening news came on, lawyers were coming out of the woodwork to assure the public that their clients had done nothing wrong and that when all was said and done, they'd be exonerated. Some blamed the FBI for being overzealous; others said the U.S. attorney was looking for headlines to advance his career.

In time for the ten o'clock news, one station had contacted Tyrone, asking what he thought about the accusations made earlier by the defendants' attorneys.

"That's just the way the criminal mind works," he stated. "The 'code of ethics' adopted by professional criminals holds that you must deny everything, admit to nothing, demand proof and, most of all, make counter accusations to put the focus on someone other than yourself. But given the spectacular physical evidence gathered in this investigation, they may want to rethink their code."

The regular ten o'clock news was interrupted with a special bulletin: "This just in. Senator Sylvester Patterson from Brookhaven was found dead in his car, which was parked inside his garage with a swimming pool vacuum hose taped to the exhaust pipe and put inside his window. The car was still running. FBI and local law enforcement officers are on the scene."

The cocky lawyers and confident defendants left the federal court-house the next day much differently than they had arrived. There were no smiles or blanket statements of innocence. They were replaced by "no comments" and sad, worried expressions as pho-tographers and cameramen clicked away.

"Can you tell us what happened?" one of the reporters asked an attorney.

"I don't think it would be appropriate to make a comment at this time," he said glumly.

"Are you confident your client will be exonerated?" another reporter asked.

"We have nothing to say," replied one of the Perry Masons of the industry.

"How about you, sir?" a TV newscaster asked.

"Get that microphone out of my face!"

By then, a sharp investigative reporter from the *Clarion Ledger* was putting two and two together. He was a well-respected jour-nalist who had more sources than the FBI did, and he began to follow the link between the recent houseboat explosion that the FBI agents had been so interested in, the two recent suicides of members of the legislature, and so on.

The *Jackson Free Press* had also printed some inside informa-tion, but being a weekly publication with limited circulation, it got little attention. In the coming weeks, though, every local media outlet would report shocking information about the case.

So many people had read or heard about the case prior to Chuck Shyster's upcoming trial that there were discussions about a potential request for a change of venue. However, national organizations such as CNN, NBC, FOX, CBS, ABC and *The New York Times* had all reported on the scandal in the state of Mississippi. There was nowhere left in the country that hadn't heard about it—and nowhere to move the trial that would have changed the circumstances.

Chapter 25

Discovery

*"Discovery consists of seeing what everybody
has seen and thinking what nobody has thought."*
—Albert Szent Gyorgyi

Motions for discovery were filed by all the top lawyers in the state. The list appeared to be a who's who of the State Bar Association. But the attorneys soon discovered that sometimes you have to be careful what you ask for.

The indictment against Chuck Shyster cited his prostitution ring and extortion efforts, but he was not one of the politicians. Their indictments were less explanatory concerning those issues and did not mention that the evidence included sexually explicit videos of the legislators. When the defendants' lawyers found out what they were up against, some dropped out.

U.S. Attorney Tyrone was planning to show those DVDs when the time came. As he explained to the assistant U.S. attorney, "I expect that as a result, many if not all of the accused will want to enter pleas, especially with statements from other legislators admitting to the scheme and copies of bank records showing deposits on the same day votes were cast in legislation."

He had no problem showing the evidence—and in fact was looking forward to it. "But I'm not making any deals until after the kingpin's trial. I want to see Chuck Shyster convicted and given the maximum punishment to send a message to the others."

Of course, the U.S. Attorney's Office didn't need any of their help to put Shyster away for life. "But I want the others to fear what the judge will give them if they force us into a trial. They won't receive a sentence like Chuck's likely to get, but making an example of him will take away any desire they have to stand in front of an angry federal judge who'll have little respect for legislators, most of whom are lawyers themselves, casting the legal profession and political institution in such a bad light," Tyrone reasoned. "Besides, I'm sure they know that a federal judge is appointed for life by the president and has no reason to be influenced by or bow down to state politics."

"But you'll be willing to entertain plea bargains once Shyster's convicted?" the assistant U.S. attorney asked.

"Yes, to save time and not tie up juries in so many trials. But I've already set the standard in my mind. Prior to showing the discs, the offer will have to be to plead guilty for a total of ten years, serve five years then remain on probation for the five suspended years, pay a fifty-thousand-dollar fine and resign from office, agreeing never to seek a political position again. But I won't tell the defense attorneys about those terms until *after* Shyster's sentencing. Let them look at the video and give thought to what kind of deals they can make afterwards," he said with a cunning smile.

"You're providing them actual copies of the DVDs?"

"No. We're setting one day for viewing, listening to the wiretap tapes and so on, so it doesn't become a logistical nightmare and we only need the technicians once. Besides," Tyrone smirked, "we don't want any of that footage ending up on YouTube."

Wayne wasn't allowed to go to the hearing but he just couldn't stay away. He put on an old ball cap and a pair of sunglasses, and rode around the building, watching as the cars stopped out front and the high-paid lawyers got out with their clients. *It looks like Sunday at the big church downtown, with men dressed in suits pouring into the building,* he thought. *But these don't have Bibles with them—just lawyerly-looking briefcases in their hands and legal files under their arms.*

The media was having a field day, with reporters hanging around, waiting for cars to stop and empty their loads, then trying to get comments from anyone making their way through the crowd. The line to enter the building was slowed down due to the old, skinny man in a wrinkled brown security uniform who stood at the metal detectors. He was nicknamed Barney, and the lawyers cussed under their breaths as they were inconvenienced by his asking them to take all metal objects out of their pockets before entering.

All of the defense attorneys were to come in to view the videos privately with their clients. However, to save time, the attorneys got together and agreed to watch the videos in a room with all of them present. Tyrone thought it was a mistake on their part, but had no objections.

The U.S. attorney only had to show a couple of seconds of one disc before hearing the lawyers gasp, "Oh, my God," and the defendants scream, "Turn it off!"

The technician Tyrone used to operate the video system had a broken leg and a cast up to his hip. Each time he'd turn on a new disc, he'd take his seat slowly but surely in the back of the room, behind the defense team. It took him a long time to reach the front of the room to turn off the DVD when the protests rang out. By then, the entire group had seen some very revealing footage.

The rest of the lawyers wanted to know if there were similar images of their clients, and if statements tied these acts to any other evidence of malfeasance in office or attempts to influence legislation. Tyrone simply stated, "Yes."

After the third video, all the lawyers wanted to talk to Tyrone privately. However, sticking with his plan, he refused to meet with any of them to make a deal until after Shyster's verdict and sentencing.

When the long day finally came to a close, long faces drooped as the defendants and their lawyers exited the building with their heads down. One of the reporters out front commented, "The expressions are very different coming out of the building than they were going in."

It was obvious that the lawyers had discovered some things they weren't particularly happy about discovering. It meant they'd have to go back to the drawing board and try to put together a defense against the damning evidence or convince their clients to throw in the towel. One thing was sure: These lawyers weren't going to walk away from the trials with the success of O.J. Simpson's "dream team" and become instant national icons. At best, they'd be objects of ridicule and derision, win or lose.

There was no doubt in Tyrone's mind that additional motions would be filed, especially ones to prevent evidence from being entered.

"But the FBI is very good at what they do and there are some damn sharp lawyers in my office to guide us in our offensive efforts as the case develops," he told the assistant U.S. attorney.

Outside the building, when the last defendant pulled away, the news vans packed up and there was nothing left to see, Wayne took a ride alone to the reservoir, looking out at the vacant slip that once held a beautiful houseboat.

———

Not long afterward, the deal offers started to develop and U.S. Attorney Tyrone felt more like Monty Hall on *Let's Make a Deal*.

The negotiations were flying like crazy and he was being offered what he wanted but sat on them for the time being. However, he was glad that Shyster, the worst of the worst, wanted a trial—and he couldn't wait to give it to him.

"I want the press there to see every part of this trial, and it'll be a training session for our young agents to be able to watch the process as it's happening," he told the assistant U.S. attorney. Of course, a rule would prevent agents who worked on the case from hearing the entire trial, but those who weren't involved could certainly stay and enjoy.

"I'm looking for bigger and better things from this," Tyrone said, relishing each moment. "We're going to expose the criminal element in the state legislature through one of their highest-profile lobbyists."

He wouldn't even mention the fact yet that the FBI already had another top lobbyist working for them who could be responsible for the second wave of cases long after this upcoming trial ended, maybe a year or so down the road. His federal judge appointment was practically in the bag.

Chapter 26

The Trial

*"Though the vicious can sometimes pour affliction
upon the good, their power is transient and their
punishment certain; and that innocence,
though oppressed by injustice, shall, supported
by patience, finally triumph over misfortune!"*
—Ann Radcliffe

Shyster was the only individual in the criminal racketeering enterprise who still hadn't faced the potential consequences. The others had seen the evidence and wanted closure as soon as possible, but had to wait on him to be taken down publicly—and only a defiantly corrupt individual like Chuck could face the public, given his deeds.

Of the five categories of defendants, Shyster was the lone occupant of the first, trying to win the case against him and thumb his nose at society and the prosecution. Categories two, three and four had done everything they could at this point: respectively, take their own lives in lieu of facing the fiddler, make a deal with the prosecutor to save what was left of their disgusting skins, or help as much as they could to right their wrongs and see that justice would prevail, accepting full responsibility for their actions. All of their fates rested in the hands of God and the judge.

The last category consisted only of Wayne Lott, an unindicted victim who refused to give up, choosing instead to follow the path his father had shown him—and he still had work to do.

With Wayne's help and the help of other witnesses, the U.S. attorney would have to prove to a jury beyond a shadow of a doubt that Shyster committed these crimes. In the event he was found guilty, Will Lott, the victim of one of his crimes, would have to rise up and tell the judge that Shyster needed to receive his just reward. Only then could an ending take place.

Chuck had made his contribution to the long list of political corruption in the country, and once all the evidence had been presented, it was time for him to learn his destiny. The jury had been out for only two hours before returning to the courtroom, which was in itself a good sign.

"Has the jury reached a verdict, madam foreman?" the judge asked as the last juror took his seat.

"We have, your honor."

"Very well. The defendant will now stand and face the jury."

Shyster stood, looking at the judge with anger in his eyes as if that one high court official had caused all of his problems.

"Please read your verdict," the judge continued without expression.

"On charge one, conspiracy to commit murder, we find the defendant...guilty as charged. Charge two, extortion, we find the defendant...guilty as charged. Charge three, bribery, we find the defendant...guilty as charged. Charge four, racketeering, we find the defendant...guilty as charged. Charge five, violation of the White Slavery Act, we find the defendant...guilty as charged."

Shyster stood stone-faced, without the decency to even bow his head in shame.

"Mr. Shyster, the jury has found you guilty on all five charges.

You'll be remanded to the custody of federal marshals and incarcerated without bail until such time as this court receives a pre-sentencing report and hears from victims as well as witnesses on your behalf thirty days from this date," the judge said firmly as his gavel struck the pallet. "Court adjourned."

Reporters rushed outside to try to be the first to get the news back to their editors, but everyone else was solemn. There was no rejoicing in the crowded courtroom that day. The case had no winners, only losers: The jurors had lost time with their families and their work; the defendant faced a long prison sentence; the victims were not fully restored to their original status; and, worst of all, the public sadly saw what society had become.

The defense lawyers had lost. The prosecution had won the battle but was in no way winning the war and had suffered severe casualties along the way. Only a future with revised values would right the wrongs revealed in this case.

Maybe the judge's sentencing would deliver a warning to would-be criminals and a message to citizens to be more selective in the future and to stand guard at the state Capitol to protect the core values it represents. Or maybe history had already cursed them for building it on the grounds of the former state penitentiary, somehow transferring the personalities of ghosts of the past onto their present-day lawmakers.

Thirty days later, the sentencing hearing was called to order. The federal probations investigator had provided a report to the court outlining the history of Chuck's life. On paper, he had been a model citizen.

The court would consider his past free of criminal convictions. However, it would also consider the heinous crimes committed by a person hiding behind a cloak of power, who was almost single-handedly responsible for the ruins of scores of people's lives.

It would consider the multiple offenses and the mandatory sentencing guidelines, but would have to choose to either run the sentences for each offense concurrently or consecutively. Ten years on each offense concurrently would mean a maximum of ten years, not taking into consideration time awarded for good behavior. Ten years consecutively, however, would mean a maximum sentence of over sixty years. He'd be more than a hundred years old when his sentence was complete, if he didn't die in prison.

The deterioration of public trust he caused, the multiplicity of the charges, the lack of remorse he showed, and his unwillingness to name his casino ties seemed to be tipping the legal scales in one direction. But would a life sentence and loss of freedom be so bad considering that his victims would forever face what they had suffered at his hands? The judge was the only one who could answer that.

The witnesses on Chuck's behalf were few: the pastor of his church and family members. No friends, business acquaintances or public officials would put their integrity on the line for this parasite. In contrast, there was a long line of legislative witnesses against Chuck willing to take the stand—and thanks to the Victim's Rights Act, Will would be able to confront Shyster himself or submit a letter. Rumor had it he'd choose a live appearance.

Will had not sat in the courtroom listening to the other testimony, as his son had. Just before it was his turn to take the stand, he pushed open the tall, wooden double doors at the entrance of the courtroom and rode in on his wheelchair, followed by his daughter-in-law, Julie. There wasn't a person on any of the benches who wasn't focusing on him.

He worked his way down the middle aisle, thinking about all the letters he had received from church and family members asking him to forgive and forget and wondering if he had the strength to do that today.

When the wheelchair rounded the front pew, much to the surprise of all concerned, Will pushed the blanket off his legs, placed

Chuck Shyster was gang raped, forced to perform oral sex and beaten up in prison less than a month after his arrival. One of the inmates involved in the sexual attack was infected with AIDS. Chuck continues to be tested monthly but so far shows no sign of being HIV positive. The prisoners who did it commented on how much they liked his hair. They were facing life sentences and had nothing to lose for their conduct, other than having to serve short stints in solitary confinement. Chuck now has a new haircut and is slowly recovering from his injuries.

Bob is still working the undercover case with the female lobbyist and things are progressing nicely. Wayne one day hopes to learn his last name.

Agent Tischner was transferred to the Oxford office and promoted to special agent in charge. He is currently overseeing an investigation called Operation Boomerang, which targets corrupt county supervisors and mirrors an old case of a similar nature that occurred about thirty years ago. After this stint, he says he plans to retire, move to Virginia and raise boneless chickens.

Wayne Lott went on to become a successful assistant U.S. attorney, continuing to prosecute cases of corruption and making his old man proud. He finally junked his old Geo Prism and got a new black Kia Amanti with all the bells and whistles—including a baby seat for his and Julie's first child, Dawn.

Will Lott completely regained his ability to walk. He had thoughts of re-entering law enforcement but instead decided to write a book during those times when he wasn't bouncing his new granddaughter on his knee. He took a long trip in his motor home to Key West, where he visited his favorite places along Duvall Street—especially the Hog's Breath Saloon, where he could find peace of mind and inspiration for written scenarios, as well as his favorite snacks: fried chicken wings and conch fritters. His book was based on his previous experiences, though they were embellished and names were changed so as not to embarrass any fine, upstanding politicians. He hoped that the exposure from his book would raise enough questions that a new Democratic appointment for U.S. attorney would be motivated to pursue the type of corruption he wrote about.

U.S. Attorney Tyrone did a good job on the case, but only after it was handed to him, and still had no intentions of pursuing widespread corruption that even a blind man could see. Instead, he spent his time pursuing a promotion.

Several of the old-time legislators chose not to run for office the next term and after the case ended, lobbyists found their jobs much harder. Even a hint of a potentially unethical offer brought on suspicion and often terminated the conversation. Political speculators theorize that one of two things will happen: Business will go on as usual, eventually climbing back to the previous level of corruption, or the new U.S. attorney would have politicians and lobbyists so scared that they'd pat down everybody they met and spend much of their hard-earned money buying electronic security devices to detect bugs—in turn causing the feds to spend our tax dollars on new technology to detect bug detectors or jam the frequencies, and creating a vicious circle.

Given all the possibilities, it seemed the case hadn't really ended at all. It was just the beginning of the long road that lay ahead…

Author's Notes

*"An unconditional right to say what one pleases
about public affairs is what I consider to be the minimum
guarantee of the First Amendment."*
—Justice Hugo L. Black (U.S. Supreme Court)

The *Lawmaker* is a work of fiction that was inspired by many events in my life, some of which were associated with my former employment as Director of Charitable Gaming at the Mississippi Gaming Commission. Although fictitious, the story touches on real issues that are at the forefront of discussions today regarding campaign contributions, legal loopholes, bogus charities and the potential adverse effects that gaming coupled with corruption could have on society.

This book, unlike most legal thrillers, was written from the perspective of a seasoned law enforcement officer. It should be noted, though, that I am neither for nor against gaming. However, after growing up in Tunica, Mississippi, where the Reverend Jessie Jackson described "Sugar Ditch"—and the poorest county in the United States, with despicable living conditions—I see that casinos have drastically improved living conditions there. Many great highways and thousands of jobs have been created by the industry, and tourist dollars have significantly contributed to the infrastructure, as well as the building of resort hotels across the state, which would not have been possible without the casinos.

As far as charitable gaming (bingo) goes, I believe in its original intent: for churches and veterans' groups to raise money during the Depression when no donations were available. But I do not agree with what it has become as it spread throughout the country: a source of exorbitant salaries for the directors and supervisors. At least other states are doing something about it with daily arrests and illegal machine seizure. In my opinion, Mississippi is barely even slapping the back of the abusers' hands with civil fines and administrative sanctions that require charities to pay for their employees' wrongdoings.

I don't know if any casino in Mississippi has broken the law or has had that intent. I have no doubt, however, that if an owner wanted to start a scam and needed a partner in state government or the lobbying industry, one would present him- or herself rather quickly and without reservation, perhaps only with the words, "Show me the money." Mississippi politicians might even follow the Illinois governor's approach and give casino owners what they want if donations are made to their campaigns.

Though one might think I have an agenda or ax to grind, I left the Gaming Commission on my own free will, disgusted by the influence that present and former members of the legislature had on limiting its activities to enforce the law. I feel it is my responsibility to bring these issues to light and I highly encourage residents from every state that has legalized gambling or bingo operations to look at them closely and ask themselves, "Who really benefits from this?" I praise the gaming industry for the good it does, but I curse my state's lack of enforcement, which, at least in my mind, creates suspicions of bribery, corruption and other appearances of impropriety.

To me, Missouri has the best laws, which require members of

the charity to run bingo operations without benefit or compensation. Not only do supervisors *not* get a huge salary, or any salary at all, none of the helpers are compensated, either. They volunteer so that their cause can earn money and continue its charitable purpose.

The Mississippi legislature considered a bill last year that would have increased the compensation given to bingo hall supervisors—though there were already some who were almost tripling the annual gross income of the average household in the state. One clause would have limited agents' "peace officer" powers, meaning they couldn't pursue crimes such as embezzlement, grand larceny, state RICO, or any other scams common to the business, only misdemeanors. I congratulate those members of the legislature who saw through this and didn't pass the bill.

All characters and events in this book are strictly fictitious. The state committees, agencies and commissions are real, and I believe they could perform a much-needed job were it not for legislative meddling. Most of the comments or stories relating to bingo in this book are true, verifiable and documented. The rest is pure fiction.

As far as I know, the events of this story involving attempted assassination and blackmail based on sexual activities are not real. To my knowledge, no casino mobsters even exist in Mississippi. I believe casinos are a legitimate industry and will remain so *with proper controls*. What I am against is the lack of enforcement in *any* industry, which will lead to corruption. Laws must be enforced. If they are just for show, they should be taken off the books. Let law enforcement salaries be paid for the purpose of tracking down murderers, child molesters, rapists and other criminals, instead of "regulating" the status quo while those criminals run the streets and continue to make us victims of their crimes.

The records do not lie: Examine them if you think the Gaming Commission is enforcing the law with their in-house officers, but don't be fooled by claims of "regulating" or letting other agencies do their jobs for them. This is not just a problem in Mississippi; something needs to be done in all states and countries, including Peru, Bolivia, the United Kingdom and Canada. Their stories can be found on the Internet. Many states and some countries are aggressively pursuing convictions for illegal games and unlawful machines, depriving charities, and other corruption through arrests and seizure (especially in charitable gaming), but not Mississippi.

Some of the establishments, media organizations, streets and towns mentioned in *The Lawmaker* are real and their names are used only for authenticity and to help readers identify with the setting. They are not intended to be portrayed in a negative light.

About the Author

Rick Ward was born in Tunica, Mississippi, on August 1, 1953, long before casinos cluttered the river. He has an Associate degree in law enforcement from Mississippi Gulf Coast Community College, a B.S. in criminal justice from the University of the State of New York, and a Master's in education from the University of Hawaii. He is a graduate of the Mississippi State Police Academy, the U.S. Army Military Police School, and the FBI National Academy.

Rick began his law enforcement career in 1975, becoming a uniformed police officer in Mississippi. Three years later, he became an undercover state narcotics agent then the chief investigator for Desoto County, Mississippi. After a short tour back in uniform as a police officer near Jackson, he re-enlisted in the U.S. Navy in 1983 as a master at arms and was promoted through the ranks to lieutenant physical security officer. He left the navy again in 1995 but remained in the reserves and worked for the state attorney general investigating white-collar crime and political corruption.

In 1998, Rick became a division director for the Mississippi Gaming Commission; his division was responsible for the largest number of arrests before or since. In late 2000, he became a Federal Employment Compensation Act fraud investigator under contract for the U.S. Army Corps of Engineers.

After a six-month tour with the Southern Command as a navy reservist interdicting narcotics traffickers in El Salvador, he went to the northeast region for the navy. Rick was on a reserve assignment in New York City during the September 11 attacks on the World Trade Center, and voluntarily accepted a full recall offer to active duty three weeks later. He was placed in charge of security and law enforcement for all bases in the entire Northeast before going to headquarters in Washington, D.C. for two years. He retired in late 2005 as a lieutenant commander, but continues to work for the navy as a Security, Law Enforcement and Anti-Terrorism/Force Protection expert consultant under a defense contract.

Rick's actual experiences have inspired him to embellish real-life events and write fictitious scenarios that he believes will be enjoyed by readers interested in legal thrillers, crime and politics told from the perspective of a seasoned, well-rounded retired senior law enforcement officer.